SIMON PEPPERCORN

LOG IN TO MAGIC SPACE

BY

WENDELL SPEER

Magic Space

TO MY SON, LUKE

Text copyright 2009 by Wendell Speer
Cover and interior art copyright 2009 by Wendell Speer
All rights reserved.
Published by Magic Space
14749 Croft St., Dade City, Florida 33525
Magic Space is a trademark of Magic Space

Visit www.magicspace.com

Library of Congress Control Number: 2009909196

ISBN 978-0-615-32034-2

Printed in the U.S.A.

First printed in 2009

TABLE OF CONTENTS

CHAPTER ONE

PART I – MISS TOAD

"*SIMON!*"

A knight of unknightly stature galloped onto a tournament field. He tried to sit tall in stunted armor of shiny silver. Instead of lance and shield, he held a short, wooden rod. A dozen knights positioned themselves to charge, but the newcomer's powerful white stallion reared high and shot off toward them. Two lance lengths away, the Silver Knight pointed his rod. "ELECTRO!" he shouted.

A beam of light flashed from the stick and separated into a dozen firebolts. The burning streaks zapped and frazzled the oncoming knights like shafts of lightning. Before a new group of warriors could give challenge, a thunderous roar ripped through the forest, and the ground, trembled violently.

Two enormous giants, Blunderboar and Cormilan, stomped into view. Covered in armor, except for their heads and bare feet, they carried humongous clubs. But the little knight knew the power of his weapon.

"*SIMON PEPPERCORN!*"

The Silver Knight urged his horse before the new opponents and quickly dismounted. Blunderboar swung his club, but the little warrior waved his wand and floated upward. He smacked the clumsy giant's nose as hard as he could. The gargantuan threw both hands over his face, dropped his club, and cried out so loudly that many tents across the field blew away.

The Silver Knight flicked his wand at Blunderboar's weapon. "SCROLL UP!" he commanded. The club rose quickly and hovered high over Cormilan's head. "SCROLL DOWN!" The warrior swished his wand toward the ground. The big wooden club zoomed down and smashed into Cormilan's hairy foot. Now both giants cried in pain. They stumbled away into the forest, their screams echoing after them.

Mounted knights galloped back onto the field followed by peasants and others who had taken refuge in the castle. The hero climbed onto his horse and trotted toward the judging platform. Before the king's court, he tugged off his helmet and revealed the head of a twelve-year-old boy with sandy blond hair and bright blue eyes. The queen rose from her throne and started to speak.

"*Simon Peppercorn!*"

Suddenly, queen, king, platform, castle, knights, and tournament field all faded away.

"*Simon! Wake up, Simon Peppercorn!*"

The smile quickly dissolved from the boy's face. He was no longer sitting high on a war horse, but was seated at a table in a middle school classroom. Instead of a beautiful queen, before him stood a woman who must have been less than five feet tall and more than five feet wide. Her bulging eyes were crowned with bushy eyebrows, and buck teeth pressed her quivering lips several inches from her face.

Simon raised his head. He looked around as if he had

awakened in a foreign world. Layla Belladonna, the girl sitting next to Simon, looked at him in exasperation. "I tried to wake you up ten times, fool, but you *never* listen to me."

Miss Todd — the History teacher — leaned over Simon, tapping the table with her pointer. "Simon Peppercorn, you're *always* off in some other space. Why you daydream so much, I simply *do not* understand."

"I'm sorry, Miss Toad. Miss Todd, I mean," Simon muttered. The whole class broke out laughing.

"I know why!"

The voice came from the second table behind Simon's. "It's because he's Simple Simon, Miss Toad. Miss Todd, I mean." The whole class laughed even louder — none as loudly as the boy who had just spoken. Simon jumped to his feet and stomped back to the boy's table. The little pinprick he'd been feeling inside his chest lately burned again.

"I've had enough of you, Arthur Sunshine!" he said. The boy flew out of his chair to meet Simon. Arthur was taller, but Simon was strong for his age. The boys held each other in tight grips, neither able to get the advantage. Miss Todd aimed her pointer at them.

"You boys separate right now, or you'll stay after school," she said. "I don't think you want *that* on the last day." Then the bell rang. Simon and Arthur let go of each other. Miss Todd got it right — neither of them wanted *that*. Arthur snatched up his backpack and brushed past with a final shove.

As Simon was grabbing his stuff, a tall, pale girl with dark hair walked past and rolled her eyes at him. "You're so stupid, Simon Peppercorn," said Morgan Lafayette. Simon turned red. At least it was the end of the school year. But sometimes the end of one thing is the beginning of another.

Simon felt relieved to get on the bus and escape. He couldn't stand to be cooped up in school all day. It was more fun to be in the woods with his dog, or at the skate park falling off his skateboard. And between the worlds of school and outdoors came the bus ride home. Simon always sat alone in the front, away from the other kids who lived on Old River Road. *They* wanted to shout and fight in the back seats and force Miss Beetle to stop ten times along the way.

Simon preferred to pretend he was sailing over rough seas in a pirate ship. Or he would stare out the window at himself racing a chariot over desert sands. "Simon! Simon, you're home!" Miss Beetle said. Simon's house was the last stop on the route. The ardent adventurer turned his head from the lion hunt outside the window. His grandparents were sitting in their rockers on the big front porch.

"Thank you, Miss Beetle," Simon said. "I'm going to miss you all summer."

"Oh, Simon, don't be silly. I live just down the road. I'll see you when you come to mow my lawn."

"I know, but I like riding the bus. You break me out of that dungeon and take me on a chariot ride."

"Is it a chariot now?" Miss Beetle laughed. "Last week it was a submarine." She gave him a thumbs up sign. "May you feel the magic!" she said, closing the bus door.

"Huh?" Simon said, not certain what he had just heard. As he opened the creaky gate, a scrawny, short-haired mutt

4

darted from the side of the wood frame house. He would have sprung over Simon's head and onto the road, but the boy dropped his pack and caught the flying dog in his arms. Doggy had wandered up to the house on the day after Simon was born — according to the grandparents. They said he scared away the sprites that unsettled the chickens, so they let him stay. Simon always suspected it was his pet that got after the chickens, and not sprites.

"Don't jump at me like that, you crazy mutt!" Simon shouted in Doggy's face. The hound growled back at him with yellow teeth. Then he licked Simon's face with a large, purplish tongue. "Eeeeyuck!" Simon shouted. He dropped Doggy to the ground and wiped a blob of dog slobber off his face. "I can't believe I let you pull *that one* again." Doggy leapt onto the porch with what appeared to be a snicker on his face.

"Hi, Grandma — hi, Grandpa." The grandparents both had silver hair and radiant faces. Grandpa always sat with a bundle of twigs that he whittled at with an ancient pocketknife. Grandma kept a pile of sticks and straw at her side that she twisted into baskets or old-fashioned brooms. All Simon had ever heard about his parents was that they disappeared when he was a baby. He accepted the fact as if it was what parents do.

"Dinner's going to be late today," Grandma said, much to Simon's surprise. "Don't forget to do your homework," she added.

"Got to do your homework — unless you have a magic pen," Grandpa chuckled. He winked at Grandma.

Today's the last day of school — I don't *have* any home-work," Simon said, going through the screen door. In the kitchen, he saw balloons and a paper banner hanging across the upper cabinets: *HAPPY BIRTHDAY SIMON*! A chocolate cake with a dozen candles on it dominated the table. "I completely forgot," Simon said out loud. "Today's my birthday!"

Two wrapped presents sat beside the cake, one quite large and the other very small. Simon ripped the paper off the large one. It was an old book with a flaky leather cover. Simon could barely make out the gold lettering of the title. "*Magic of the Templars*. Cool," he said. "I bet they dug it out of that spooky attic."

Simon lifted the other gift and weighed it in his hand. "Knowing her, it's probably empty." He opened the box and pulled out a miniature skateboard. "Just as I thought — another techdeck." A note lay on the bottom of the box. Simon unfolded it, " 'A little board for a big fly.' That's dumb," he said to Doggy, who was sitting in a chair, staring at the cake. "She usually calls me worse names than fly. And if you touch that cake, *you're* going to get it with a *fly* swatter!"

Simon put the techdeck in his pack and picked up the book, knocking off one of Grandpa's sticks, which lay underneath it. As the stick hit the floor, sparks shot out the end. "Wow!" Simon said. "He must've rigged that to light the candles with." He put the stick back in its place and headed for the back of the house, passing his fourteen-year-old sister's room. As he suspected, Sammie was sitting at the computer.

"Happy Birthday, little bro!" She didn't turn around, or let up on her rapid typing.

6

"Thanks for the present," Simon muttered.

"You weren't supposed to open them yet. And you'd better clean up your room, Birthday Boy. You're twelve years old now. Time to join the *real* world."

His room *was* a mess, but to Simon it had its own logic. He threw his school things on the bed and left with his pack.

"Looks good to me," he said to Sammie.

"Morgan's coming over for help with her homework again. Want me to ask her to stay for supper?"

"You better not — if you know what's good for you!" Simon said, blushing. He and Doggy rushed out the door.

"Happy Birthday, Simon!" the grandparents said in unison.

"Don't be off too long, Dear," added Grandma.

Simon headed out the gate without a word. He was really mad at Sammie for inviting Morgan over on his birthday. "Why did Sammie have to help Morgan with her homework, anyway?" he thought. "Hey — what the heck? What homework? Today was the last day of school. Why is everybody talking about *homework*?"

CHAPTER ONE

PART II – THE WANDING LORD

Just up the road, Simon cut off on a trail into the woods. He grabbed up a fairly straight stick about four feet long and a brown, dried palmetto frond that fanned into a shield. With weapons in hand, he charged up to a twenty-five-foot-tall cabbage palm. It had green fronds and long, saw-toothed branches that curved up from the trunk like dozens of swords.

"I'm not afraid of you, Green Knight — no matter how tall you are, or how many swords you have!" Simon shouted. He lunged forward, swinging and thrusting his weapon. "Take *that*, you wicked villain!" Doggy yawned and rolled his eyes as if he had seen this battle before. Simon delivered a blow that snapped his sword in half. He threw the part he still held at the Green Knight. "Strike, brave giant! Chop off my head with your battle axe — if you think you can penetrate my powerful shield."

As the tree contemplated its next move, a rustling of dried leaves on the forest path broke the silence. Doggy jumped up, growling. He rushed forward to protect his master. A tall, muscular man dressed in camouflage rounded the bend in the trail. The woodsman gripped a camp shovel in both hands. "Well, well. Sir Simon Peppercorn," he said. "You see more action helping me tangle with a gator than dueling with errant knights."

Waldo Burncastle, an old friend of the family, was a professional alligator trapper. But sometimes he would go into the dark waters of the narrow river and drag out the beasts just for the fun of it. "Most I ever did was grab one around the tail after you had him worn out," Simon said.

"Takes a lot of guts just to do that," Waldo said. "Not many kids around these days who feel the magic of the woods like you do. Your father would be proud of you." Simon had once asked Waldo about his parents, but only heard the line about them disappearing.

Waldo pulled his hand out of his pocket and held it toward Simon. A long, reddish brown arrowhead lay in his open palm. "Wow, that's a beauty!" Simon said.

"Archaic period. At least five or six thousand years old. Happy Birthday!"

"*Really*? Thanks, Waldo. But you shouldn't be digging out here. You know what'll happen if you get caught."

"Ah, they don't never bother me — as long as I fill the holes in. I'll bring it over this evening."

Simon led Doggy on a narrow trail that led to the river. He held onto his leafy shield and picked up a fairly straight oak twig over a foot long. A few steps later, an armadillo darted off into the bushes at the sight of the odd little dog. Simon pointed his stick in its direction and shouted, "After that armored dillobeast, my faithful squire!" Doggy sat down unfaithfully and looked into the bushes and then back at Simon. "You lazy scoundrel!" Simon said. "I should turn you into a two-headed snake for not obeying your master."

Simon turned away from his mutinous mate and, "AAR-RGGGHHH!" He stopped dead in his tracks — his face was about three inches from a humongous banana spider. Its body was nearly the same shape and color of a banana and had brownish orange markings around the edges. Two rows of white dots ran down the spider's yellow-gold back. It's long, spindly legs were creepy-fuzzy and decorated with rusty orange and yellow bands.

The creature stared at Simon with beady, black eyes. The boy pointed his oak twig at it. "DISAPPEARO!" he shouted. The stubborn beast remained visible where it sat. "Anti-disappearing charm, eh? Then take *this*!" Simon swept the long-stemmed palmetto frond through the air, capturing the spider and its web on the fanned-out leaves. He tossed it as far as he could into the bushes and commanded it with his wand to fly. "I saved your life again!" he said to Doggy, who showed no sign of appreciation.

The adventure seekers continued through the woods on a narrower path. Simon turned a tree stump into a wild hog and several trolls into cabbage palms. Soon he and Doggy made their way into a clearing where a great oak tree spread its limbs through the air. The ground was blanketed with dried oak leaves and a few small clumps of gray Spanish moss the wind had blown from the tree. A fairly smooth but weathered rock a little larger than a basketball stood prominently in the clearing. It reminded Simon of a tortoise gopher.

Simon stepped up to the ancient rock and tapped it three times with the oak wand. *"Rise, I command thee!"* he shouted. To his surprise, a strong wind began to blow, swaying the limbs of the massive tree. The stone rose several feet into the air and spun rapidly! Multi-colored sparks emitted from it in every direction. The spinning soon stopped, and a bright green turtle hovered where the stone had been. Its eyes glowed like dazzling emeralds — the segments of its shell were brilliant gold. A translucent globe of silver particles surrounded the apparition.

Before Simon could cry out in surprise, or shock, he saw Doggy stretch upright on his back legs, lift off the ground, and also spin. Most amazing of all, Simon felt himself rise and twirl. When he stopped spinning, he saw his pet standing on two feet like a person. In fact, Doggy now looked incredibly human-like, and he was wearing a white, hooded robe and had a sword hanging at his side.

Simon sensed something different about himself, too. He noticed that he stood in the same kind of robe as Doggy, but he didn't have a sword. He still held the oak twig in his right hand, though now it was perfectly straight and smooth, as if it had been whittled into shape.

Doggy knelt on all fours before the hovering turtle (Simon thought he looked more natural that way). "Master, we have arrived," he said with reverence. He looked sternly at Simon. "Kneel before the Wanding Lord." Simon obeyed without thinking. He dropped to his hands and knees and lowered his forehead to the ground.

"Rise, Warrior Wizards!" the Wanding Lord commanded. His voice was old, but powerful. Simon and Doggy rose to their feet.

Simon suddenly realized how crazy the situation was. A rock just turned into a talking turtle, and his pet — now in the form of a dog-person — spoke to him. And he, Simon, was wearing a weird robe, and the freaky turtle called him and Doggy *Warrior Wizards*. "Whah — I — uh — umm," Simon muttered.

"Fear not, lad. You have begun the Awakening to Magic Space," said the Wanding Lord.

"But, but," Simon stammered, "but, my — my dog looks weird — and he just talked to me, and... uh." (technically Doggy had spoken many times before — to get chocolate chip cookies).

"Careful how you speak of a Master Magus Warrior Wizard," the Wanding Lord said. "Master Magus Dogbert Ambrosius is centuries older than you. Respectfully refer to him as Master."

"*This is crazy!*" Simon shouted. "What's going on? I must be dreaming."

"No, Simon. It's as if you are waking up from a dream," said Dogbert, in a familiar voice. "Now you can join the real world of magic. I have been waiting with you to be your guide."

"Why so surprised? You have already taken steps along the Way," continued the Wanding Lord.

"What way? What steps?" Simon said, confused.

"Magical play in your imagination, your dreams and daydreams — and Magic School. In those states, the Magical Interfaces, you are very good at magic," said the glowing turtle.

"But, that's only dreams," Simon said. "It isn't real. I don't know *anything* about real magic."

"When you are dreaming, is not everything in your dream real to you?" the Wanding Lord said.

"Well, yeah," Simon began, "but —"

"Then what makes you think it is less real than what you call the real world?" said the turtle.

"That's what we Magicals call Hard Space," Dogbert joined in, "but the most powerful magic happens in Magic Space."

"What's Magic Space? How do I get there?" Simon asked, suddenly intrigued.

"Enough talk!" said the Wanding Lord. "Now you must decide if you will take the path of a Warrior Wizard and transition to Magic Space. If not — give your wand to Master Dogbert. Otherwise, present it to me."

Simon hesitated for a moment, but he knew what he would do. He did spend most of his time daydreaming and playing at magic. He had always wished he could have a real wand and make whatever he wanted happen with it. But what was Magic School? This obviously wasn't the time to ask.

Simon stepped up and dropped to one knee. He held the wand forward in both hands — as he imagined a knight would present his sword to a king. Then beams of brilliant green light shot from the Wanding Lord's eyes. The rays stopped at each end of Simon's wand and then quickly dissolved away. The glittering turtle took the stick in his little hand and swished it about in the air. "Excellent!" he said. "Precisely fourteen inches — the exact length of a Warrior Wizard's wand. You may rise."

As Simon rose to his feet, the Wanding Lord raised the wand. Long streaks of lightning shot from it and spread out in the sky. Simon's eyes stretched wide. "Wandfire has passed through your wand," Dogbert said, wringing his long-nailed hands in excitement. "It has been initiated by the Wanding Lord — a rare privilege. Now you can use it to perform the spells you learned in Magic School."

"What do you mean — Magic School?" Simon said anxiously. "The only magic at my school is getting through a day without any homework."

"That will be explained in time. It is part of your Awakening," said the Wanding Lord. "Take the wand, Simon. Repeat the demonstration of Wandfire. Empty your mind and just let it happen."

Simon took the wand and hesitated. But then his courage and his desire to do magic swelled up inside. He pointed the wand toward the sky and — nothing happened! Simon lowered the stick in disappointment.

"Your intention must be clear and strong, your mind free and focused. Try again," said the Wanding Lord.

Simon focused on the wand with great determination as he thrust it upward. "Wandfire, Wandfire!" he said to himself. A few sparks sputtered from the stick like a dying sparkler. Simon felt the burning pinprick inside his chest. At the same time, he felt mysteriously energized.

"You need to focus with all your might, but without trying — if that makes sense," Dogbert advised. It didn't
make sense, but Simon was more determined than ever,
though he feared he might fail. What if they took the wand
away forever?

Simon took a deep breath and stretched out the wand —
he closed his eyes this time. In his mind, he saw great streaks
of lightning. He thrust his arm upward and let go of the picture. Immediately, he felt a warm pulse in his chest. It shot
through his arm and out of the wand. He opened his eyes in
time to see a single small lightning bolt fading away over the
tree tops.

"Marvelous, Simon! Marvelous, indeed!" boomed the
bright green turtle. The Wanding Lord smiled broadly, his
emerald eyes flashing. Dogbert skipped around — also smiling. At least he seemed to be. It was hard to tell, the way his
tongue hung from his mouth.

"That was a dud compared to your fireworks," Simon
said.

"Don't worry, Simon," said Dogbert. "Many Warrior Wizards can't even do that. You have a special trait that —"

"Enough of words — now a Transformation spell," said
the Wanding Lord. He twisted inside his sparkly globe.
"Point your wand at the tree stump there and visualize what
you wish it to become. Then say TRANSFORMUS and the
name of the object."

Simon took aim at the half-rotted stump and focused
intensely. "TRANSFORMUS HOG!" he shouted. Dogbert
howled like a dog. A black and white hog stood where

Simon had been, grunting excitedly! The animal ran up to Dogbert and nudged him hard with its snout. The Wanding Lord gazed at the hog and shot red beams from his eyes. Instantly, Simon was on his hands and knees, bumping Dogbert with his head. He picked up his wand and scrambled to his feet.

"Marvelous, Simon! Marvelous!" exclaimed the jubilant turtle over Dogbert's raspy giggle. "Nicely spelled, indeed! The intensity was nearly perfect — if only your projection had followed through."

"It will be easier to spell when your awareness of your power merges with your magical memory. That's what your Awakening is," Dogbert said, trying hard not to snicker. "Then you'll become a true Warrior Wizard."

"Why do I have to be a stupid *Warrior* Wizard? Can't I just be a regular wizard and have fun?" Simon said, still shaken.

"In your daydreams, Simon, do you battle with terrible knights?" the Wanding Lord asked.

"Yeah, but —"

"Do you fight giants and dragons?"

"Yeah, but —"

"Do you save a girl you have a crush on from danger?"

"Yeah, but — hey, how do you — but —"

"You must use your magical powers to their greatest potential in Magic Space — or not at all," said the Wanding Lord. Simon could think of nothing more to say. In his heart, he knew it was the truth. "You shall now perform an Affecting spell on Master Magus Dogbert," the Wanding Lord continued.

Simon looked at Dogbert with a sly grin. "Can I turn him into a cat?"

"No, no, that would be a Transformation spell," Dogbert said hastily. "An Affecting spell changes one's behavior, or actions."

"Somebody has to teach me how," Simon said.

"Again — you must rely on your intuition and intention," said the Wanding Lord. "You have spells in your magical memory, but you can also improvise."

"And don't let your focus be distracted," Dogbert added, with a slight grin still on his face. "It's just like when you're lost in a daydream and nothing else gets through to you."

Simon felt that he more or less understood, but he still had his doubts. He faced Dogbert and pointed his wand, eyes closed. After a few seconds, only one thought remained. He opened his eyes and saw nothing but Dogbert. "LAUGH OUT LOUD!" he spelled.

The sparse hair on Dogbert's head stood on end. The master burst into a fit of hysterical laughter, grabbed his belly with both hands, and bent double. Then he fell to the ground, rolled about, and beat the earth with his fists. The master magus sat up, still laughing hard, and tried to pull the few hairs on his head. "Doggone hair!" he sputtered out between spastic heaves. "Or should I say — dog hair gone?" The Warrior Wizard got a real kick out of his joke and laughed even harder.

The Wanding Lord shot a ray of blue light at Dogbert — the laughter quickly dissolved to a whimpering giggle. "Excellent again, Simon. Your Awakening is well under way.

You will soon be ready to transition to Magic Space and undertake your Venture."

"What venture?" Simon asked, suspicious.

"Your powers must be tested on a journey in Magic Space," said the Wanding Lord. "You will learn more at the appropriate time. Keep in mind that your Awakening and initiation are most secretive."

The colorful turtle and his sparkly globe began to spin. The shiny particles of the orb dispersed in every direction and disappeared.

When the sparks cleared away, Simon saw the big, mossy stone standing half buried where it had been before. "*Wow*! I'm a wizard! I can do magic!" he said. "And you, you're a, you're a —"

"A Master Magus Warrior Wizard, to be exact," said Dogbert. "And now *I'm* the boss. Let's go home — it's getting late." Simon found the new relationship a bit hard to swallow, but it didn't really matter. He could make incredible things happen with a wand, and he was going to Magic Space, where he could do even bigger magic.

"Why have you been disguised as a funny dog all these years?" Simon asked, as he and his master made their way along the trail.

"A *what*?" Dogbert said, offended.

"Well, I'm surprised you weren't a German Shepherd, or a Doberman."

"A wise Warrior Wizard doesn't draw attention to himself," Dogbert said. "I've been here to wait with you for today — and to protect you."

"Protect me from what? I don't think I've been given the full picture," Simon said.

"We will return to the Wanding Stone tomorrow. You'll learn more then," Dogbert said.

"Can you at least tell me something about Magic School?"

"You'll know more about that soon enough, too. But I can tell you that it's a Space of its own. It's like what Hard Heads might call a virtual space —"

"Hard Heads?" Simon interrupted.

"People who don't truly believe in magic and never completely let go of Hard Space," Dogbert continued. "Children who show a strong ability for magic are guided to Magic School."

"So, why don't I know I've been going?" asked Simon.

"Your magical memory has been blocked so you wouldn't try to use magic before the right time," said Dogbert, "and to avoid certain dangers."

"AARRRGGGHHH!" Simon shouted. He stepped back quickly into Dogbert, pulling spider web from his face. Simon pointed his wand at the big banana spider that was scurrying up the remainder of the thick, yellowish web. "SPAZZ OUT!" he spelled without thinking. The spider twisted and convulsed in a powerless frenzy.

Dogbert pulled his wand from his robe and spelled at the spider. "RESTORE!" The creature stopped moving. It then crawled away to the top of the web and sat still. Dogbert stood tall in front of Simon. "Relinquish your wand!" he demanded.

"*What?*" said Simon, astonished.

"Do not question your master," Dogbert said. "A Warrior Wizard does not harm other creatures needlessly." He held his hand out. The boy's wand flew out of his hand and into that of his master. Dogbert tucked it into his belt.

"It was just a stupid *spider*," Simon said. "There're *millions* of them in these woods."

"Everything has its place in the world — and in every Space," said Dogbert. "When you allow fear and dislikes to control your actions, the consequences can be very negative — and destructive."

Master and initiate walked on in silence through the fading light. Simon knew that Dogbert was right. His whole world had just begun to change, and he was happy that his best friend ever was there to guide him, even if he did still resemble a scrawny, old mutt. They soon approached the road and stopped cautiously. "I'm really sorry about the spider," Simon said remorsefully. "I won't bother them again."

Dogbert remained firm. "You cannot judge a creature by appearances, especially in Magic Space where you are not used to the sights. Magic is not just fun and games, Simon. Being a wizard is very dangerous, especially a Warrior Wizard. You can back out and remain in Hard Space — if you wish."

"NEVER!" Simon blurted out. "I'm not a Hard Head!"

"Tomorrow afternoon, we go back to the Wanding Stone. You can let things sink in until then. By the way, that Spazz Out spell came spontaneously. It shows that your Awakening is progressing." Dogbert suddenly thrust his hand upward — he and Simon went into a spin. When they stopped, the boy was dressed in his normal clothes, and Doggy was back to his four-legged self.

"I think I like you better *this* way," Simon grinned. "Now, can I be the master again?" Doggy growled menacingly, but Simon knew that he was joking, too.

Simon was exhausted when he and Doggy entered the house. The only thing he wanted to do was go to bed and think about all that had happened. What Doggy wanted was a piece of chocolate cake and a bowl of milk. In the kitchen, Simon's grandparents, Waldo Burncastle, and Miss Beetle were chatting away. Simon barely heard a thing as they wished him birthday greetings. Luckily, Sammie and Morgana were not there.

Simon choked down half of a chicken leg and a few bites from his slice of cake. Doggy finished off both, besides his own supper. After receiving a few presents, Simon excused himself and headed for his room. "I should've known," he thought.

Sammie was sitting at the computer. "Sweet dreams, little bro," she said without turning. "Morgan couldn't make it. She decided to stay home and study."

"Whatever — goodnight," Simon muttered.

It felt so good to climb between the sheets and sink his head into the pillow. As soon as Simon's head settled, a light gush of wind swept across his face. Simon turned his head and saw Doggy spinning into Dogbert. His master, in Warrior Wizard robe, sat on the edge of the bed.

"Who am I?" Dogbert asked warmly.

"Master Magus Warrior Wizard Dogbert Ambrosius," Simon slowly said.

"Remember that — and remember who *you* are at all times."

"Tell me — about — Magic — Space," Simon said, eyes half closed.

"It is like another dimension. It is the Space where most of your dreams and imaginings take place. It is the world where legends, fairytales, and myths happen. It has day and night, but it is timeless. Those who transition there have adventures hardly imagined in Hard Space."

"Awesome," said Simon, as his eyes fell shut.

"But it is also filled with danger — and dark magic," Dogbert continued. He touched his wand to Simon's forehead and quietly chanted something under his breath. Then he raised his hand and spelled, "G2G!" Master Dogbert disappeared.

CHAPTER TWO

THE MAGIC EYE

Simon and Doggy arrived at a small skate park in the small Florida town. Simon tried an ollie, but his board hardly came off the ground. He skated up a pyramid ramp and attempted to do a frontside tailslide down a rail, but he lost balance and ended up on his backside.

As Simon was getting up from the ground, he heard Doggy growl. He looked around in the direction his skateboard had skidded and saw Arthur Sunshine standing there holding it, spinning the wheels. Arthur was accompanied by Angel Ramirez, Cato Collins, and some kid Simon didn't know. "Can't even do something *simple*, Simon?" Arthur sniggered. His friends backed him up with a burst of laughter. Simon's blood boiled. He clinched his fists and took a step forward.

"Go ahead, Peppercorn — if you think you can take on four at a time," Arthur said. Simon was ready to give it a try. If he could get one lick in at Arthur, it would be worth getting his butt kicked. Then he remembered the wand and pulled it from his belt. "What are you going to do with that stick, turn me into a toad — like your favorite teacher, Miss Toad?" Arthur said. Another uproar erupted from the gang.

Simon raised the wand, but Doggy ran forward. The skinny dog flashed his teeth and snarled. Arthur pretended not to be frightened. "Ah, let's get out of here before the mutt gives one of us rabies," he said. He dropped the skateboard on the ground and pushed it back at Simon. Doggy eased a couple of steps closer and growled louder than before, but the bullies hurried away.

Simon pushed off on the board and skated to the pyramid again. This time he did a frontside boardslide down a rail and stayed on his feet. Encouraged, he tried another ollie. Instead of crashing to the ground, the skateboard jumped into the air and continued to rise. Simon freaked out — as he steadied himself, his feet felt solid on the board. He used them to steer it and flew even higher.

Simon circled above the skate park, his arms outstretched for balance. He saw Doggy on the ground barking up at him. "Look, Doggy, I can fly! I can fly! I can —"

"Simon! Simon Peppercorn! Wake up, Simon!"

Simon slowly raised his head. "Sleeping in school again," he mumbled to himself.

"Just because you passed your final exam, you can't expect to *ever* transition to Magic Space, *if* you don't stay awake till the end of class," Miss Todd said.

"Huh? Did she say Magic Space?" Simon said quietly. He quickly looked up. A huge toad-like creature with very human features, Miss Todd's features, stood in front of him holding a wand. Miss Todd(ish) had on a long, flowing robe of green velvet decorated with yellow stars and orange moons in different phases. Her forehead was higher than a toad's, and her lips and protruding teeth were more or less human. The teacher had pale, greenish gray skin, and her short arms ended in stubby, slightly webbed fingers.

Layla nudged Simon with her elbow. "I've been trying to wake you up again, fool! Master Todd's going to turn you into a skunk if you don't stay awake today." Simon looked at Layla. She was wearing a deep blue silk robe. He looked at his own clothes and saw that he was wearing the same type of robe, though styled a bit differently. He looked over his shoulder and saw that all the kids in the class were dressed in blue robes. "*Magic School*! *Awesome!*" he said.

Simon's attention was caught by a bright glint from the dim front left corner of the room. He turned to see an ancient globe hovering there. The oceans of the model Earth were of real water. There must have been a storm in the Pacific — the waves were raging wildly. A small, glowing moon and tiny, whizzing sparks circled the globe. One of the sparks flew at Simon. "I remember! I remember Magic School!" he suddenly shouted. The rest of the students looked at Simon oddly.

"*Finally*! I just hope you remember all your spells after you log in to Magic Space," said Master Todd, "or you'll be in for *big* trouble." At that moment a flashing orange insect flew in front of the teacher's face. Her tongue flicked out and pulled the bug into her mouth. All the kids giggled, except Morgan, who squirmed in disgust. In the back of the class, Demarcus Williams was folding bits of paper into small insects. He touched the tip of his wand to one. The paper construction came alive and flitted off. "It's just *that* simple.

I hope you understand," continued Master Todd.

"It has to be simple for Simon to understand," said Arthur, who was already standing at his table in anticipation.

Simon jumped from his seat and rushed at Arthur with wand in hand.

He pointed at the boy and spelled, "SPAZZ OUT!" Arthur began shaking and twitching. After a few seconds, he quit moving. Then he held his hand up and snapped his fingers. A large orangutan now stood where Arthur had just been. The ape grabbed Simon in its long, hairy arms and squeezed tightly. Simon squeezed back and raised high on his feet, lifting the orangutan off the floor.

Master Todd aimed her wand at the fighters. "SEPA-RATO!" she spelled. Simon and the orangutan flew back away from each other. The ape flipped backwards over the table where Angel Ramirez sat alone and knocked Angel to the floor. Arthur and Angel slowly climbed up to their chairs.

"You should *both* be expelled from Magic School!" Master Todd shouted at Simon and Arthur. Her tongue shot out and curled around another of Demarcus's insects. "However," she smacked, "it is graduation day — and I would *hate* to see three years of hard work go to waste. Furthermore, Arthur — you receive the highest grade for Shape Shifting. And you, Simon — you get extra points in Affecting Spells. Demarcus — you get honors for Transformations."

Just then a pink and yellow bug, with a long snout and wings that spun over its head like a helicopter's, buzzed over Master Todd's head. She pointed her wand at it. The thing sizzled, crackled, and fell into the teacher's open mouth. She swallowed with a single crunch. Again, everyone giggled — except Morgan.

"Now," continued Master Todd, "Lexi Magenta — you have only Affecting Spells to complete." She turned to a very cute girl with golden, curly hair. "You may choose anyone in the class for your subject. Use one of the Cyber spells taught by the Magical Techie who visited. Those spells were formulated to help young Magicals relate more easily to Magic Space. We old-school Magicals like them as well."

Lexi stood and waved her wand at everyone, giggling. She finally pointed it at Michael Mountjoy, who sat alone next to Simon and Layla. "Stand up, dude," Lexi said. She flicked her wand like an orchestra conductor and giggled.

The lanky boy stood up and faced Lexi. His dark, close set eyes peered down his long, thin nose toward her. He pushed his stringy black hair back toward the hood of his robe and placed his hands on his hips. "Give it your best shot — *dude*," Michael said.

Lexi aimed her wand at the boy's chest and concentrated for a moment. "LAUGH OUT LOUD!" she spelled.

As the words left Lexi's mouth, Michael dropped to the floor. Master Todd burst into uncontrollable laughter. Her whole body shook like a massive bowl of JELL-O. Several rolls of fat undulated up and down her body like ocean waves. Her extra chins rolled from side to side. Large tears rolled down her enormous cheeks. Finally, she snorted loudly, wiped her flabby arm across her face, and stopped laughing as suddenly as she had begun.

"That wasn't the *least* bit funny, Michael Mountjoy!" Master Todd said. "You are lucky I'm in a good mood today, or I would make you repeat the year. Well done, Lexi. An excellent diversionary spell. You don't have to stand there like a pillar of salt. You have passed all your tests." The girl returned to her seat — giggling nervously.

"Well," Master Todd continued, looking at Morgan, "your spells were perfect, Miss Lafayette. You have only Levitation to complete."

Morgan rose quietly and moved away from the table. With her look and serious demeanor, she stood out from the rest of the class. Everyone fell silent as she slowly extended her arms out to the side.

"LEVITATO!" Morgan spelled. She floated above the table top.

"*Perfect!*" said Master Todd. Morgan's feet then rose slowly as her head lowered, until she was suspended in a lying position. "Very nice — *very* nice. You may come down."

"DESCENDO!" Morgan spelled. She returned to a vertical position and drifted back to the floor. Most of the class could levitate fairly well, but Morgan made it look so mysterious. Everyone clapped their hands — except Layla.

"Any half decent witch can do that," she whispered to Simon.

"That brings us to you, Layla. The last test of the exams is your Transformation spell," said Master Todd. She walked back to Demarcus's table and picked up one of his paper creations and almost popped it into her mouth. Instead, she waved her wand over the remaining paper bits. All of the little creatures came to life and flew quickly away.

The corpulent teacher placed the paper scrap in front of Layla. Next, she pointed her wand at the purpleboard in front of the room. "APERIO!" she spelled. A bright yellow window the size of a plasma TV appeared on the board. Creepy-crawly and flying creatures moved about in the virtual screen.

Master Todd followed a sluggish, fuzzy thing with the tip of her wand. "That — as you all should know," she said, "is a cattopillar. It metamorphoses into a bright green cattofly with a long, furry red tail, fairy-like wings, and whiskers that it can stretch out and rap around its prey with an unbreakable grip." She pointed the wand tip at a cat-like creature flying about on the screen. "I advise Shape Shifters *not* to shift into a small animal — such as a mouse — in the vicinity of a cattofly. They are *vicious* with a meal."

"What would it do to a rat like Arthur?" Simon asked. Arthur started to rise out of his seat, but Master Todd pointed her wand, and he slunk back down.

Master Todd took Demarcus's paperwork and set it on an empty table in the middle of the room. "Come forward, Layla, and transform this morsel into a large cattopillar."

Layla jumped up from her table. "Piece of cake," she said. She pointed her wand at the paper scrap. "TRANSFORMUS GIANT CATTOPILAR!" she spelled. The piece of paper faded to a dull green shade. It slowly twisted and stretched into a fat, furry, worm-like creature like the one on the board. But the cattopillar didn't stop growing. It got bigger — and Bigger — and BIGGER! Soon the wormy thing covered the table and was drooping onto the floor. It spread upward and outward, longways and sideways. The students had to jump up from their seats and back up against the walls. Rows of flying brooms that hovered near the ceiling jetted out through the open windows.

Before she could react, Master Todd was pressed against the purpleboard unable to raise her wand. The monstrous thing soon had everyone pinned. Simon found himself pushed against an open window, afraid he'd be squeezed out of the room. Finally, he opened his mouth wide and bit into the warm, mushy side of the fuzzy beast. He immediately discovered that cattopillars have amazingly thin skin. As his teeth ripped a hole in the squishy worm, his mouth filled with a gooey bright green bitter stinky substance.

The nasty gook slowly filled the room and oozed out the open windows. After a while, the cattopillar looked like a slimy deflated balloon. All the kids were screaming and flicking worm gook from their hair and faces. Lexi Magenta was particularly upset about the icky condition of her long, blond curls — now thin and matted.

Simon spewed a mouthful of the mess all over Arthur and Angel. Then he looked around and saw Morgan leaning out another window. She was hurling a huge mouthful of the worm gook onto the ground! "She must've bitten into it, too," Simon thought. He quickly turned his gaze so as not to embarrass the girl who was always quick to embarrass him. She would manage somehow to blame *him* for the catastrophe.

Master Todd finally regained composure and shook her wand in the air. A small bell appeared over the middle of the room and clanged loudly. All the kids — dripping with green slime — went silent. Their angry eyes turned to Layla. Before anyone could say a word, Master Todd waved her wand in a wide circle. "RESTORE!" she spelled. The deflated cattopillar skin shriveled up to a small scrap of paper on the table. The green gook faded from the kids and everything else — except for a small glob on Master Todd's cheek.

Simon stuck out his tongue and noticed that it was bright green. He looked back at Morgan and saw that she was sticking *her* tongue out at him. It was bright green, too. The girl smiled quickly at Simon and took her seat. He blushed and stumbled as he sat.

"Well!" exclaimed Master Todd. "I only meant large enough for the class to see, but not *that* closely."

"I'm sorry, Master Toad — Todd — I mean," Layla said. The whole class giggled, even Morgan.

"Levitation, Potions, and Spells — you have passed them all," said Master Todd, ignoring Layla's gaff. "You have the potential to be a very good Wicked Witch Hunter. *If* your exuberance doesn't get in your way in Magic Space."

Master Todd stepped behind her desk and with her wand tapped a large crystal ball. A milky white cloud filled the orb. "Now we have reached an important moment. The Magic Eye has evaluated your results, taking into account the sum of your three years in Magic School. Eight of you have graduated to undertake the Magic Space Venture. The remainder will be transferred to Master Magus Mortimer Belltower for

Magic Summer School — or graduation as Hard Space Magic Practitioners."

Cheers and moans arose from the students, depending on expectations. Master Todd swirled her wand. "TRANSFERRO CHAMBER 13!" she spelled. All but eight of the students disappeared. Those who remained glanced around at each other with big smiles, though Arthur cast Simon a nasty look.

"You have been told about the Venture," continued Master Todd. "Your Master Magus Guide will refresh your magical memory as needed." The glob of cattopillar gook had dribbled further down her cheek and was now barely hanging there. "If you are unsuccessful and *survive* — you will still be allowed to practice lesser magic in Hard Space. If all goes well — you may be called upon to do service in either Space." Layla looked at Simon in apprehension.

The glob of gook dripped from Master Todd's cheek. She swiped it from the air with her fingertip and slurped it into her mouth. Then she tapped the glass ball with her wand. It became clear again. "You will now be assigned your designated Magical Craft by the Magic Eye."

The head of an old wizard with a long lavender beard and long lavender hair appeared in the Magic Eye. "Your purpose in transitioning to Magic Space is to practice and increase your knowledge of the Magical Arts," said the ancient head.

"You will undertake a journey, which shall end on the first full moon after your transition. During this time, you are certain to encounter dark forces, dangerous creatures, and non-Magicals in need of aid. How you respond to situations will determine your success. Positive evaluation will earn you the title of practitioner in your designated craft."

The wizard's head disappeared from the crystal ball. The image of Demarcus popped up in its place. "Demarcus Williams — Ordinary Wand Wizard," continued the old voice. "Your primary role is to aid and protect non-Magicals in distress. You may in time practice the arts of a Healer Wizard. The sword you shall not wield, though a dagger you may."

Demarcus's head disappeared from the crystal ball, and Angel's took its place. "Angel Ramirez — Dragon Slayer. Your duty is to defend Magic Space from dragons and other dangerous creatures. You shall carry a wand, but its use will be limited, as dragons are mostly immune to magic. The chief instrument of your craft is the sword. You must win your own in order to complete your Venture."

Angel's head was replaced by a girl's. "Heather Fairfield," said the wizard, "— ordinary Wand Witch. You are the female equivalent of an Ordinary Wand Wizard. The same comments apply."

Arthur's head appeared next. "Arthur Sunshine — Shape Shifter. You were born with the natural ability to change from human to other animal forms. You shall wield the wand, but not the sword. Your role in Magic Space is to aid witches and wizards in the battle against dark magic and to serve as messenger and spy. You may act alone to aid non-Magicals in need and to confound the Dark Forces."

Three heads popped up after Arthur's. "Lexi Magenta, Layla Belladonna, and Morgan Lafayette — Wicked Witch

Hunters. You have shown great potential in all areas of magic practiced by the highest order of white witches. In addition to the duties of an Ordinary Wand Witch, you have the greater responsibility to aid Warrior Wizards and to seek and destroy the power of Wicked Witches."

Finally, Simon's head filled the crystal ball. "Simon Peppercorn — Warrior Wizard. You shall wield both wand and sword. Sword you must win. Your responsibilities include those of all your magicmates. Beyond that, you shall seek combat with Wicked Wizards and all sorts of terrible beings: giants, trolls, goblins, dragons, and other dangerous creatures. The Warrior Wizard also protects Hard Space from intrusion by all dark enemies from Magic Space."

The wizard's head replaced Simon's in the Magic Eye. "Not often are initiates chosen for this exalted craft. It is a high honor, Simon Peppercorn."

"It's not fair! *I* should be a Warrior Wizard!" Arthur shouted.

"Do not question the Magic Eye," said the wizard. "The voice of Fate has spoken. May you feel the magic!"

The ancient head disappeared from the crystal ball. Master Todd stepped closer to the students again. "Now then — you will be supervised in Magic Space in two groups, though you may not be together at all times, and your Guides may switch off, or leave you on your own. Group One will be composed of Demarcus, Heather, Lexi, and Angel. However, Angel, you will almost always be with a Master Dragon Slayer.

"Group Two, of course, will be Simon, Layla, Morgan, and Arthur. It is time now to meet your Guides. May I introduce Group One to Master Magus Wicked Witch Hunter Philomena Todd." She did a clumsy curtsy, and nearly tumbled to the floor. The members of Group One sat frozen in disbelief — until Lexi giggled and began clapping her hands. Everyone else followed her example.

After Master Todd had sufficiently glowered in the attention, she raised a stubby hand to signal a pause. "And now," she said, "it gives me great pleasure to introduce to you the Guide of Group Two — the highly venerated Master Magus Warrior Wizard Dogbert Ambrosius." Master Todd swept her arm around and Dogbert appeared beside her.

"That old dude looks a *lot* like your dog!" Layla said to Simon. She turned her head to see Simon's reaction, but his head was lying on his crossed arms. She elbowed him in the side as Dogbert approached their table. "Wake up, Simon!"

CHAPTER THREE

LOG IN TO MAGIC SPACE

A wide sunbeam poured through the window. Simon slowly forced his eyelids apart. Doggy was sitting on his belly licking his face. "Stop it, Master," Simon said. "We have to go to the Wanding Stone." He jumped out of bed and began dressing. "I finished Magic School, and I remember it — some of it, anyway." He grabbed his backpack and rushed to the kitchen.

Simon gulped down a bowl of cereal. He and Doggy split the last piece of birthday cake and hurried out the door. The grandparents were sitting on the porch in their usual places. Several old-fashioned brooms leaned against the railing. "Simon, Sweetie, be a good boy and take a broom to Miss Beetle for me," Grandma said. "She's done worn out the last one. Then you'll have all summer for high adventure."

"Can't it wait till —" Simon cut himself off. He was never disrespectful to his grandparents. "Okay, Grandma — it won't take long, anyway."

"Tell her we'll see her at the crafts show this evening," Grandpa said. Simon was already heading across the yard, followed by Doggy. He decided to cut across a couple of pastures to save time. Halfway across the first field, Simon was attacked by a horsefly. It kept buzzing around his head like an electron around its nucleus. He swatted at the pest with the broom. "Get out of here, you stupid fly!" he said. "*Fly?*" Simon put the broomstick between his legs and gripped it with both hands. Doggy hadn't transformed yet, so he probably wouldn't, or couldn't, say anything against it. Simon jumped hard off the ground. "Fly!" he said. "Fly!" He shouted several times, jumping harder and harder. But the broom seemed to have its mind set on nothing more than sweeping.

The boy stopped to catch his breath. "Focus," he thought, "don't think, just focus." He took a couple of deep breaths. His mind calmed down, and he pictured himself flying on the broom. Again, Simon jumped and shouted, "Fly!" He bounced up and forward a few feet, feeling much lighter than before. Encouraged, he tried again and bounced across the field uncontrollably. On the last bounce, Simon rose into the air at least ten or twelve feet.

The broom zigzagged around the pasture and buzzed low over several cows. Simon held on tight, but he slipped upside down and lost grip with his legs. The broom circled over Doggy with the boy dangling by his hands. Doggy barked once, his tail pointing at the broom.

Simon felt his feet hit the ground, and then his butt, as he fell, tumbled, and rolled in the grass. He stopped with his face an inch from a fresh cow patty. "I kind of remember flying on a broom in Magic School — but it stinks." Simon lifted his face away from the cow patty. "I prefer a skateboard." Doggy listened in silence, frowning.

Miss Beetle didn't answer. As much as he admired the friendly bus driver, Simon was glad she wasn't home. He left the broom beside the door and took off up the road. He and Doggy soon cut off onto a path in the woods. The young initiate wanted to try to transform his clothes into the War- rior Wizard robe, but the master barked. Simon supposed it was a warning to wait.

He and Doggy reached the clearing under the sprawling oak tree without running into banana spiders. Simon pulled out his wand and tapped the Wanding Stone three times. The old rock lifted into the air and began to spin. Multi-col- ored sparks flew into the air as on the day before. At the same time, Simon felt himself go into a spin. When he came out of it, he and Master Dogbert were standing before the Wanding Lord.

Simon and Dogbert knelt together. "Master, we have arrived," both said.

"Rise, Warrior Wizards," said the Wanding Lord. Back on his feet, Simon felt strong and confident in his Warrior Wiz- ard robe. "What have you to report, Simon Peppercorn?"

"I dreamed I was in Magic School. I mean — I thought I was dreaming. I remembered that I was learning magic, and I could do the spells. I don't know if I remember them all, but I remember that I remember," Simon said, excited. "But, maybe I'm dreaming now."

"The dreaming is over, Simon," said the Wanding Lord. "Your Awakening is final. Your magical memory is opening well — things will come to you, if you trust your intuition. Are you confident now with Transformation spells?"

"Yes," Simon said uncertainly.

The Wanding Lord indicated the dead tree stump. "Demonstrate, please."

Simon hesitated and felt his nose. Then he pulled out his wand and pointed at the stump.

"TRANSFORMUS ROSE BUSH!" he spelled.

"Just like Grandma's!" Dogbert said gleefully. He skipped over to the thorny bush that replaced the dead tree stump and sniffed one of the abundant pink blooms.

"Marvelous! Marvelous!" said the Wanding Lord. "You shall now demonstrate your control of Wandfire."

Simon pointed his wand upward and pictured a lightning bolt shooting out of it. He let go of the image. A long, bright bolt beamed into the sky and faded slowly. Simon felt the burning sensation in his chest again and a warmth that spread to every part of his body.

"Marvelous! Marvelous, indeed!" said the Wanding Lord. "Repeat the demonstration." Simon did exactly what he had done before with his wand. As the lightning bolt reached its maximum height, the Wanding Lord raised his arm. A ray of electricity shot from his extended finger and joined into Simon's. The double streak of fiery light stretched far into the sky and emitted many branches.

This time, Simon was so energized he felt as if he'd been bathed in electricity. The Wanding Lord finally lowered his arm and the lightning dissipated. "Marvelous, Simon! Marvelous!" said the Wanding Lord. "Wandfire originates from the greatest source of power within certain wizards. When activated, it takes magical abilities to a higher level."

"You mean I've got a *fire* inside me?" Simon said.

"The burning point you feel inside, Simon — it is the Elfin Spark," said the Wanding Lord. "Its recent expressions signaled that it was illuminating and adding a new dimension to your Awakening."

"Yesterday was your twelfth birthday," Dogbert said, "a significant day for the Elfin Spark to illuminate; your magical memory was unblocked; you found the perfect oak twig for your wand; you finally summoned the Wanding Lord — and you produced Wandfire. Those events confirmed that the Elfin Spark in you is activating strongly."

"Can someone tell me what an Elfin Spark is?" Simon said.

"You would know had you listened to Master Todd more often," the Wanding Lord chuckled. "It is a mysterious and magical particle in the heart of every Light Elf."

"I'm an *elf*?" Simon broke in.

"Do not interrupt," said the Wanding Lord. "In the distant past, after the Magic Wars, the Light Elves used their greatest magic and created Elfin Space. Only they could exist there. But previously, elves and humans had wed in rare instances. Their children were born with the Elfin Spark — and their children's children, to some degree.

"It is not understood why, but in most of them the Elfin Spark lay dormant, or was very weak. However, in some cases it would come to shine brightly, even many generations removed from the elf ancestor. Then it would produce a witch or wizard with the potential to do great magic. As the elf blood thinned over time, the cases of such a powerful Elfin Spark have become extremely rare."

"Master Magus Wizards and higher Magicals can usually sense who has the Elfin Spark and its potential to illuminate," Dogbert said. "So we have been watching over you as you gravitated toward Magic Space, Simon. We knew you would make a great Warrior Wizard, and Master Todd's Magic Eye confirmed it."

"Now you know the source of your magic and your Wandfire," said the Wanding Lord. "You have finished Magic School, and your Awakening is sufficient. You have reached the stage at which your future is yours to decide. I ask you again — Simon Peppercorn — do you wish to transition to Magic Space and undertake the Venture to become a true Warrior Wizard?"

It all sounded so serious to Simon, now that the time had come, but he wanted to be in the world of magic more than anything. "I *must* go," he said. "I'm ready for the Venture. How do I get a sword?"

"That would be one of your tasks," said Dogbert. "After some adventures with only a wand, you must win a blade in combat. Usually, the bigger and badder the opponent, the better the sword. And believe me, it helps to have a good one in Magic Space."

"You're going with me. Aren't you going to help me?" Simon said, worried.

"Your master's role is to guide you," said the Wanding Lord, "but you must prove yourself with your wand and your wits. You may undertake tasks with your magicmates, but if your master has to seriously intervene, you will have to return to Hard Space." The incredible creature raised his little fist and gave Simon a stubby thumbs up. "May you feel the magic!" he said.

The glowing sparks of the Wanding Lord's aura flashed brightly and scattered in every direction. Simon shielded his eyes with his forearm. When he lowered his arm, the great turtle wizard was gone. The Wanding Stone was also missing. The ground where it had stood was level and covered with brown oak leaves. Simon felt that something in his life was passing away. If only he knew what was about to take its place!

Simon and Dogbert walked in silence on a narrow trail down to the river. Luckily, hardly anyone ever came to this part of the woods. Most were afraid of rattlesnakes, or simply too lazy to walk. The winding river was narrow and dark like tea. The Warrior Wizards sat on the bank at a spot that was special to Simon. He found it very peaceful and uplifting to be there. "When and how do we log in to Magic Space?" Simon asked.

"Soon — very soon," said Dogbert. "There are many methods of transition. Some use magical power collectors, such as pyramids, and transition with the energy waves. Others practice meditation. When their minds become clear of all but the thought of Magic Space, they cross over."

"I'm not a monk — and I don't live in Egypt," Simon said.

"Magical Techies have developed a way for new initiates," said Dogbert. "You'll learn it soon enough."

Dogbert had Simon practice some Transformation spells. The young wizard turned a floating stick into a sailing ship. It floated out of sight around a bend. A small log drifted by, and he transformed it into an otter. The frisky animal splashed and rolled in the water a couple of times, only to emerge a log again. Dogbert explained to Simon that his magic wasn't strong enough yet to keep something transformed for long. His awakened power and the effects of Magic Space would change that.

"If you are hit with a Transformation spell," Dogbert said, "repeat the Restore spell to yourself until you return to normal."

"I kind of remember that from Magic School," Simon said.

Dogbert transformed Simon into an alligator for practice. After half a minute, the gator popped back into Simon, though first he managed to frighten the master with a mouthful of sharp teeth and a loud reptilian hiss. Then Simon demonstrated a good levitation — high enough to see Waldo Burncastle on another trail across the river.

After reviewing other spells, Dogbert taught Simon a new one not taught in Magic School. "We usually only allow this in Magic Space, but it's best you learn it now," he said. "Mortis Simulatis is a very powerful paralyzing spell. However, it can leave you feeling as though you've killed someone."

Dogbert pointed out a squirrel sitting in a cypress tree. "Try it on him."

Simon took aim at the squirrel and spelled, "MORTIS SIMULATIS!" The frisky ball of fur stopped dead in its tracks and stiffened. Simon felt a cold, weird rush of power. "I see what you mean," he said. The little squirrel slowly came to and scampered higher up in the tree.

"Do not confuse it with Mortis Totalis," Dogbert said. "That is the Death Spell. It should be rarely used, and initiates are forbidden to use it at all. Even the worst Magicals refrain from it — for it is easily sensed by Master Warrior Wizards, who hunt them down."

Next, Dogbert had Simon demonstrate a few spells of the Magical Techies. Then he let him make up some. "Standard spells have extra power in their words," Dogbert explained. "Some come from an ancient, magical language. But remember that intention and focus give a spell most of its power."

The session ended with a practical lesson on Wandfire. "You are authorized by the Wanding Lord to use it," Dogbert said, "but only against the most evil Magicals and dangerous beings — and only to save life. Still, it is much too powerful as a weapon, unless well-controlled with a spell."

The master pointed his wand at a tall cypress stump across the river. "ELECTRO!" he spelled. A short lightning bolt shot from the wand and ignited the top of the stump.

Simon took aim at the same place. "ELECTRO!" An even longer bolt zipped out of his wand, but it branched out and incinerated the stump and all the brush around.

"AQUASTINGUIO!" Dogbert spelled. A stream of water jetted out of his wand and extinguished the brushfire. After a few more attempts, Simon was able to fire off a short, sharp bolt, much to Dogbert's satisfaction.

"Do you have an Elfin Spark?" Simon asked his master.

"Yes, but it didn't illuminate of its own. I had to kindle it over many, many years."

The Warrior Wizards left the peace of the lazy river and headed down the trail. "It's time to feed the chickens," Dogbert said. The boy was taken by surprise.

"Is that something a Warrior Wizard should have to do?" Simon said. He was hoping Sammie would have to take over that chore in his absence.

"Magicals have even greater responsibility toward their surroundings than Hard Heads," Dogbert said, "because of having much more power to affect them. And Warrior Wizards must perform their duties no matter how unimportant they seem. Why, as Doggy, I enjoy chasing sprites from the yard."

"What about my family? Am I supposed to just disappear?" Simon said.

"Your grandparents have known for years. They are aware that you will transition to Magic Space." Simon could just imagine the look on Sammie's face when she found out. She'd be jealous to know he had a magic wand. "It's like going to summer camp," Dogbert continued. "Except that you — *what was that?*" He pointed into the bushes where he had seen a heavy rustling.

"I think it was a coyote," Simon said. The big animal scampered heavily across the trail and into the thick bushes.

"That's no coyote – it's a wolf!" Dogbert said, concerned.

"There aren't any wolves down here," Simon said.

Dogbert gripped the hilt of his sword. "Keep moving. We need to —" The wolf bolted from the palmettos and leapt high at Dogbert. In mid-air, it transformed into a huge, hairy beast with a hideous head that was neither wolf, nor human, but somehow both. The monster was eight feet tall and had long, muscular arms instead of front legs. It growled ferociously, exposing two rows of enormous teeth and pointed fangs.

The creature crashed down on Dogbert before he could draw his sword. Simon froze in terror, but he pulled out his wand when the monster lowered its head toward Dogbert. "STUPIDUS!" he spelled.

The monster shivered all over and turned its ugly head toward Simon. It sprang off of Dogbert and onto the boy, knocking him to the ground. The beast bit Simon on the neck before he knew what hit him. Blood spurted from the holes. The wolf demon raised its head and licked its mouth. It flashed its fangs again and bent down for more.

"PROPELLO!" Dogbert spelled. He had his sword in hand and used it as a wand. The wolf beast flew ten feet into the air and hit the ground with a hard thud. It jumped up and lunged at Dogbert. The Warrior Wizard stood ready with his blade. He swung it with both hands as the powerful creature brought down its arm, tipped with dagger-like claws. The sword blade sliced into the tough muscle. The monster screamed in agonizing pain. Dogbert raised his sword again and swung for the wolfish head, but the beast ducked the blow and ran swiftly away through the palmettos.

Simon stood up with his hand over his neck. Blood seeped through his fingers — his robe was covered in stains. "Show me your wound," Dogbert said, rushing to Simon's side. He made an icky face when he saw the bite. The master put his hand on Simon's neck and mumbled a few words. The bleeding stopped immediately and the fang marks faded away. Dogbert pointed his wand at Simon's robe. "PURGO!" he spelled. The bloodstains disappeared.

"Awesome!" said Simon, though still visibly shocked. "What *was* that thing?"

"It was a wolfern — much worse than a werewolf — probably drawn to Hard Space by all the Wandfire," said Dogbert. "You've learned that evil beings slip in from Magic Space sometimes. Now you know what Warrior Wizards do. Anyway, everything has changed."

The pair walked swiftly through the woods. As Simon saw the road, he heard the roar of the monster again. It was joined by the howling and vicious growls of wolves — a lot of wolves. "*Run, Simon!*" Dogbert shouted. They took off as fast as they could, wands in hand. At the road, Simon looked over his shoulder. The ferocious pack was closing in on them, led by the wolfern.

Simon and Dogbert ran swiftly down the road, still in their robes. As they neared the house, Dogbert rushed to the lead. "Follow me!" They both leapt over the fence like hurdlers, the wolves close behind. Dogbert bolted head first into his doghouse by a big elm tree. Simon was much surprised, but he followed his master. Outside, the whole elm tree glowed brightly. Lightning shot out of the branches and filled the sky. Streaks of it arced downward, forming a cage of light around the house and yard.

Simon was surprised to see that he could stand inside

the little doghouse. It was quite spacious and furnished with a bed, a table, two chairs, and a flat panel TV. A poster of Mariah Carey was pinned to the wall, and strings of sausages and a couple of hams hung from the ceiling. Simon spotted a slice of his birthday cake sitting on the table. His amazement was shattered by the sound of the beasts screaming outside.

Dogbert tapped a wall with his wand and an opening appeared. "This way," he said. Simon followed — the hole in the wall closed behind him. He noticed that he had just entered his grandparents' bedroom through their old wardrobe.

Simon hardly noticed the strange objects that adorned the place. Dogbert grabbed him by the hand and pulled him into the hall and into Sammie's room just opposite. His sister was missing from her chair — another surprise. The computer was turned on, but Simon didn't notice the image of a small island on which were old stone buildings surrounded by high walls. Dogbert rushed to the monitor and touched the screen with the tip of his wand. "MAGIC SPACE!" he spelled.

Simon felt himself sucked into the monitor. He felt as if he was vapor swirling through a tornado of light. In the blink of an eye, his butt crashed hard onto the ground. As he regained his focus, he saw Dogbert standing nearby. Simon scrambled to his feet. Before he could open his mouth, five big men popped up from nowhere, surrounding him and his master. They all wore the same robe as he and Dogbert, and each held a long sword in his hand. "Master, we are at your command," said one of the men.

"Rise, Warrior Wizards," Dogbert answered with authority. "Go there from where I have come — prepared for battle." The men disappeared. Simon stood in awe, but his mind returned to the scene he had just escaped. Horrible wolves had just chased him from his home into a different world.

"My grandparents, my sister! We have to go back," he said.

"Don't worry, Simon. The Warrior Wizards are there already. And your home has always had magical protection. You have much more serious concerns at the moment."

"What do you mean?" Simon said.

"I healed the injury on your neck, but there is internal damage. You could become a werewolf."

Simon's eyes opened wide. He rubbed his face with both hands, as if checking for hair. Magic Space suddenly seemed to be very real. "Can't you heal that, too?" he asked, fearful.

"It is beyond my magic, but there are ways," said Dogbert. "The Philosopher's Stone could do it, but finding the real thing would be extremely difficult — maybe impossible. The Elfin Spark could heal you if you were master of all its power, but that takes years."

"How much time do I have?" Simon asked. He worried that his dream of being a wizard was going to end up a nightmare.

"You should know how it is with werewolves," Dogbert said. "You have until midnight of the next full moon — thirteen days — the last day of your Venture, in fact."

"*Thirteen days!*" Simon said. His eyes opened even wider than before. "Then there's nothing we can do, is there? I'm going to turn into a *werewolf*. I guess you'll have to sic a bunch of Warrior Wizards on me."

"Calm down, Simon — I can think of one thing," said Dogbert. "In the distant town of Krakow, a large crystal lies under the castle hill."

"What good's another rock?" Simon said.

"Listen to me," said Dogbert. "It was brought there hundreds of years ago from a Himalayan kingdom. The magical stone is a great collector and radiator of earth energy — a chakra. Just to touch it would bring instant healing."

"What are we waiting for? Let's go there now." Simon rubbed his face again, certain it was getting fuzzy.

"It's not that simple," said Dogbert. "You are very special to me, Simon, perhaps more than you know, but I cannot abandon my other obligations." Simon frowned.

"I can get you to Krakow very quickly, and perhaps to the chakra, but that level of aid would mean an end to your Venture. You would have to return to Hard Space — healed, but with very limited use of magic. You must understand that."

Simon's heart sank. He couldn't imagine not being a wizard and having adventures in Magic Space — he just *had* to become a Warrior Wizard. "But, I have thirteen days ahead of me," he said. "That's plenty of time to do magic stuff and get a sword. I can complete my Venture, *and* go to Krakow to the chakra."

"That could be very dangerous," said Dogbert. "If you

were wounded, or slowed upon the way, the results would be disastrous."

"I just *can't* go back to Hard Space," Simon said. "I *have* to continue."

"The choice is yours, Simon," Dogbert said with a smile. "Your decision is the one a Warrior Wizard would make." Simon felt a rush of pride.

"The Venture can take you in many directions, but I will do all I can to keep it directed toward Krakow."

Just then, a woman's scream rang from above the cliff and around the hill. It was at that moment that Simon actually noticed his surroundings. He was standing near a rocky sea shore at the bottom of a hill. When he looked up to see where the scream came from, he saw a high stone wall with towers and tall stone buildings inside. "You'll find that adventures are never far away in Magic Space," said Dogbert.

Master and initiate climbed up the craggy hillside and came upon a pretty, young woman sitting by a well. She was with an older woman, who was dressed in black. Their gowns looked like old costumes to Simon. Both of the ladies were sobbing. "What causes you such grief?" Dogbert asked.

"It is one of the Giants of Geen," said the younger woman. "Last night he killed this lady's mistress, and just now he has murdered the brave knight to whom I was betrothed. My beloved came to free our country from the terrible giant who has terrorized us for seven years." Simon was only slightly amazed by the medieval scene and talk of a giant. After the wolfern attack, he was prepared for anything.

"That horrible giant has more treasure than all the nobles in Magic Space," the lady continued. "Even now he guards a great pile of precious stones. Yet — he holds several maidens for ransom."

"We shall challenge him then," said Dogbert.

The women looked at the puny Warrior Wizard as if he was crazy. "Five hundred brave knights have died in such vain attempt," the old woman cried. "But you will find him around the hill preparing a fire to roast your innards." Simon didn't care to have his innards roasted, but he knew now that his Venture had begun in earnest.

The rocks and boulders made climbing difficult, but the giant finally came within view. He was crouching by a small fire. The hostage maidens were tied with ropes and were sitting against a huge pile of glimmering gemstones.

"Hey, you oversized freak," Dogbert said. "I have come to put an end to your treachery." Simon was happy to see that his Venture would begin with a demonstration from the master. "I challenge you to do battle with Simon Peppercorn — Warrior Wizard!"

Simon felt as if he had just swallowed one of the large boulders on the hillside with which the giant would probably smash him, anyway. The giant stood erect — he towered over twenty feet into the air. His body was massive and strong, his face scarred and rough. He reached down and grabbed up a huge iron club.

"You distract him and I'll untie the ladies," Dogbert said. "After all — it's your fight." He popped out of view as the great club came swiping through the air.

Simon ducked just in time. He dived to the ground and rolled to avoid the next swing. Jumping to his feet, he pulled out his wand and pointed it at the giant. "STUPIDUS!" he shouted. The overgrown man shivered all over and then laughed loudly as he swung and missed again.

"That tickled. I too big for little magic," the giant roared.

Simon tried to think up a bigger spell. He remembered his practice session with Dogbert by the river. "MORTIS SIMULATIS!" The giant froze for several seconds before advancing toward the pesky little wizard. Simon fell back against a large boulder — the big stone gave him an idea.

"MAGNETO STONES!" He pointed his wand at several smaller boulders. As the iron club swept low again, the magnetized rocks flew up and stuck to it with a loud clang. The heavy weapon, with stones attached, continued its swing over the giant's head and hung suspended there. "DEMAGNETO!" Simon spelled. The small boulders fell on the giant's head and shoulders. One dropped on his foot — he released his club and grabbed his throbbing toes.

Simon pointed his wand at the club. "SCROLL UP!" he spelled. The heavy club rose over the giant's head, directed by the wand.

"PULSO GIANT!" Simon spelled again. The big iron bat hit the enormous head repeatedly. The angry giant, more confused than harmed by the blows, reached up and took hold of the weapon. He swung with all his might — the boulder Simon had just jumped behind crumbled to dust. The boy dashed behind another huge rock.

Dogbert, who was picking choice jewels from the treasure pile, called out, "If you got him off his feet, he couldn't swing at you."

Simon wasn't sure if he took the hint correctly, but he aimed at his opponent and spelled, "LEVITATO!" The befuddled giant rose about twenty feet into the air. Simon looked back at Dogbert for further instruction, but the Master Magus had gone back to pilfering the treasure.

The boy looked back to the giant again, who seemed to be defying gravity. At that moment the air beneath the giant's feet gave way and he fell. Simon jumped from behind his boulder. "TRANSFORMUS BOWLING BALL!" he spelled.

The giant's feet landed on the round, smooth stone and set it rolling down the hill. The humongous dude danced wildly, teetered, waved his arms helplessly, and rode the ball down on his tiptoes. Halfway down the hill, the ball hit a large stone and ended the giant's balancing act. The pitiful fellow flew into the air and hit the ground rolling. He flipped and bounced and rolled until he came to a stop on the rocky beach below.

As the giant lay sprawled on the ground, three knights in full armor galloped up on mighty horses. One of them dismounted, drew a long sword, and raised it over his head with both hands. Simon gasped in disbelief when the sword came down. "That would be King Arthur," said Dogbert, now standing beside Simon.

CHAPTER FOUR

GOOFANG

"*King Arthur? Incredible!*" Simon said. "But it wasn't *fair*. I don't care *who* he was. How could he *do* that?"

"It's your word against his. He'll have a different version of the story," Dogbert said. Simon and Dogbert winded their way through the single narrow lane that snaked up the hill. "There are many versions of Magic Space, Simon. In a sense, every Magical has his own."

Simon didn't pay much attention. He was observing the incredible medieval sights. The small shops had signs hung out indicating their products and services: armor & weapons, magical supplies, palmistry, self-playing musical instruments, wands and staffs, healing and spell reversal, flying brooms and carpets, bloodletting, magical pets. There were also normal establishments: a bakery, apothecary, cobbler's shop, pots and pans.

The people crowding the passage were dressed in robes, gowns, and cloaks of brightly colored cloth, though some were dirty and threadbare. A small jester in red tights, purple shirt, and a green hat with bells on it, ran into Simon and almost knocked him over. "Watch out, fool!" said the jester as he scuttled away.

A tall knight in a suit of armor creaked and squeaked out of an armory shop, his helmet under one arm. The armor maker bustled around the knight with an oil can, squirting at the metallic joints. The jester came running by again. He smacked straight into the knight and toppled him to the ground with an awful ring of metal.

"Cursed scoundrel!" screamed the knight. Simon rushed over and helped him lumber slowly to his feet. "I'll thrash that witless fool with a dragonskin whip when I get back to court," bellowed the knight.

Simon handed the heavy helmet to the angry warrior, who didn't even seem to notice him. As he walked away, the knight called out, "You, there — come back here! Thought you were my squire, but I suppose he ran off to chat up the maiden at the cauldron shop. I'll thrash him with a dragon-skin whip when I get hold of him."

Simon slowly approached the knight, hoping he wouldn't be thrashed with a dragonskin whip. "With Master Dogbert, I see. You'll make a fine Warrior Wizard, you will. I've known plenty of them, and the best come from Dogbert Ambrosius."

"Thank you, sir," Simon said modestly. Over his shoulder, he saw Dogbert bowing deeply. The knight was one of those who had accompanied King Arthur. However, he didn't acknowledge having seen Simon on the hillside.

"Come, Sir Bedivere, I'll need to hammer out some of those dents," said the armorer.

Farther on, Dogbert stopped in front of a sign that read: *MORDECHAI'S TREASURE EXCHANGE — PRECIOUS STONES*

AND METALS, GOLDEN AND SILVER SHINIES. "I have some business with an old acquaintance," said Dogbert. "You look around, but don't go far. And keep an eye out for your magicmates."

Simon still marveled at the sights as he wandered up the hill. In spite of the Magicals, knights, fancy ladies, and noble gentlemen, he was surprised at the number of beggars that tugged on his robe and cried for a handout. He had thought everyone in Magic Space would be rich and happy. In fact, he didn't have a single cent himself to give the miserable folk.

A withered old woman in a black robe with the hood pulled over her head stood in the entrance to a shaded alley. She beckoned Simon to come to her. Simon felt bad about having nothing to put in the large, wooden bowl the woman held in her arms. She smiled warmly at him, anyway. "Come, young one. Look deeply and see what lies ahead."

Intrigued, Simon peered into the bowl. It was filled with water. The liquid began to swirl, and Simon felt as if his head was spinning. When the water stilled, Simon saw an image of himself standing in a cave. Sunbeams poured in through the large entrance, lighting up huge piles of treasure.

Simon looked around the cave and saw a blond girl sitting on a splendid chair. The maiden began playing on a golden harp. Simon stepped closer to watch her play. Just a step away, he noticed that the girl had a beautiful face. Then the music intensified, and the girl's face began to change form. Simon saw an ugly old hag sitting in front of him. He wanted to run away, but his feet were as heavy as lead. His eyes felt even heavier. Simon thought he would soon collapse on the floor of the cold, dank cave. Then he heard a voice over the deafening harp.

"EVAPORATO!"

Simon's eyes opened wide as the water in the bowl disappeared in a cloudy vapor. The old woman and the bowl also turned into mist and vanished. Morgan was standing at Simon's side, holding a wand. She was dressed in a robe similar to his, but cut differently and somewhat whiter in shade. "*Morgan*! Where did you come from?"

The girl's eyes became wide and glassy. "I am Morgana," she said in an eerie voice.

"Morgan, what are you —"

"I am Morgana!" she repeated firmly.

"Okay, then — Morgana. How long have you been here?"

"You're so stupid, Simon Peppercorn," Morgana said in her normal voice. "You wouldn't trust a scryer if you had paid attention in Magic School."

Simon felt stupid, of course. "Well — thanks, anyway," he said, wanting to change the subject. "At least I know I can beat a giant. I had to fight one called the Giant of Geen."

"Most giants are too dull to use magic. What could be so hard about fighting one?" Morgana said. Simon ignored the slight. He recounted his battle as they moved up the narrow street, hoping to make some kind of impression. The young witch, though, seemed more interested in the sights they passed.

"You should have seen how high I levitated him," Simon rattled. "When his feet hit that boulder, he —"

"Master Spurlock!" Morgana said. Simon looked in surprise. Master Pippin Spurlock, their Charms and Enchantments teacher, was standing in front of a magical pets shop, as if just hanging out. Unlike Dogbert, he was tall and had lots of hair. In fact, he had a very lion-like appearance. Very powerful in magic, he was a Master Magus, but not a Warrior Wizard. His robe, therefore, was sky blue.

A small, squirmy monkey sat on Master Spurlock's shoulder. "Just transitioning an initiate to Magic Space," he said. The hyper monkey leapt onto Simon's head and gripped tightly with its hands and feet — Master Spurlock disappeared. Simon reached for the monkey, which now tugged hard on his hair, but he couldn't pry it loose. He bumped into many people as he struggled up the passage, pulling at the furry hitchhiker.

Simon almost fell in front of a rickety cart full of potatoes pulled by a hunchback. He weaved among the crowd, many of whom stopped to watch the amusing sight. A troupe of Arab merchants carrying baskets of fruit, fragrant spices, and rolls of cloth, crowded into the street from an alley.

A girl dressed in a silk robe and a veil over her eyes squeezed past Simon with a large bunch of bananas balanced on her head. The impish monkey grabbed a banana in one hand and peeled it with his teeth. His other hand kept pulling hard on Simon's ear. As boy and monkey twisted through the last of the Arabs, the monkey tossed the banana skin away and wrapped its arm over Simon's eyes. Simon grabbed the critter's tail, but he still couldn't pull it off.

Blinded by the furry arm, Simon bumped into Sir Bedivere, who happened to be coming down the way, flailing his squire with a dragonskin whip. The bungling knight stepped on the banana peel and fell with a terrific crash, banging up his armor. Simon spun around several times, pulling at the monkey's tail with renewed effort. Finally, the tiny ape's hands and feet lost their grip. Simon slung the pest around by the tail and threw it to the ground.

Arthur Sunshine rose from the spot where the monkey had hit, rubbing his butt with both hands. Simon's blood boiled with rage when he saw Arthur. He pulled his wand and aimed at the Shape Shifter. "SCROLL UP!" he spelled. Arthur rose quickly into the air until Simon stopped moving his wand. Simon swirled the wand and Arthur flipped upside down in the air. "SCROLL DOWN!" Simon spelled. He zigzagged his wand toward the ground.

Arthur fell with the movement of Simon's wand. He hit the ground hard, shook his head, and then sprang to his feet, shape-shifted into a spotted leopard. The vicious cat flashed its fangs inches from Simon's face. The young Warrior Wizard stepped back and raised his wand. At that moment Dogbert and Morgana pushed through the crowd.

Dogbert pointed his wand at Arthur. "RESTORE!" he spelled. Arthur popped back into human form. The master led his young initiates away from the crowd. "If you are going to fight among yourselves, you will be cast back to Hard Space and have your magical powers taken away forever!" he said angrily. "Magic Space is filled with wonders, but you are on a *Venture*, and many dangers abound. You are sworn to protect and assist each other — not squabble like silly pixies. Now shake hands and be done with it."

Simon took Arthur's hand and gave it a firm squeeze. It felt like a monkey's paw. As the group wound back down the hill in silence, Simon felt ashamed that he had let his master down. It was still strange to him how their roles had changed. But at least Dogbert didn't make him fetch sticks, or demand he lie down and roll over.

The mood lightened when the company stopped at a food stall and Dogbert treated his young initiates to large, fluffy omelets made from eggs the size and shape of footballs. They also ate delicious fruit pies, but no one could recognize the fruit with which they were made.

Best of all was a stop at the Magic Space IceCreamery. No one worked inside except an old witch, who sat by the door to collect money. Instead, golden scoops hovered over large cauldrons filled with unusual flavors. They flung the delicious ice cream into crispy cones that floated elusively around the room. Simon grabbed a cone out of the air and was served a large ball of Raspberry Rush. The frozen treat was warm when it touched his mouth, but it gave him the worst brain freeze of his life! Elanor got a scoop from the cauldron labeled *I SCREAM*. When she took a lick, it shrieked like a siren. The little witch had to gulp down the whole multi-flavored glob to shut it up. The magicmates finally got their fill of thrills and flavors and left the tasty shop. However, Arthur tried to sneak out without paying and was battered over the head by several angry scoops.

At a shop called Potions and Magical Medicaments, Dogbert bought four small, silver flasks and gave one to each of the youngsters. "It's Japper Juice — made from japper berries," Dogbert said. "Take no more than a tiny sip, and only when you are very tired. It's the energy drink of Magic Space, but only Magicals are permitted to consume it. You may try a bit now, but just wet the tip of your tongue."

Simon was surprised at how pepped up he felt. Even Morgana seemed a little spunkier than usual. As they passed through the gates of the town, Dogbert pulled three leather pouches from his robe and handed them around. "Here you are, a little spending money — compliments of Simon. Sometimes fighting a giant makes a little cents. No dollars, just cents — get it?" he chuckled. Nobody got it, but Simon glanced at Morgana to see her reaction. She turned her head away.

The three magicmates opened their pouches and pulled out brilliant gold and silver coins in two sizes. *MAGIC SPACE* was stamped on one side of them around the image of a unicorn. The other side had the words *GOLDEN SHINY* or *SILVER SHINY* imprinted on it. "Golden and silver shinies," Dogbert said, "the currency of Magic Space. The smaller ones are half shinies. Four silver shinies equal one golden shiny." The young Magicals were delighted by the flashy money. But Simon's thoughts were elsewhere. He couldn't help wondering about the price he would pay if his Venture should fail.

At the foot of the hill, a narrow strip of sand stretched toward the forest in the distance. "We must pass quickly," Dogbert said. "The tide's coming in, and soon the mount will be cut off completely from the mainland."

Simon, Arthur, and Morgana turned their heads back to view the magnificent hill — the Mount of St. Michael — with its walls, towers, tiled roofs, and a beautiful glow that formed a halo around the mount. From the point where they now stood, they could see a huge flag waving over the hill. It was made up of a white unicorn in a blazing sun on a purple background.

As Simon turned for a last look, his feet sank heavily into the boggy sand. He struggled to pull free, but his feet went deeper and deeper. Before he knew it, he was up to his waist in the quicksand. He freaked out, but was too ashamed to call out for help.

Simon was compelled to turn his head yet again toward the place where he defeated a giant on his own. The view gave him a sense of great peace. "LEVITATO!" he spelled. He felt himself slowly loosening from the grip of the greedy sand. After he rose to a foot above the ground, he noticed Morgana standing nearby, wand in hand.

"Poor Simon," Morgana said in a strangely sweet tone. She reached over and took him by the hand and pulled him a few feet away. She tapped him on the head with her wand. Simon's feet dropped to the ground. He and Morgana walked toward the others in silence.

Seeing that Simon was wet and sandy, Dogbert pointed his wand at him. "PURGO!" he spelled. The robe became instantly clean and dry, and Simon felt as if he had just had a hot shower. "We must march on," said Dogbert. "We'll make camp in the forest."

Some of the trees looked rather familiar, but the leaves were more colorful. Some were filled with fragrant blooms — others with unusual fruits. The warm light that filtered from overhead gave everything a vibrant glow. The air was unusually crisp and sparkly.

A band of heavily armed knights on spirited steeds passed the Magicals on the trail. They wore white tunics emblazoned with a red cross. Simon recognized them immediately as Templars — he could hardly contain his excitement. Their leader stopped to secretly confer with Dogbert. The master magus addressed him as Sir Richard.

Later, a small herd of satyrs, creatures with the body of a goat, but head and torso of a person, crossed the trail in front of the company. They nodded politely and disappeared into the forest. Some of their group were playing a soft, entrancing tune on small, wooden flutes.

Other fantastic creatures flew by or scampered around the new arrivals. But not all were cute and cuddly. A flock of winged animals swooped down from the treetops and circled just over the heads of the Magicals. "*Cattoflies!*" said Morgana, pulling her wand. The creatures were as large as raccoons. They were bright green and had long, bushy, red tails and greenish, transparent wings similar to those of a dragonfly.

"They've got yellow stripes down their backs," Simon said, dodging the lashing whiskers of one.

"They're polecattoflies," Dogbert said as a purple mist filled the air.

"That smells worse than cattopillar gook tastes," Simon said, gagging. Dogbert waved his wand in the air and the purple haze disappeared, though the stench remained. A polecattofly dived at Arthur and flew upward with him wrapped in its whiskers.

"STUPIDUS!" Morgana spelled at Arthur's smelly captor.

Arthur fell about ten feet to the ground. The cattofly glided head first into a tree and dropped into some bushes. Simon hit one of the attackers with a Spazz Out spell. It shrieked loudly like an alley cat in a street fight, twitched violently in the air, and flew off erratically into the forest. Still on his hands and knees, Arthur shape shifted into a large, red dog. He ran around barking ferociously and snapped at the swarm of polecattoflies, which buzzed around just out of reach.

"Enough of this game," Dogbert finally said. He pointed his wand upward. "REPELLO POLECATTOFLIES!" The nasty creatures screeched loudly and flew out of sight. The magicmates gathered around their master — shaken.

"UGGHHH! You *stink!*" Arthur said to Simon. He had shifted back to human form.

"You're the one who stinks!" Simon said, holding his nose. "Too bad that polecattofly didn't get away with you."

"You *both* stink!" said Morgana, holding her nose, too. Simon and Arthur both looked at the girl with grimaces.

"You all stink!" said Dogbert. He pointed his wand at his initiates. "PURGO!" he spelled. Everyone let go of their noses and breathed deeply. The kids glared at their master. "I rather enjoy the aroma," he said with a grin.

The magicmates all pointed their wands at Dogbert. "PURGO!" they spelled together. The stench went completely away, and the few hairs on Dogbert's head fluffed up, as if freshly shampooed.

"So that's why you always ran from a bath," Simon said.

Dogbert blushed. "Come along," he said hurriedly. "We

need to cover more ground before it gets completely dark."

As evening fell, Dogbert led the company off the trail and stopped in a small clearing near a stream. "Isn't it dangerous here — with those polecattoflies around?" Arthur said.

"Shall I fly us to a Holiday Inn?" Dogbert asked.

"Oh, yeah, let's go!" Arthur said, excited.

"Not happening. Get used to it," Dogbert said. Simon looked at Morgana and rolled his eyes. He thought he detected a slight grin. "I'll hide us in a Druid's Fog. It'll make us invisible to most creatures," Dogbert continued. He waved his wand in a circle. A grayish blue cloud about twelve feet across formed over the company and then faded away. "We can see out, but no one can see in."

The magicmates looked doubtfully at Dogbert.

"Walk a few feet away, Simon. You can test it," Dogbert said. Simon walked slowly backwards. After a few steps, his friends disappeared. All he could see before him was the dim forest. He stretched his hands out in front and slowly inched forward.

"*Arrhhh!*" Simon shrieked. His arms had disappeared to the elbow! He stuck his foot forward and it disappeared inside the circle, too. Morgana suddenly jumped out of the Druid's Fog and scared the wits out of Simon. Arthur joined in the disappearing game, but after a while the youngsters tired of the play. Dogbert transformed the ground inside the campsite into a soft mattress. Morgana aimed her wand at the middle of the area.

"FLAMMAERO!" she spelled. A huge, logless fire popped up from nowhere, sending a great cloud of sparks into the air. It soon settled into a cozy campfire.

The master transformed some pieces of wood into a pitcher and four cups. He tapped the pitcher with his wand, and it disappeared. After a few seconds, there was a splash in the stream. A moment after that, the pitcher re-appeared in Dogbert's hand, full of water.

Everyone settled around the small fire and drank the delicious liquid. No one was really hungry after all the goodies they had eaten on the Mount of St. Michael. Arthur rolled over on his side, and the golden shinies in his pocket jingled. His eyes lit up immediately. "Can you transform something into gold? We never tried in Magic School."

"It takes very powerful magic to transform things permanently, especially something magical like gold," Dogbert said. "We call that Transfiguration. Very few wizards are able to do it. In fact, many have destroyed themselves with undesired transfigurations in the attempt."

Silver lights began to streak through the woods like shooting stars. Many of them seemed to bang into the trees and drop to the ground with a thud. The magicmates watched them in wonder. "Silver Dingbats," Dogbert said.

"Are they dangerous?" Simon asked.

"Only to themselves, unless one hits you accidentally." One of the dingbats hit a nearby tree and ricocheted into the camp in front of Morgana. The bright, silver glow faded to a dull, silvery blue. Dogbert touched the limp creature with the tip of his wand. The silver shine returned as the dingbat rose up on spindly legs, looking dazed and confused. Morgana picked it up and tossed it into the air. The silver dingbat flew away. It may have been the same one that smashed into a tree a few seconds later. Soon the clumsy creatures had flown off into the night, or knocked themselves out cold.

"Master Dogbert —" Morgana hesitated. "Have you always looked — have you always had — a canine appearance?"

"Have I always looked like a dog, you mean?" Dogbert said. "Oh, I was once handsome, indeed. But it is very difficult to learn higher magic, unless one has pure intentions and is free of selfish desires. That is nearly impossible in a normal human form — unless one has an illuminated Elfin Spark." Dogbert glanced over at Simon, but the boy was lying on his back, looking up into the stars. Morgana stood up and levitated several feet into a horizontal position. She crossed her hands on her chest and there she went to sleep — as Wicked Witch Hunters prefer.

Simon noticed that groups of the bright, twinkling stars formed shapes which moved across the sky. He was sure he saw the outline of a galloping bull drift by, chased by the starry shape of an archer with drawn bow. "Thank goodness, the moon isn't as fast as the stars," he thought as he drifted into a deep, deep sleep.

In the morning, Simon woke up before his magicmates and discovered that Dogbert was gone. With nothing else to do, he took the master's water pitcher down to the stream. He hoped he could catch a fish in it for breakfast, or at least bring back some of the refreshing water.

To Simon's delight, there were quite a few fish swimming in the stream, but none looked familiar to him. One variety, with green and yellow stripes, had *arms* that pulled them swiftly through the water. As Simon knelt with the pitcher, ready to scoop, he noticed that certain other fish were swimming backwards. "How stupid," he thought, "those'll be easy to catch." Indeed, as one of them swam by, he easily caught it in the pitcher.

Simon stepped back from the bank to get a close look at his catch. The pop-eyed little fish thrashed its tail in the water and raised its head above the surface. "Let me go! Please, let me go!" the scaly victim pleaded. Simon wasn't surprised to hear the fish talk. "Let me go — I'll grant you three wishes."

"Really? I don't believe you," Simon said.

"Well — not really," replied the fish. "But I would if I could. Is it a deal?"

"How's that a deal if I don't get anything out of it?" Simon said. "But, if I keep you I'll have some breakfast."

The terrified fish's eyes popped out even more. He sank beneath the surface for a breath of air and quickly came up again. "Could you eat someone you've had a conversation with?" asked the fish. "By the way, my name's Goofang. What's yours?"

"Simon Peppercorn," Simon answered automatically.

"There now!" said Goofang. "We've introduced ourselves. Surely you wouldn't eat a friend." He went down in the pitcher again for another gulp of air. Simon knew he'd been had.

"Okay — you can go," Simon said when Goofang resurfaced. "But first you have to tell me why you swim backwards."

The clever fish looked at Simon as if he was crazy. "Isn't

it obvious?" he said. "I want to see what's behind me. One can't be too careful, you know. It's easy to get eaten by a river sprite."

"But, whatever you see is in front of you — not behind you," Simon said.

"Oh, no. When you move in one direction, the other direction is behind you," Goofang said.

"Well, then," Simon reasoned, "if you see what's behind you — you don't see what's in front of you."

"Now *that's* ridiculous! How could I possibly not see what's in front of me?" argued Goofang. Simon was beginning to wish a river sprite had already eaten his captive.

Goofang submerged and splashed up again. "I suppose next you'll tell me you can see a hidebehind."

"A what?" Simon asked, wishing he hadn't.

"You noobies from Hard Space never know *anything*," Goofang said, with an air of superiority. "It's a vicious monster that hides behind its victim and eats it alive."

"I've never seen one of those," Simon said.

"*Of course, you haven't.* How could you see it, if it was hiding behind you?" said Goofang. "Hidebehinds are so quick they can turn faster than you can, so you *never* see them. They're *always* behind you."

"What if three of them attacked me and two friends? Wouldn't I see the one that attacked the friend in front of me?" Simon said intelligently — he hoped.

"I've never heard of *that* happening," said Goofang, "but if it did, you couldn't be sure it was a hidebehind, as it wouldn't be *behind* you."

Simon was too exhausted to continue. "Okay, you can go now. Just look out for a swimbehind." He emptied the pitcher into the water. The little fish took off downstream, frantically twisting to see if there was anything swimming behind it — or in front of it — you decide. Simon filled the pitcher with water, but he made sure there wasn't a fish inside.

Back at the camp, Simon found Arthur and Morgana sitting with Dogbert. The Druid's Fog had been lifted. "You didn't bring back anything to eat?" Simon asked the master.

"I've had more important things to attend to. We'll get something on the way."

"Why didn't you catch some fish while you were at the stream, stupid hick?" Arthur said over a loud rumble from his stomach. Simon ignored the remark. He wasn't about to recount his meeting with Goofang. "Can't you transform a stick into a hotdog?" Arthur asked, turning to Dogbert.

"I could, but you had just as well eat the stick. Its internal structure would still be that of wood," explained Dogbert. "You can all have a small sip of Japper Juice. It will quell your hunger for the time being — but just a drop."

Simon and Morgana obeyed their master, but Arthur took a big swig from his flask. Immediately, his eyes bugged out and his hair stood on end. He jumped up and down, flapping his arms wildly. "I was afraid of that — hold him down," Dogbert said.

Simon and Morgana jumped toward Arthur, but he shape shifted into a large falcon and flew rapidly into the air. Dogbert shape shifted into an eagle and took off in pursuit of the falcon. The two raptors flew in circles high above the ground. Arthur evaded Dogbert very well, but the master managed to pull out a couple of tail feathers.

Arthur spiraled down toward the stream and hit the water with a great splash. "Goofang probably thinks it's a swimbehind," Simon thought. After two seconds, Arthur leapt from the stream as a big, pink salmon — Dogbert hit the water as an otter.

Simon and Morgana ran down to the stream and watched the chase. Morgana saw the backward-swimming fish and turned toward Simon. "Don't ask," said Simon. She probably would have, anyway, but just then a sleek Siamese cat streaked by like a whirlwind, followed by a border collie.

The cat ran a couple of circles around a huge oak tree. On the third round, it ran into the gaping jaws of the dog. The collie trotted up to Simon and Morgana and dropped the heavily panting cat. The feline hit the ground and popped back into Arthur. He lay sprawled on the ground, trying to catch his breath, whereas the dog turned into Dogbert.

"You should've eaten the stick," Simon said with a wicked grin.

"If you disobey me one more time, you will be restricted to shape shifting into a *rat*, or a *skunk*!" Dogbert said. Simon wanted to comment, but decided against it, seeing that Dogbert was not in the mood for humor.

"Yes, Master," Arthur said humbly.

"You will be spending time without me," Dogbert said, "and bad things can happen. You don't need to make it worse by doing stupid things. Speaking of that, your fourth magicmate has transitioned alone and has found herself in trouble. We have to go to her right away."

"Can't we fly there?" Simon asked. He was really looking forward to hitting the air, after the broom and skateboard flights.

"No," said Dogbert. "I prefer to keep you on the ground, but there's a place to get some food along the way." He transformed the magicmates' wooden cups into canteens and filled them with spring water.

The master was true to his word. After following a new trail for about half an hour, the company came upon a small clearing. An old hag stood there behind a cauldron that hovered over a small fire. She was heaping huge portions of stew into wooden bowls. A group of stocky dwarves armed with battle axes, several witches and wizards, and a few knights in armor stood in line to be served. Others sat on giant mushroom stools, or on the grass, enjoying the aromatic food.

A small girl, no more than eight years old, stood beside the smiling hag, handing out bowls. She also took back dirty dishes from those who finished their meal. Every time the lass took a bowl in her tiny hand, she pointed a small wand at it and spelled, "PURGO!" Then she would place the clean dish on a pile.

The magicmates finally reached the cauldron. Arthur pushed ahead of the others and hurried off with his stew. Morgana was intrigued by the quiet, little girl, who seemed to be very proficient with her wand. "Is that your daughter?" Morgana asked the old woman.

The bent, wrinkled crone smiled, though rather sadly. "She's my mommy."

"*Your mommy?*" Morgana wondered if the woman had heard correctly.

"My mommy," repeated the woman. "We have been placed under a terrible curse by a powerful Wicked Witch. Mommy grows ever younger every day. And I get much older. Soon we will both be no more than magic dust blowing in the wind."

Morgana took her food and moved away silently. Simon was amazed, but equally hungry. He was afraid there wouldn't be any stew left for him, but to his surprise, when he peered into the cauldron — it was completely full!

"It's a cauldron of plenty; it never runs out, but we can change the fare," the tiny mother said to Simon with a wise smile. She tapped Simon's bowl with her wand. The delicious smell of the stew changed into another fragrance, equally delicious. The appearance changed also. Simon felt certain he was holding a bowl of his grandma's Irish stew. He joined his magicmates and quietly ate his food, watching Dogbert have a secret conference with the chief dwarf, Sir Bedivere, and three Warrior Wizards.

Later in the march the trail widened somewhat. For a while, the company encountered some of the same characters they had seen at the cauldron — or others like them. A number of Magicals flew overhead on brooms, or flying carpets. Soon, though, the trail was left by everyone but Dogbert and his initiates. The walk through the forest was tiring, in spite of the golden sunlight's uplifting sparkle. But the sweet serenity of the woods was about to give way to a forest of a different sort.

SWANWHITE

The company emerged from the trees onto a vast plain. Many rows of standing stones stretched in slightly curving lines far into the distance. They ranged in size from three feet high to over twelve feet — some were even taller. Around seventy or eighty large stones stood in a circle in front of the long rows.

"What kind of magic could put all those stones there like that?" Simon finally uttered.

"Higher magic — Merlin's magic," said Dogbert.

"Merlin," Morgana whispered.

"The standing stones of Carnac," said Dogbert. "They were a legion of Roman soldiers. Merlin was too scared to fight, so he turned them to stone."

"There must be *thousands* of them!" said Arthur.

"Some of them were always stones," said Dogbert, "and some of *those* are enchanted sensors. They signal changes in the legionary stones — in case they ever reanimate. Now spread out and search for your naughty friend."

The magicmates fanned out among the magnificent stones, which had a life-like force about them. It wasn't long before Simon came upon a large, flat stone that stood like a four-foot-high table. Layla was lying sound asleep on top of it in her Wicked Witch Hunter robe. Simon shook her vigorously, but she barely stirred. He called for the others.

"Is she dead?" Arthur asked.

"Just exhausted," said Dogbert. "Simon — give her a drop of Japper Juice." Simon squeezed Layla's lips open and dropped in the liquid. Her big, dark eyes popped open, and she sat up straight.

"Welcome back, Layla," Simon said.

"I am Elanor!" the girl said in that eerie, snappy way that Morgana had changed her name. "It's about time you came looking for me," she said in her normal voice. "Where've them nasty little imps danced off to?"

"What are you talking about?" said Arthur.

"Gorics," said Dogbert.

"I don't care what you *call* them. I popped up here and a bunch of ugly little midgets made me dance with them all night long till I couldn't stand up no more. Then they just stood around me laughing like fools till I conked out."

"Gorics are a type of fairy who don't like their dancing interrupted. They are only two or three feet tall, but they're as strong as giants," said Dogbert. "You're lucky they didn't take your wand — *and* your robe."

"I'm sure they wouldn't want *that*," Morgana said. Elanor didn't catch what Morgana meant, but it was too late to respond once she did.

"You did something very dangerous and irresponsible," Dogbert said to Elanor. "You could have ended up in a much worse situation. Magic Space is no place for the undisciplined Magical." The master glanced at Arthur, who shifted about and dropped his gaze to the ground.

"I'm sorry, Master Dogbert. Please, let me stay! I got nervous waiting for Master Belltower. I was afraid he wouldn't come for me, and I just had to come to Magic Space. *Please!*" Elanor cried. Morgana rolled her eyes and crossed her arms.

"You will be permitted to stay," said Dogbert, "but another serious violation and it's back to Hard Space."

"Thank you, Master Dogbert — thank you so much," Elanor said humbly. This time Simon rolled *his* eyes. Elanor swung her legs from the stone table to jump down, but it began vibrating violently, and she was shaken off. The company noticed that many of the standing stones across the field were shaking and humming in a high pitch.

Dogbert pulled Elanor to her feet. "Run to the stone circle as fast as you can!" he shouted. The magicmates took off. They reached the circle of stones in a flash. Simon and his friends turned around to see all the stones in the field now shaking. Most of them were coming to life and transforming into Roman legionaries.

The soldiers emitted a loud battle cry. Dogbert raised his wand and outlined a ring inside the stone circle. "FIRE-WALL!" he spelled. A bluish electrical glow sparked around the stones and dissolved away. "That will make it almost impossible for enemies to get inside."

"*Almost?*" Arthur said.

He was answered by a rumbling roar from the woods surrounding the plain. Sir Bedivere and a large contingent of mounted knights charged from the forest with their lances leveled as the Romans advanced. Some of the horsemen carried the Magic Space flag. At least a hundred dwarves rushed onto the field from a different direction, swinging battle axes. The knights rode straight toward the larger soldiers, who had been larger stones — the dwarves engaged the smaller ones.

As the battle began, many Warrior Wizards and other mounted knights charged from different parts of the woods. Simon was delighted to see a dozen Templars ride onto the field. Some Warrior Wizards flew into the fray on broomstick, or magic carpet. Several flew in with no ride at all.

Every Roman struck by weapon or wand spell turned quickly back to stone. Dogbert ran from the stone circle and brought down every legionary he encountered with his sharp blade. He used the sword as a wand to blast Petrifio Totalus spells at the larger of the enemy — the enchantment worked well to petrify its victims.

Dogbert and his allies advanced down the field in heroic battle. The legionaries were slow and stiff after so many years as stone, but they struck down a number of dwarves and some of Sir Bedivere's knights. The magicmates strained to see the fighting in the distance, which became more difficult as the battle pushed farther away. Simon finally couldn't take it any longer. "I'm going to help Dogbert," he said.

"You better stay put," said Elanor. "You saw what kind of trouble I got in for not listening."

"He said we'd be safe here — I didn't hear anything about staying," Simon said.

"I ain't taking no chances. I'm staying here," said Elanor.
"I better stay here to protect her," Arthur said weakly.
Just then, a great flash of fire lit up the sky. The magicmates looked up to see three large dragons circling high overhead. Several Warrior Wizards flew up from the battlefield, as if to keep the dragons under watch. Suddenly, one of the fire-breathing beasts dived rapidly toward the field of combat. He scooped up an eight-foot-tall legionary in his powerful jaws and sped toward the sky again, swallowing his prey.

A Warrior Wizard in the air aimed his wand at the foot of the Roman soldier, which was about to be gulped down. "PETRIFIO TOTALUS!" spelled the wizard. The now high-flying dragon rose a couple more feet and then dropped like a bomb from the weight of the massive stone that lay in its belly.

The magicmates watched the beast crash heavily in the forest. A great fireball rose into the sky. Everyone on the battlefield looked up to view the blazing ball. As the skirmish resumed, the remaining two fire drakes flew off behind a large, dark cloud that lingered in the distance.

"Like I said — I better stay here," Arthur said.

Simon took off running. After a few steps, he heard a voice behind him. "Simon, wait up!" said Morgana.

The allies had been slowed by the larger and more numerous Romans when Simon and Morgana reached the battle. The young initiates stood behind stones and jumped out quickly to fire off Petrifio Totalus spells when it seemed safe enough. Soon some of the knights and dwarves had to regroup behind Simon and Morgana. A wounded Warrior Wizard was carried back by two sturdy dwarves. "Can we help him?" Morgana asked.

"Take him back to the stone circle," said one of the dwarves. "The energy there will sustain him until a Healer comes." The dwarves and knights rushed back to the fight.

"Help me carry him," Morgana said to Simon.

"You're a witch — use magic," Simon said. Then he ran off after the dwarves.

Morgana pointed her wand at the Warrior Wizard. "LEV-ITATO!" she spelled. The old wizard rose into the air flat on his back. The young witch steered him back to the stone circle with her wand.

Simon ran toward the battle, but he was nearly trampled by a large war horse. One of the Templars had retreated to charge with his lance. The knight spurred his steed and rushed at a twelve foot Roman. At the same time, Dogbert hit the legionary with a spell, unaware of the charging Templar. The wooden lance crashed into a pillar of stone and shat-tered. The knight catapulted off his horse and landed hard on the ground.

Simon ran to help. He eased off the warrior's helmet — it was Sir Richard, with whom Dogbert had spoken the day before. "How can I help you?" Simon asked. The battle was now raging all around.

"Swan Maidens," said Sir Richard.

"Swan Maidens?" Simon said. He thought the brave knight had gone batty.

"Swan Maidens," Sir Richard repeated. Simon noticed

that the Templar was gazing into the sky. He looked upward.
Groups of large, white birds were approaching. As they flew
lower, Simon could see that some of them were giant swans.
Each had a woman in light armor on its back — others were
not birds at all. They were women in capes made of white
feathers.

Simon counted nine groups of the Swan Maidens —
about nine in each. The women on the swans carried bows.
They released a hail of sharp arrows at the Roman soldiers
and greatly increased the number of standing stones. The
maidens in the flying capes landed on the battlefield and
joined the fray with long swords.

The Swan Maidens were slender and beautiful, but
Simon had never seen such fierce women. Their apparent
leader landed by Simon and Sir Richard, her cape flowing in
the breeze. She was at least six feet tall, with long, golden
hair hanging in one braid behind her head. "Swanwhite,"
said Sir Richard. "Far from your battle hall, are you not?"

"I have answered the call of my friend Dogbert Ambrosius. He has a nose for a good fight," said the Swan Maiden.

"Precisely why I am here. Now — if you'll assist me to
my feet." Swanwhite pulled the big knight off the ground as
if he was a swan feather.

"And who is this handsome young lad — your shield
bearer?" said Swanwhite. Simon turned red.

"I'm Simon Peppercorn, a Warrior Wizard," he said.

"Then let us join in battle together, wand bearer," Swanwhite said. She and Sir Richard drew their swords and
entered the fierce battle. Simon kept up, effective with his
wand.

The tide of the battle turned again as another company of knights and dozens of dwarves reinforced the allies. But some of the larger Romans, who had just finished transforming, also entered the fray. Simon saw Dogbert take one of them down with a single sword blow. Sir Bedivere defeated another.

Swanwhite and her Swan Maidens were equally effective with their blades and bows. The Amazon leader came face to face with one of the tallest giants on the field. "Observe, young Warrior Wizard, how the sword of a Swan Maiden yields greater power than the wand of a wizard. See the fall of the Manio Giant!" Swanwhite pointed her sword at the giant. "STUPIDUS!" she spelled — like a witch.

The great soldier stumbled backwards and nearly dropped his enormous sword. Swanwhite rushed him, swinging her blade with both hands. The giant regained his footing and blocked the sword with his shield. The two exchanged several shocking blows — Swanwhite was quick and elusive. The giant almost took her head off several times, but she was the better at defense, until —

An unfortunate dwarf, wounded by a Roman sword, fell at the brave woman's heels. She tripped backward over him and tumbled to the ground, losing grip of her sword. The Manio Giant exploded into ear-splitting laughter as he stood over Swanwhite. He drew back his sword. Simon nearly froze in fear for the heroic maiden. He pointed his wand at the gigantic soldier. "PETRIFIO TOTALUS!" he spelled. The giant twisted his upper body to face Simon as his legs turned to stone. He flailed about from the waist up, swinging his sword at the boy.

The giant screamed out at the top of his voice, and all the combatants within fifty yards stopped to watch.

Swanwhite sprang from the ground with her sword. She dodged a blow from the giant's weapon and thrust her own into his belly. No sooner had she withdrawn the blade than the Manio Giant became one large block of stone. "You will be a great wand wizard, Simon Peppercorn, but do not call yourself a true warrior until you have mastered the sword," said Swanwhite. She smiled broadly and flew back into the renewed battle.

Simon ran to catch up with the skirmish line, which had pushed back toward the last of the legionaries. He soon caught up with Dogbert. "You were supposed to stay in the stone circle," the master said firmly.

"You said it would be safe there — nothing about staying. Warrior Wizards are supposed to fight," Simon said.

"There's just some cleaning up to do now, and caring for the wounded," Dogbert said. Simon had already seen some Healer Witches in light green robes fly onto the battlefield.

"Is Swanwhite some kind of witch?" Simon asked.

"She's a Swan Maiden *and* a Warrior Witch — very rare," Dogbert said. "You will have the chance to..." Dogbert fell silent. A great, thunderous trembling rippled the ground. A few of the taller stones tumbled over. Simon saw the head of an enormous giant over the treetops. It seemed to him impossible for a person to be so tall. The massive man's head had to be sixty-five feet above the ground.

The giant had long, shaggy hair and a thick, bushy beard. He carried an uprooted pine tree over his shoulder for a club as he labored onto the battlefield, roaring like a lion. A formation of Swan Maidens on their great white birds flew above the goliath and shot arrows at him. The tiny barbs barely stung enough to get his attention.

Sir Bedivere and his knights charged the giant at full gallop. They chopped at his thick legs, but left nothing more than bloody scratches. The knights soon retreated, after the giant kicked a couple of their company into the branches of a tree.

Simon wished desperately that he could do something, but even Dogbert stood by — helpless. Then a white stallion galloped onto the field from the forest, weaving through the standing stones. A rider in gleaming white armor sat high upon the fantastic horse. There seemed to Simon to be a golden glow above the knight's head.

The warrior rode directly up to Dogbert and bowed his head. He drew his sword, and the master magus redrew his. "I was afraid you wouldn't make it," Dogbert said, bowing also. Simon's jaw dropped to his chin. At that moment the great giant advanced. Dogbert and the White Knight pointed their swords at him. Electrical bolts shot from both blades and met in the air before striking the giant in the chest. The huge man stood in his tracks, shaking and convulsing.

Simon remembered his wand initiation and practice by the river. He raised his wand and focused — a stream of Wandfire flashed out and struck where the other beam was sizzling away. The whole sky, already growing dim, lit up brightly. The great giant convulsed more violently. He dropped his club and stumbled about, swatting at the electrical bolts with both hands.

After a few seconds, the gargantuan shifted into slow motion. He finally stood tall, stiffened, and turned totally to stone. The Wandfire dissipated, as if knowing its job had been done. Everyone on the battlefield stared in silence at the petrified pillar.

The White Knight pointed his sword at the sixty-five foot column. A narrow electrical beam shot from it and hit the tower of stone with a mighty force. The enormous rock tilted slowly and broke into four large pieces as it hit the ground. The White Knight sheathed his sword. He reeled his horse around, nodded to Simon, and galloped off. Loud shouts and cheers rose up across the field. All those around him stared at Simon in awe.

The combatants drifted off the battlefield. Simon and Dogbert walked back to the stone circle. On the way, they saw a lot of dwarfish creatures popping up on top of the stones, dancing and singing in a strange language. "Elanor's friends — Gorics," Dogbert said. He spoke secretly with one of the merry creatures for a moment.

Inside the stone circle, Morgana, Elanor, and Arthur were busy helping Healer Witches and Wizards tend to the wounded. A crowd of warriors formed outside. A group of Swan Maidens was there with Swanwhite. Sir Bedivere and Sir Richard, each with several of their knights, sat upon their horses. A few exhausted dwarves sat in a circle around a small fire. Swan Maidens, Warrior Wizards, and Wicked Witch Hunters patrolled the air over the plain.

Most of the wizards and witches on the ground had their wands lit up with fireballs. Dogbert levitated to the top of one of the stones in the circle. "I spoke with Peric, prince of the Gorics," he said. Everyone listened attentively. "His people will re-align the stones to their liking. After all, it is their field. I thank you all for your bravery and sacrifice in this great battle today. A powerful force has been stopped that would have brought havoc to Magic Space. I learned that subtle vibrations were detected by the monitor stones. I suspected then that someone was probably breaking the complicated spell that kept the legionaries petrified."

"It must've been Merlin!" shouted Sir Bedivere. "It was he who cast the original spell." The mounted knights protested angrily against Merlin the Magician.

"It certainly wasn't Merlin. He is trapped in a curse of his own making from which he cannot escape," Dogbert said. "I suspect a powerful master of the Ars Notoria, the Dark Arts, is at work — one who desires to destroy the forces of Good in Magic Space for personal gain. I urge you all to remain alert for such greater acts of the Ars Notoria, and let us join forces whenever needed to protect Magic Space." The crowd applauded and shouted in favor of Dogbert's speech. "I will end by introducing to you my newest initiates. Step forward, magicmates."

Arthur, Elanor, Morgana, and Simon lined up outside the stone circle. Dogbert levitated Arthur into the air. "Arthur Sunshine — Shape Shifter." The master lowered Arthur and levitated the girls. "Elanor and Morgana — Wicked Witch Hunters." The young witches drifted to the ground and Simon rose into the air. "Simon Peppercorn — Warrior Wizard, vanquisher of the Giant of Geen on the Mount of St Michael."

Sir Bedivere squirmed uneasily in his saddle. Sir Richard dismounted and knelt before Simon as the boy's feet touched the ground. "You are a hero today and the bravest lad I have seen in combat," said Sir Richard. "I would present you my sword if your order allowed it," said the Templar.

Sir Richard withdrew and Peric, the Goric prince, came forward with a large sack slung over his shoulder. He dropped it on the ground before the magicmates. With a swish of his hand, the sack fell open. It was filled with glittering golden shinies. "You may each take a handful — even Magicals must pay their way in Magic Space," said the impish Goric.

Simon, Elanor, and Morgana each took a handful of coins and stuffed them in their robe pockets. Arthur reached in with both hands and pulled them out overflowing with the brilliant money. Peric looked at Arthur with a sly grin. He turned his gaze to Elanor. "You may return to celebrate with us any time you wish," he said with a bow. The other Gorics whistled and clapped, perched on top of their stones.

"Not till you learn hip hop!" Elanor said, cowering behind Simon.

Swanwhite strode up to Simon — she ignored his friends. "Wandfire is a very powerful force, Simon Peppercorn, though it may destroy as much within as it may without. Be pure of heart, and you will become master of wand and sword, but most importantly, of yourself." Simon felt jittery inside.

The Swan Maiden reached into a white, feathery bag and pulled out a cape — also of white feathers — like the one she wore. "Few men have been honored with the gift of a swan cape and the freedom of the air it imparts," said Swanwhite. She unfurled the sleeved cape and put it on Simon. The sleeves drooped far over his hands, and a foot of the hem dragged the ground.

Swanwhite placed her hands on Simon's shoulders. The cape quickly shrank to a perfect fit. She took Simon's hand in her own and raised his arm into the air. "With your permission, Master Magus," she said to Dogbert. The Master Magus Warrior Wizard nodded approval.

Simon suddenly felt himself lifted into the air beside Swanwhite. He thought his arm would be pulled completely off, but after a moment his whole body became as light as air. He was flying on his own! Swanwhite released Simon's hand, and they flew side by side, circling over the plain. Other Swan Maidens and Warrior Wizards flew behind in escort.

Simon moved his arms in different positions. With them outstretched in front of him, he could better control his direction. Stretched outward, they helped him turn and bank more easily. When he pressed them to his sides, his speed increased. This beat any other way of flying he could imagine.

Simon wanted to fly up into the stars and grab one, but Swanwhite took him by the hand again and guided him back to the ground. Morgana, Elanor, and Arthur stood with their mouths gaping. Swanwhite finally took notice of them. She reached into her swanbag and pulled out golden apples for each of the magicmates. She also tossed one to Dogbert. "These magic apples will nourish you as well as a king's table," said Swanwhite, "and even better, for they grow whole again after biting — and they taste like whatever food you imagine."

Arthur immediately bit a chunk out of his apple and chewed away. "*Cheeseburger!*" he said.

"*Navel orange!*" Elanor said, trying hers. Morgana took a bite from her apple, but didn't comment. Simon was too excited to eat. How could he think about food when he was just given such power to fly? The magicmates thanked Swan-white for the apples.

"I am sure we will meet again, Simon," said Swan-white. "May you feel the magic!" She gave him a thumbs up and kissed him on the forehead. Then she joined her warrior women and ascended into the evening sky. Simon watched until the formation disappeared — like one of the starry constellations that moved swiftly across the heavens.

"Who you crushing on now, Simon?" Elanor said. Simon remained silent, but Morgana gave Elanor such a piercing look that she backed up toward Dogbert.

Others came to compliment Simon and welcome the young initiates to Magic Space. A Healer Witch filled their flasks with Japper Juice and gave Elanor a flask of her own. Sir Bedivere would have greeted them merrily, but he tumbled off his horse with a great clang and lay on the ground cursing his squire. The boy was behind a large standing stone learning a dance step from some Gorics. Some of the host dispersed into the night — others made camp among the stones. All the wounded were healed well enough to join their mates in their camps.

Dogbert and his initiates were left alone to spend the night in the stone circle. The company dined on all their favorite foods from the magic apples — Simon finished with banana pudding. Morgana carefully started a small fire with her wand while Simon retold all the events of the battle. His magicmates were filled with awe when they heard about the Wandfire and the White Knight.

Later, Arthur filled Elanor in on everything that had happened from the Mount of Saint Michael on, though he made Simon's defeat of the Giant of Geen sound like an accident. To Simon's surprise, Morgana took up for him. She said that he was very brave to fight such a giant alone. When Arthur came to the part about Dogbert handing out pouches of golden and silver shinies, he reached into his robe pocket to give his treasure a jingle. "*Hey*! Somebody stole the gold that that little dude gave me," he said. All he found was the meager leather pouch. The others checked their pockets and found all their Goric coins.

Dogbert gave Elanor his canteen and the pouch of coins he had saved for her. "That's how the Gorics' magic works," he said. "If you take more than they offer, it disappears." Arthur sulked silently while his friends had a good laugh.

Dogbert made a loud sound that reminded Simon of Doggy when the pooch wanted a ham bone — Simon thought something serious must be up. "It does not seem to be a coincidence that Elanor was logged in here," Dogbert said. "She may have been spied on in Hard Space and known to be — well — impulsive." Elanor looked away from Dogbert, ashamed. "I believe she was drawn here to

Carnac as bait. The Wicked Wizard who broke Merlin's spell, as I suspect, probably wanted us here when the stones transformed."

"Why would he want to have his enemies here?" Morgana asked.

"To create a big diversion with his new army. But I don't think he expected to face such a force," said Dogbert.

"That still doesn't explain why he wanted *us* here," Simon said.

"If I am correct, he wanted *you*," said Dogbert. Simon suddenly felt as if his insides had turned to stone. His magicmates looked at him with concern. "Simon is endowed with the Elfin Spark and it is highly illuminated. That is why he has the gift of Wandfire." The magicmates now looked in astonishment.

"There's something you still haven't told us," Morgana finally said. Dogbert knew what was on her mind.

"There are very advanced wizards who believe that the Elfin Spark can be extracted from a beating heart. Then it could be harnessed for unlimited power and total mastery of the Ars Notoria."

"How can they get something out of a beating heart when it's still in a body?" Elanor asked. Morgana glared at her as if she was the most stupid witch in the world. "Oh," said Elanor.

Simon was glad that Dogbert didn't mention his wolfern bite. He didn't want to upset his magicmates, or frighten them with the thought of such a demon.

CHAPTER SIX

THE CASTLE WHERE TIME
STANDS STILL

High on a treeless mountain, surrounded by dark, ominous clouds, a crumbling castle sat heavily, hidden from the view of anyone passing in the desolate valley below. A winged dragon circled overhead — a sentinel against the silvery shine of twinkling stars up higher in the sky. The dragon's dank and dreary lair lay in a cavern deep beneath the castle, treasureless, for this was the type of drake that hired itself out for the flesh of its victims alone — the type for whom gold held no allure. The fire-breathing beast shared the thin air with black-robed wizards on broomsticks who, though tentative allies, were still to be distrusted.

The air inside the castle was no less suffocating than the sulfurous stench of the dragon's foul breath that surrounded the frigid fortress. The atmosphere, though, seemed suitable to the six horrid creatures in dusty black robes with hoods pulled low over their heads, who sat at a long, splintered table in the middle of a sparse, dimly lit room.

The figure at the end of the table was much larger than the others. His hood was pulled so low that only a shadow seemed to fill it. But his hands were placed on the table.

Paws, rather, they were covered with thick, coarse fur and tipped with long, sharp claws. The other five creatures had faces of a very wolfish nature, much like the fiend that bit Simon, but slightly more human and, at the same time, more vicious and sinister — Wolfern Wizards.

A decrepit old hag in the tattered black robe of a Wicked Witch stumbled from the feeble fire on the hearth to the table. An ancient iron kettle preceded the old woman in mid-air. It followed a path described by her finger. The kettle stopped just over a gold chalice sitting before the large beast at the end of the table. The old witch moved her finger and a thick, boiling liquid poured into the cup. As the chalice filled up, the hag twitched her finger upward, but the liquid continued to pour out — it overflowed onto the table.

The shadow-faced creature flung his hand toward the one tiny, dingy window in the room. The kettle flew across the air and smashed through the thin glass out into the night. A great stream of dragon fire flashed in the darkness. "*Witless fool!*" shouted the creature. He grabbed up the steaming chalice and drank down the bubbling contents. The old hag hobbled weakly away.

"I summoned you here to partake in the greatest spell-breaking Magic Space has ever seen," said the evil wizard, "and to have you perform the simple task of capturing a little boy."

"But, Master Bloyse, who would have thought that a mere Warrior Wizard like Dogbert Ambrosius could spoil such an ingenious plan?" said the dark figure nearest to the master.

"Don't be foolish, Battlefang. Dogbert Ambrosius is a very powerful master magus, and cousin to Merlin Ambrosius himself. He may have known secrets about the stones I didn't suspect," said Master Bloyse.

"But you are a greater wizard, Master," said another of the Wolfern Wizards. "Dogbert fell right into your trap."

"Don't try to flatter me, you idiot," Master Bloyse growled. "He was ready with a great army. He had to know something was in the making. Perhaps he had a spy in my inner circle."

"Impossible — certainly not us — we could never betray you — we are faithful servants," muttered the underlings.

"Is that why you didn't enter the battle and capture the boy?" said Master Bloyse. "Is that why you hid in a cloud?"

"But we explained, Master," said Battlefang. "The air was full of Warrior Wizards and Swan Maidens. And the boy hid within the fighting. It was impossible to get near him."

"Enough of this cowardly sniveling," said Master Bloyse. "A new strategy must be employed. We will wait until the boy is out from under the watchful eye of his master. He must be left alone on his Venture at times. You, Battlefang, have the honor of bringing him to me. The rest of you can create diversions to occupy Dogbert Ambrosius. Do not fail me, Battlefang. I *must* have the Elfin Spark! You *must* bring me Simon Peppercorn!"

Dogbert and his initiates traversed a narrow, winding trail through the light-filled forest. Simon hadn't slept much that night, though totally exhausted. A lot had run through his mind. He had fought together with an incredible knight using Wandfire. He had flown through the air with the incredible Swanwhite, and now he had a swancape and could fly without a stupid broom. As tired as he was, Simon felt uplifted by the fresh forest air and the sweet sound of multi-colored songbirds — his thoughts returned closer to the ground when he heard a voice.

"This is the old Elfin Trail," Dogbert said. "It was traveled by the Light Elves long before people arrived to these parts."

"Are we going to meet any of them? I want to learn some of their healing magic," Elanor said.

"You probably won't," said Dogbert.

"Didn't they go away after some big war?" Arthur asked.

"They went to Elfin Space," Morgana said coolly.

"Can Magicals go there?" Elanor pursued, ignoring Morgana.

"Some can — after many years of practicing magic," said Dogbert, "sometimes sooner, but very, very rarely."

Simon noticed that Morgana had lagged behind the others. He looked back down the trail to see her standing still, gazing into the woods. When he went back to see what was wrong, he spotted a milky white horse half hidden by the trees, its head to the ground. Simon stepped on a twig and the horse raised its head. It was then Simon noticed the long, silvery white horn extending from the animal's head.

"*Unicorn*," Morgana whispered. The fantastic creature turned its head toward the young Magicals. Simon and Morgana stood transfixed for a few moments until the unicorn turned away and vanished into the forest. Morgana beamed.

"Come on — we better catch up with the others," Simon said.

Dogbert was waiting with Arthur and Elanor by a bend in a narrow river.

"The marvels are endless," he said, as if he knew what the stragglers had just witnessed. The company continued along the trail by the river in silence. Three dwarves floated by on a river raft loaded with bulky sacks. A large boat soon followed, powered by unmanned oars. It was filled with many witches and wizards in variously colored robes, all laughing and singing, or doing magic tricks to amuse each other. The flag of Magic Space flapped lightly in the breeze.

A little farther along, the forest began to thin until the company came upon a clearing. A tall castle built of shiny white blocks stood by the river. It was surrounded by a moat on the other three sides. Twelve towers rose from the walls. The four on the corners were much taller than the others — Warrior Wizards kept lookout on all twelve. A large crystal pyramid floated in the air over the castle. "Wow! Whose castle is this?" Arthur asked.

"It is the Castle Where Time Stands Still," said Dogbert. "You have an appointment with the Keeper of Time. He likes to greet my new initiates. Afterwards, continue in the same direction on the trail. I will find you, but for now I have things to do elsewhere."

"What time is our appointment?" Simon asked.

"There is no time in the Castle Where Time Stands Still. You will be summoned." Without further word, Dogbert raised one hand into the air. "G2G!" he spelled. The master magus disappeared.

Time, or no time, the magicmates stood before the castle for what seemed like hours. None of them had a watch. They wondered if they should try to get in by magic. "Why don't you levitate to the roof and look for a way in?" Arthur suggested to Simon. Seeing a Warrior Wizard with a crossbow aimed in his direction, Simon thought better of the idea.

The deafening bark of a pack of hounds resonating from the forest finally broke the boredom. But only one large animal burst through the woods. It darted across the clearing. The ear-splitting yapping seemed to echo from the creature's belly. The thing was no dog, however. It had a vicious serpent's head, a body like a leopard's, the back haunches of a lion, and the feet of a deer.

The beast was soon followed by an armored knight on horseback. The knight galloped past the magicmates, but he halted suddenly and came back. "Sir Palomides, at your service, though not exactly," he said, lifting his visor.

Simon was the only one to answer. "Simon Peppercorn — Warrior Wizard. What do you mean — not exactly?"

"I am in pursuit of the Questing Beast, which you have just seen. But, alas, he shan't be caught. It is my fate to pursue him endlessly," said Sir Palomides.

"Won't you stop when you die?" asked Elanor, as only she would.

"Nothing dies forever in Magic Space," Sir Palomides said gravely. "I see you wait to enter the Castle Where Time Stands Still. If only I could have a moment of distraction from that *horrible* beast!" The weary knight let out a long sigh, closed his visor, and rode off into the woods.

"Let's go on. They probably forgot about us," Arthur said. But at that moment the drawbridge slowly lowered over the moat. A brilliant light radiated from the opening and nearly blinded the young Magicals. As their eyes got used to the glare, they saw a tall wizard at the entrance to the castle. He was dressed in a light blue robe and a long, pointed hat of the same color.

The old wizard had long, silvery white hair and a matching beard that flowed down his chest. He motioned for the magicmates to enter. As Simon crossed the drawbridge, he noticed that the wizard had a young, glowing face.

"Welcome to the Castle Where Time Stands Still. I am the Keeper of Time." The drawbridge closed again and the light inside intensified, though it was very soft and dream-like at the same time. The magicmates found themselves standing in an enormous hall with a ceiling so high they couldn't see the top.

A great gyroscope in the middle of the hall spun rapidly. Balls of light, with the appearance of planets, moons, stars, and even small galaxies, emanated from the gyroscope and revolved around the room. Some dissipated into nothingness — others flew around as if held by the gyroscope's gravity. The celestial objects looked solid, but they passed through the magicmates on their orbits.

Simon felt as if he was in the ceiling of a planetarium. He noticed some of the same constellations above him that he had seen in the sky while camping. They drifted by overhead at about the same speed they had when he lay watching them in the woods.

"What exactly do you do here?" Morgana asked, just as amazed as the others.

"We control time," said the Keeper. "Well, technically speaking, we control magic."

"How can you control magic?" Elanor asked. She tried to avoid a planet, but it passed right through her.

"Time vibrates through the Spaces," said the Keeper, "and magic piggybacks on it. You see how powerful magic is in Magic Space. But we manipulate it here so it won't be strong in Hard Space as it vibrates on."

"Why are there different Spaces, anyway?" Arthur asked. He reached out to grab a comet, but it passed through him.

"Did you sleep through Magic School, too?" the Keeper smiled. "Long ago, Hard Space and Magic Space were one, but after the Magic Wars, the Light Elves created Elfin Space for themselves. There was much less high magic in the Space they left behind. As technology advanced, magic declined — and so did belief in it. The unbelievers became more dependent on hard technology than magic. And as technology became more and more dangerous, the Magicals separated from the Hard Heads until two different Spaces evolved."

"But there is *some* magic in Hard Space, and Magicals, too," Morgana said. "And a lot of people do believe in magic."

The Keeper held up his hand, and a bubble-like sphere appeared before him. He stepped inside it, signaling the magicmates to join him. The sphere rose off the ground and floated through the vast space of the castle hall. "Sometimes a bit of powerful magic slips through. Most Hard Heads call that a miracle, but even most of those who witness such wonders soon convince themselves that it didn't really happen, or that it was a freak of nature."

"Then why not let in more? Maybe then they'd believe it," Arthur said. The globe traveled through a meteor shower and past a door with a sign that read: *MAGICAL TECHIE LAB — TOP SECRET, KEEP OUT!*

"Most Hard Heads would be too overwhelmed, easily manipulated. And Wicked Wizards and Witches from Magic Space couldn't be kept out. Hard Space would be destroyed in no time," said the Keeper.

"So that's why Magicals are brought here, or controlled in Hard Space?" Simon asked.

"Eactly. This way a balance is maintained. It's difficult enough fighting the Ars Notoria in Magic Space. If Hard Space was open to higher magic, it would be impossible to protect the Hard Heads, especially from themselves, if they had access to it."

The kids all gasped as the globe nearly collided with a wall. However, the big orb passed right through. The new room must have been much bigger than the castle itself. Zillions of small crystal balls were suspended in the air of the vast space. But they didn't float alone — hundreds of wizards drifted among the clear balls, or walked around on the floor, closely observing them.

Now and then, one of the little balls glowed brightly, and a wizard touched his wand to it. The tiny sphere then grew to the size of a grapefruit. The Keeper touched his wand to one. Simon gazed inside and noticed a baby, maybe a year old, inside a playpen. The giggly toddler was levitating about a foot in the air. "That's one way we know when magic is happening in Hard Space," said the Keeper.

The gentle wizard flicked his wand, and they were in another room. It was very similar, but with fewer and larger crystal balls. Some of those would glow bright green. When the Keeper enlarged one to the size of a basketball, Simon saw inside it a Mayan pyramid, in front of which stood a Wicked Witch holding a broom. The Keeper touched his wand to the ball. "BACKSPACE!" he spelled.

The old hag disappeared from the ball. The Keeper touched the orb again. This time the same witch was standing inside a dolmen of very large stones. Immediately, a trio of Wicked Witch Hunters popped up beside the bad witch. "They slip through once in a while," said the Keeper, "but you see that we react very quickly."

The Keeper took Simon by the hand and stepped out of the globe with him. "Excuse us for a moment," he said to the others. They walked through another wall, or it seemed to Simon that they did. He saw that they were in an old-fashioned room. A number of wizards were sitting at small, wooden tables. They were all bent over, working away at something.

"What are they doing?" Simon asked.

"Making watches," said the Keeper.

"*Watches*? What for?"

"Why, to tell time with," said the Keeper. "We have a top

secret deal with a company in Hard Space — best watches available! Our operatives in Hard Space need spending money, you know."

The Keeper stepped up to a rack of watches on the table of a Wizard Watchmaker who worked alone in a corner. He lifted one of the time pieces and handed it to Simon. There was no crystal on the watch — the face was a silver disk with gold marks for the minutes and hours. The hands were two thin, red lines. It didn't look special to Simon, especially the simple leather band.

The Keeper tapped the watch with the tip of his wand. The gold and red lines disappeared. "A present for you," he said. "In times of need, it can shield you from danger if you call upon it. It can also reflect spells back at those who cast them. Just remember about intention. In extreme need, it can be used to turn back time, but there are very serious consequences for that — so beware."

Simon looked at his reflection in the simple watch. "The Elfin Spark may hasten you to great magical powers, Simon, but it can also attract great danger," said the Keeper, "from inside and without. It is not the power one possesses that makes a great wizard, but how it is used."

They rejoined the magicmates in the globe and floated into another chamber. It seemed like being inside a big, white cloud. There was nothing in the space but nine throne-like chairs. Each rested on four small crystal pyramids and had a larger one hovering upside down over it. The chair in the middle was raised higher than the others. It had blue pyramids — the only ones with color.

"Seats of Knowledge," said the Keeper.

"What are they for?" Morgana asked.

"Young Magicals who spend a lot of time in Magic Space have to keep up with school," said the Keeper. "Math is math in any Space. But a Seat of Knowledge puts it in your head without any effort — a great invention of our Magical Techies."

"You mean you just sit there, and the chair does all the work for you?" Elanor said.

"That's all there is to it," said the Keeper.

Why is one of them higher than the others?" asked Morgana.

"We call that the Time Machine, but what it really does is makes a person age quickly. Sometimes it's better to be twenty than twelve, but it's not used often." The Keeper raised his hand, and the company was suddenly back by the huge gyroscope. Simon tried to duck Saturn, forgetting that it would just pass through him.

The Keeper of Time pointed at the entrance, and the drawbridge lowered. On the way out, the Keeper held Simon back. "Due to the Elfin Spark and the nature of your Venture, I will teach you a very secret and really cool spell," he said. "But you may use it only once, or I'm sure you'll get into big trouble."

"Is it a Magical Techie spell?" Simon asked.

Back at the drawbridge, the Keeper of Time put his hand on Simon's shoulder. "The power of good may not always triumph in Magic Space, or any of the Spaces. You have come along at an important time, Simon Peppercorn, for there is much for a Warrior Wizard to do." He gave the thumbs up. "May you feel the magic!"

CHAPTER SEVEN

LILIANA

The magicmates hiked in silence on the trail until they came upon a narrow path that led into the woods. In the lead, Morgana glimpsed something white cross the little path. "Let's go exploring," she said, heading off into the forest.

"We better not — Master Dogbert told us to keep to the Elfin Trail," Elanor said.

"Do what you want. I'm going," Morgana snapped.

Simon knew there was no sense in arguing with Morgana. "We'd better stick together," he said. "Come along, or wait here till we get back."

"There's safety in numbers — I'm going, too," Arthur said.

"If we get lost, it's all your fault, Simon Peppercorn! That girl's got you wrapped around her wand," said Elanor, falling in behind the others.

"You're crazy," said Simon. "I just want to keep us all together."

Elanor looked at Arthur and rolled her eyes. "You're too scared to say anything, Arthur. Why don't you just shape shift into a big chicken, because that's exactly what you are."

Simon noticed that Morgana was scanning both sides of the path.

"What're you looking for?" he asked, after a limb Morgana had pushed out of her way slapped him across the face.

"I saw something white. I thought it might be a..."

"GRRRRRHHH!" came a roar from the bushes. The magicmates cowered into a huddle against a big tree. Something big and heavy was crashing through the forest.

"It's going to eat us!" Elanor cried. "I said don't come this way." Simon was about to give the signal to run, but just then a large animal bounced onto the trail and towered over the magicmates. The odd creature had pink and silver stripes, but instead of fur, or smooth skin, it was covered with armor plating. It was similar to an elephant, though its ears were tiny. Its head was disproportionately small and narrowed into a floppy white snout, which now hung over Simon's head. The beast was finished off with a long, pointed white tail that swung in rhythm with the floppy snout.

"GRRRHHH!" the creature growled again, whipping its snout around. Simon and Morgana pulled their wands. Elanor huddled closer to Arthur, who was pleased, as he was doing his best to hide behind her.

"Get back," Simon shouted, "or I'll blast you to pieces!"

"Please, don't eat us!" Elanor pleaded, turning one eye toward the animal.

"Oh, good gracious — *eat you?*" said the creature. "Why, not at all. Imagine a Dillobeast eating *meat*!"

"Dillobeast?" Simon said, surprised.

"You expected maybe a gophergoat?" said the dillobeast.

"No, I just... a what? Oh, never mind," said Simon.

"What do you want then, if you're not going to eat us?"

said Elanor, shoving Arthur out of her way.

"I wanted to frighten you — that's all," said the dillobeast. "You look like noobies from Hard Space. We dillobeasts have to frighten you. That's what some of you do to us in Hard Space." He looked straight at Simon.

"You mean to say there are dillobeasts in Hard Space?" Arthur said.

"Most certainly. You just see us differently there, and most of you get a thrill from scaring the wits out of us," said the dillobeast, swinging his snout and tail in opposite directions. "That's why I frightened you just now."

Arthur became angry. *He* had certainly never frightened *anything* out of a dillobeast. He shape shifted into a large, black dog and barked ferociously at the creature. The poor thing's eyes widened in terror. It took off into the forest like an elephant scared by a mouse. Arthur shifted back to human with a self-satisfied grin on his face.

Morgana waved her wand at Arthur. "You shouldn't have done that!" she scolded. "You know we are not supposed to bother creatures that don't try to harm us." Arthur ducked behind Elanor again.

"Don't hide behind me, fool," Elanor said. "That's a mean witch!"

"He had no right to scare us like that. I was just getting even," Arthur said.

Morgana spun around silently and set off down the path again. This time the silence was tense, but soon, as was often the case, the enchanting tunes of unusual songbirds had everyone at ease. The magicmates stopped under a tree with red, heart-shaped leaves. Small, green birds with gold wings and silver breasts were perched on every limb. All had tiny arms extended from under their wings and held flutes of various lengths to their mouths. They played a beautiful melody together like a feathered ensemble.

The path soon led back to the river, though before long, it wound back into the woods and ended at a small hill in front of which stood a group of seven stones. Four of the stones were ten to fourteen feet high. The other three were four to six feet tall. All of them had a very human-like appearance — like unfinished sculptures.

"I hope those aren't Merlin's victims," Arthur said.

Morgana walked up to one of the taller pillars. She snapped off one of several hardened shafts that protruded from the rocky figure. "Mountain trolls," she said.

Mountain trolls?" Simon said, "in the middle of a flat forest?"

"Maybe they're wood trolls," said Elanor.

"Don't be stupid. Wood trolls don't turn to stone," Morgana said.

"Those look like arrows," Arthur added. When they all got closer to inspect the stones, a screaming growl erupted from behind the two largest stones, which were petrified into one.

"That better not be another stupid dillobeast," Elanor said.

Then a horrible looking man over seven feet tall jumped into the open. He swung his fists over his head and screamed even louder.

Simon pointed his wand at the troll, for that's what he was. "Shut up!" Simon shouted, without casting a spell. The troll immediately burst into tears — to the amazement of the magicmates.

"Dude — you're just like the cowardly lion," Elanor said.

"I am not l-lying," sniffled the troll, "but I am a c-coward." He fell to his knees and sobbed even harder. Simon and his friends looked at each other in disbelief, while a puddle of tears formed around the troll. The ugly fellow seemed to be quite young. He was broad and muscular, with stringy hair and dark, deep-set eyes.

Simon pointed his wand at a big leaf on a nearby tree. "TRANSFORMUS KLEENEX!" he spelled. The large, green leaf turned into a soft, white tissue. Simon pulled it from the tree and gave it to the troll. The big crybaby took the tissue and blew a huge glob into it. Simon transformed several more leaves and handed them to the troll. Those were soon blown to pieces, too. All the magic mates started transforming leaves, though Arthur's came out as sandpaper. Soon the poor fellow was able to speak through teary sniffles.

"What's your name?" Morgana asked.

"Fr-Fr-Fr," the troll stuttered.

"Fr Fr Fr? That's a funny name," Elanor said.

The troll burst into renewed sobs. Morgana gave Elanor an icy look.

"It's okay," Simon said. "Try again."

"Fr-Fr. Fr-Fr. Fr-Frollo," the poor troll finally muttered through a sheet of Arthur's sandpaper.

"What are you doing here? And why aren't you turned to

stone? It's broad daylight," Morgana said. Elanor shoved a handful of tissues into Frollo's hand — just in time. He balled his eyes out for a while and then blew another slimy wad into the paper. His nose now looked like a bright, red light bulb.

"I'm a m-m-mountain troll. B-but, I never c-could turn to st-stone. I tr-tried this morning, I swear. Wh-when I was l-little I rolled out of our c-cave in the middle of the d-day. But nothing hap-happened to me," Frollo said between sniffles.

"Who are these, umm, these stones? Were they trolls?" Simon asked awkwardly.

"My family," Frollo said. Everyone thought he would burst into tears, but just a few drops rolled down his cheeks. However, he rubbed another huge, greenish glob from his upper lip. Arthur held out another sheet of sandpaper, but Morgana slapped it from his hand.

"MAXIMIZE!" she spelled, super-sizing a tissue she held ready. Frollo took the sheet, but forgot to wipe his face.

"What happened to them?" Elanor asked.

"Goblins attacked us to take our gold. We were looking for a place to hide just before sunrise," said Frollo. The mag-icmates all looked around for goblins, frightened. "They came at us with swords, but my old ones beat them off with clubs. Then the goblins shot arrows, and the sun came up. Now they're stone dead," Frollo whimpered.

"Why didn't you get shot?" Arthur asked, stepping out of reach of Morgana.

"I told you I wasn't lying — I'm a coward — I ran away." More tears rolled down Frollo's face.

"I thought trolls don't talk so good," Elanor said from behind Simon.

"I had a teacher — a dwarf," Frollo said. "We dig gold and sell it to dwarves. It was easier for me to deal with them since I could go out in the day."

"Why are you here away from the hills?" Morgana asked.

"I was still a shame to my family. The other trolls thought I was a freak," Frollo said. "My mommy heard about a wizard who lives near the sea. She hoped he could heal me. My auntie and uncle came, too. Now look at what happened because of me." He burst into tears again. "And I c-can't even t-turn to st-stone," Frollo wailed.

Soon the tears nearly dried up again. "Do you have other family where you came from?" Simon asked.

"My other br-brother, and grandparents, and an un-uncle," Frollo said.

"We'll help you get back home," Morgana said. Elanor looked at Arthur and rolled her eyes, but neither of them dissented.

Frollo jumped to his feet and smiled for the first time. Two of his teeth were missing — the rest were large and crooked. He explained that he and his family had come on the Elfin Trail, but from the opposite direction as the magicmates.

"We're heading that way, anyhow," Simon said. Frollo promised that he could find a shortcut through the woods back to the main trail. Before long, the company was totally lost and scared to death that goblins would attack them.

Frollo proved to be very good-natured and talkative — very talkative. It turned out that he was only sixteen years old, and his little brother and sister were also killed by the goblins. He taught the magicmates much about troll life. Most important was that trolls don't eat people, unless there is nothing else available.

Simon was soon wondering about the navigational skills of their new friend. He was about to take the lead when Frollo suddenly stopped in his tracks. Everyone else bunched up behind the small giant and saw the reason he had halted. An old hag in a black robe was standing in front of a shack, stirring a cauldron with a wooden ladle. She was singing an unintelligible song with the worst voice Simon had ever heard.

Frollo covered his ears and ducked behind a tree. "She doesn't look dangerous — let's ask for directions," Morgana said.

"How do you know she ain't a Wicked Witch? She might turn you into a toad," said Elanor.

"You stay here and let the goblins find you, then," said Morgana.

"Let's just go," Simon said. "There're more of us than her, anyway."

The old witch had the same warty, wrinkly face as most old hags, though that can't be taken as a sign of being evil — some do have a nice personality. This one didn't look up until the magicmates stopped right in front of her. Frollo remained hidden behind his tree.

"Granny Emerald just loves company," the hag said sweetly. She raised her head. Her broad smile revealed a mouthful of brilliant emerald teeth. "And she gets so few visitors lately, what with a band of naughty goblins on the loose."

"You know about the goblins? Aren't you afraid of them?" Simon asked.

"What could goblins want from a poor old granny like me?"

"How bout them shiny, green teeth?" said Elanor.

The smile quickly dissolved from the friendly old face. "They've never tried to take them before!" snapped Granny Emerald.

"So you get goblin visitors, after all?" said Morgana.

"They pay very well for certain potions," the witch said, "all in golden shinies." Her eyes sparkled as brightly as her teeth when she spoke of gold. "But I can't refuse to sell it to them."

The hag's voice turned sweet again and the sparkle left her eyes. "Just think what a bunch of goblins could do to poor, little old Granny Emerald." Simon eyed the old shack over, as if he expected a gang of goblins to spring out of it. "But I do love gold," Granny Emerald continued, the sparkle in her eye again. "Doesn't *everyone* love gold?" The hag glanced at Arthur, who shifted uncomfortably.

"Could you tell us how to get back to the main trail?" Simon asked, partly to change the subject. "We got a little side-tracked."

"I think it best you stay with me for a while," said Granny Emerald, "until some brave knight or Warrior Wizard gets rid of those goblins. Or you could trade that sneaky troll behind the tree to them for safe passage. I can summon them." The

114

horrible hag pulled a wand from her robe and raised it high.

"No!" shouted Morgana, lifting her own wand.

Granny Emerald lowered her wand. "Nasty temperament for such a young, little witch," she said.

("That's what I'm screaming," Elanor thought.)

"Don't you know that trolls are natural enemies of Magicals? Especially a freak like that," said Granny Emerald.

"Frollo's not a freak — he's just different," Simon said. "And we promised to help him get back to his family."

"His family's been killed by the goblins for their gold. They'll make him show them where it came from — and I'll be rewarded handsomely!" Granny Emerald snarled. She flicked her wand unexpectedly toward the shack. "STRINGO!" she spelled. A long, coiled rope flew from the porch and wrapped tightly around the magicmates, except Elanor, who saw it coming and dived to the ground. The others were bound too tightly to use their wands.

Elanor rolled once and jumped to her feet with her wand pointing at the old witch. "L-O-L!" she spelled.

Granny Emerald exploded with laughter. She bent forward and slapped her knee. "Hee, hee, hee, heeee! That's a good one," she sputtered between guffaws. "I do like you, Missy. Come into my hut. I'd love to have you for dinner." The crazy hag bent forward again, delirious.

Elanor aimed her wand at Granny Emerald again. "You won't get me in your ratty old hut. You ain't nothing but a great big butt!" A Transformation spell suddenly shot from Elanor's wand and — POOFFF!!!! A big wrinkled, saggy butt with skinny legs and arms, barely covered in black, tattered rags, stood behind the cauldron where Granny Emerald had been.

The old butt ran frantically around the yard like a chicken with its head cut off and then disappeared into the woods. All the magicmates laughed, and Frollo giggled behind his tree. Elanor pointed her wand at her companions. "LIBERATO!" she spelled. The rope fell loosely to their feet.

The magicmates were still laughing when Frollo rejoined them. Just then, a loud, low BOOM! echoed through the forest. The company all began to cough and gag. They held their noses and waved their hands in front of their faces. *"That really stinks!* Let's get out of here!" Arthur said. The company headed off quickly into the woods, worried and cautious about goblins.

"I think I was here before," said Frollo. "Let's go that way." Simon let his seven foot friend take the lead again. He and his magicmates kept their wands drawn, in case they should meet goblins — or the Butt Witch. After a while, the company came to a small, devastated stone cottage by a small path they had found. The doors, windows, and roof were missing, as well as the top part of the walls.

"We can rest here for a while," Simon said. No one argued. They all dropped to the floor, exhausted. The magicmates pulled out their magic apples.

"I'm so hungry, I could eat dog poop," Arthur said. Everyone bit in for a much needed lunch, but Arthur immediately spit out a mouthful of apple mush. His face was twisted in disgust as he kept spitting. Simon, Elanor, and Morgana laughed loudly.

"Forgot that it tastes like whatever you imagine, Arthur?" Simon teased.

Arthur rinsed his mouth from his canteen. "Oh, shut up. It's ham and cheese on rye now," he said, chewing a new bite.

"I'm having strawberry shortcake," Elanor said with her mouth full.

Simon bit a large chunk from his apple and held it out to the troll. "Here, Frollo — you need to eat, too."

The gentle giant took the fruit as if it was a handful of gold. "Gee, thank you, Simon. I never saw a little person give food to a troll before." Frollo gobbled down the chunk of apple.

"What'd it taste like, Frollo?" Elanor asked.

"Apple," Frollo replied.

"Didn't you hear what I said to Arthur?" Simon said. "It tastes like *anything* you imagine."

Frollo looked somewhat distressed. "Trolls don't eat dog poop, not even strange ones like me."

"People don't neither," Elanor smirked, "except Arthur." She gave Frollo a piece of her apple. "Now — think about something you *love* to eat." Frollo popped the food into his mouth, chewed twice, and swallowed.

"Well, what was it?" asked Elanor.

"Apple," said Frollo. "I *love* apples." The magicmates took turns feeding Frollo — they hoped he would come up with a more creative culinary choice, but the best he could do was cave bat.

After everyone had had their fill of junk food and sweets, Simon rose to get the company moving again. He hoped that

Dogbert would be searching for them. As he moved, a loud *WHIZZZ* rang through the air followed by a quivering *THUDD*. An arrow stuck in a wooden post of the back wall. Simon sank to the floor again.

"*Goblins*!" Frollo cried. "I don't think they saw you. Their magic arrows never miss what they're aimed at."

"They heard us, then," said Simon. "Everybody stay down." Frollo didn't have to be told. He was already lying on the floor with his hands over his head.

"That stupid Butt Witch probably sent them," Elanor said angrily.

Simon peered over the window ledge. He saw a thin, human-like creature about five feet tall. The goblin's head was huge, his ears were pointed, and his nose was flat and turned slightly upward. He had unusually long arms and fingers. A short sword hung at his side, and a bow and quiver of arrows were slung over his shoulder. The ugly, pale gray creature wore what looked like a canvas sack with armholes, which reached to his knees.

The goblin cupped his hands around his mouth. "We know you are young Magicals without your master. Throw out your wands and give yourselves up — or die!" he shouted. Nearly a dozen other goblins gathered around him from behind the trees. "You have two minutes to decide," shouted the leader. Another of the party shot an arrow through the window. It split the first one down the middle.

"We won't give up without a fight," Morgana said to her friends. She stole a peek through the window opening.

"Frollo's right — I remember from Magic School. Some goblins have arrows that never miss what they're pointed at."

"Just stay down," Simon said. "I'm going to try something." He stood where the goblins couldn't see him and swirled his wand around at the cottage. "FIREWALL!" he spelled. A dim, transparent blue flame filled the door and window openings and then faded away.

"I hope that works like Dogbert's," Arthur said, frightened.

"What's your answer? You have ten seconds," shouted the goblin leader.

"*Eat dragon poop!*" Simon shouted. The goblin leader waved his hand. Five of his men ran screaming toward the cottage with swords drawn.

Morgana rapidly flicked her wand through the window at one of the attackers. "SPAZZ OUT!" she spelled. The goblin flipped in the air and fell to the ground, convulsing wildly. The other four jumped at the openings in the ruined little building. They bounced back with their faces blackened, tunics scorched, and the hair singed off of their heads. The wounded goblins moaned miserably and crawled back toward their company, two of which ran forward and dragged back Morgana's still twitching victim.

"They're sure mad now," said Elanor, finally brave enough to peek out. Five or six of the goblins stepped forward with their bows and knelt on one knee. They shot a volley of arrows; some stuck in wood — some bounced off the stone onto the floor.

"I wonder why they're wasting arrows," Arthur said, as

another volley fired through. One arrow bounced off the floor and fell onto Frollo's leg.

"I've been hit! I'm going to die!" the troll cried, shaking all over.

"They probably hope we appear to an arrow, so it can home in on us," Morgana said, ignoring Frollo's whimpers.

The goblins huddled around their leader. Simon sat back against the wall to think the situation over. But nothing came to him. He began to fidget from frustration.

"*Hey*, stop that, will you?" Arthur suddenly snapped. Simon looked over at the agitated shape shifter, who was holding his arm up, shielding his eyes. A shiny little round object flitted around Arthur's face and the wall behind him. At first, Simon thought it was some magical insect, but then he noticed that it only moved when he twisted his arm — it was the reflection off his magic watch.

Simon remembered what the Keeper of Time had said, "It can shield you from danger. It can also reflect spells back at those who cast them."

Simon jumped to his feet. "If this doesn't work, try to hold them off till Dogbert comes. He has to — sooner or later." He eased toward the door.

"*Don't you go out there, Simon!*" Elanor blurted.

But Simon stepped outside with his wand pointing at the goblin leader. "MORTIS SIMULATIS!" he spelled. The goblin stiffened up, wobbled a bit, and then fell over backwards. With the other goblins momentarily confused, Simon lifted his left arm across his chest. "OPEN REFLECTOR!" he spelled. A large, silvery disk of bright light radiated from Simon's watch. The goblins all raised their bows and released arrows at Simon before they noticed their reflections.

The slew of arrows flew directly at Simon. Inches from him, they stopped, flipped in the air, and raced back at the archers. All the goblins, except the two or three who hadn't fired at Simon, were struck by their own arrows. They immediately collapsed on the ground. Two of the uninjured grabbed hold of the leader and pulled him away into the forest.

Simon shrank his shield back into the watch and turned toward the cottage. He looked for an arrow that had shot below the shield and skidded inside. Seeing that it had hit no one, he took one step and collapsed. Simon's magic-mates ran out to his side — Frollo remained shivering on the floor.

Elanor sat quickly beside Simon and rested his head on her leg. "Simon, what's the matter?" she asked tearfully.

Simon forced his eyes slightly open. "Foot not shielded — arrow grazed ankle," he mumbled as his eyes slid shut.

"Don't die, Simon! *Please*, don't die," Elanor sobbed.

"Shut up, silly girl!" Morgana commanded. She knelt by Simon and placed her ear to his chest. Next, she placed her hands around Simon's head, not quite touching him. Simon nodded his head slightly, but nothing more. Morgana poured a bit of Japper Juice down his throat. "He's still alive. We've got to get to the Elfin Trail," she said.

Arthur stuck his head through the doorway. "You can get up now, Frollo. The goblins are gone."

Frollo dragged himself up, still trembling. "Wh-what happened?" he asked.

"Poisoned arrow grazed Simon's leg," Arthur said.

"Pick him up, Frollo — you can carry him," Morgana ordered. Frollo scooped Simon up as if he was a pair of jeans.

"Wait a minute." Morgana held her arms straight out to the side. "LEVITATO!" She floated up to the treetops, looked around, and then slowly descended. "The river is over that way. We need to go there," she said, pointing into the woods opposite from where the goblins had fled. The others followed as Morgana led the way. Frollo trailed in the rear, carrying Simon.

It was already late afternoon, but there was plenty of daylight remaining. Twice, Morgana stopped to check Simon's pulse — it was there, but growing weaker. As the company trudged on, a small flock of black birds followed them, perching just ahead in tree branches. Except for their color, they were much like the green, gold, and silver ones which played the joyful flutes. These birds also had skinny arms and played little pipes, but their song was dark and sad. Elanor shooed them away with her wand, but they only flew to another tree ahead on the path.

In spite of her sadness, Elanor was uplifted by the palette of beautiful flowers that grew among the trees in large patches. She wished Master Todd was there to teach her the names and possible uses of the lovely blooms.

After some time, the company passed by a tiny meadow completely awash with magnificent flowers. As Elanor stooped to pick one, Frollo tripped over her. Simon slipped from his arms and landed face up in the sprawling flower bed. Morgana turned back with a look of scorn. "Don't look at *me*. Frollo's the one who dropped him," said Elanor.

Morgana knelt beside Simon and checked his pulse again. "Look out for them bugs," Elanor said, waiving her hand in the air. Dozens of small, colorful creatures about four inches long began swarming around Simon and Morgana. Others protruded halfway out of tulip-shaped blooms that were scattered around the small field.

"They're fairies," Morgana said as the creatures got closer. The fairies all had beautiful faces. Their tiny wings looked as if they were made of the finest silk. Two of the fairies hovered over Simon's face. Together they lifted one of his eyelids. A third, slightly taller, stood on Simon's cheek and looked into his eye. It was bloodshot and rolled back.

Two other fairies flew up to the tall one, holding up a bell-shaped flower. "We know who you are," said the tall one, using the flower as a megaphone. "Our scouts witnessed your battle with the goblins. Their poison is strong, but my people know the healing power of all the plants in Magic Space."

Just then, another fairy flew up to Simon's face with her hands filled with a thick, clear liquid. She dropped the substance onto the boy's mouth and flew away. Another flew up with the same liquid. Morgana squeezed Simon's lips open, and the tiny creature dropped her cargo inside. Then another did the same — and another. The colorful fairies were sticking their hands into flowers that looked like Lilies of the Valley and dipping out the nectar inside. When the elixir started dribbling out of Simon's mouth, the tall fairy —

apparently the leader — signaled the others to stop. Morgana watched the liquid slowly drain down Simon's throat.

The fairy leader signaled two others to lift Simon's eyelid again. This time she saw a black dot surrounded by sky blue. Then the eyelid shut forcefully. Both of Simon's eyes fluttered briefly and opened wide. Simon focused on Morgana, who had propped his head on her thigh.

The fairy leader and her megaphone bearers backed off from Simon's face. "Do not rise quickly. We must attend to your leg," said the leader. Several of the tiny creatures lifted Simon's robe over his ankle. Others flew in with a different nectar and dropped it onto the shallow gash just above his ankle. The magicmates watched the ugly cut fade away. Even Frollo leaned in to see, though at first he had been frightened of the fairies.

Simon suddenly felt as if he had just chugged a double dose of Japper Juice. He hoped he wouldn't start bouncing around like a fool, as Arthur had.

"You may rise now," the tall fairy announced. Simon sat up facing Morgana. She winked at him with the outline of a smile on her lips.

"I owe you my life. How can I thank you?" Simon said to the fairy.

"Honor your surroundings — that is all. Life is often where you least expect it," she said.

"I'm Simon Peppercorn. What's your name?" Simon said.

"My name is Liliana. I am a princess of my people. You may ask for the aid of my folk should you meet them any time, though we rarely show ourselves to other creatures."

"We're still lost," said Arthur. "Can you tell us how to find the Elfin Trail?"

"It is very near. I will send a guide with you," said Liliana. "You will be led to a well. There you shall wait for Dogbert Ambrosius. He has been indisposed."

"Man, that dude knows *everybody*. How do you know what he's been doing?" Elanor said.

"Magic," said Liliana. Then she and the other fairies disappeared, except one, who led the company away.

CHAPTER EIGHT

BEATRICE

The magicmates rested by the small pool of crystal clear water, which was bordered by a low, circular stone wall. Dogbert hadn't arrived yet, so they tried to amuse themselves. Morgana and Elanor got along quite well, working spells on Frollo to improve his appearance.

Elanor cleaned up the grimy troll with a Purgo spell and trimmed his hair above the ears with another wave of her wand. Morgana transformed his dirty animal skin into several outfits, finally settling on baggy shorts and a Rolling Stones tee shirt. She stuck pebbles where Frollo's teeth were missing and transformed them into pearly whites. Elanor finished off with a magical mudpack, which left the troll with a peachy complexion.

Darkness approached — and there was still no sign of Dogbert. Simon decided to lead the company into the woods to camp. He hoped the goblins hadn't recuperated and thought they probably wouldn't come near a well-known route, anyway. On the other hand, he didn't want to sleep where he could be easily seen. He had tried to conjure up a Druid's Fog, but ended up with a purple rain shower that left the whole group soaked. At least he was able

to transform the ground into a spongy mattress that satis-
fied everyone but Arthur, who kept rolling into the crater
made by Frollo's heavy weight.

As Simon drifted slowly toward sleep, his mind wandered to Hard Space — to his old wooden house — where
he felt certain that his grandparents and his sister slept
soundly in their comfortable beds. He wished he was lying
in his own, between clean sheets, crowded by Doggy, whose
unbearable snoring would certainly keep the sprites frightened away from the chickens.

Simon lay half awake on the warm, spongy ground. He
knew he had had a deep, long sleep, but his eyes didn't want
to open yet.

"It'd be great to sleep a little longer," he thought. But
there was a loud sound ringing through the trees. "That's
probably what woke me up in the first place." Simon slowly
rose up and noticed that Dogbert hadn't returned. He wondered if his friend and master was in some kind of trouble.

The irritating sound grew louder and louder — it roused
the other magicmates, too. Simon looked in the direction
from which it came. Three giant banana spiders were crawling his way! They were nearly identical to the spiders of
Hard Space, except that the smallest was at least five feet
high, and their coloration was more brilliant. Simon did the
first thing that came to mind.

"RUN!" he shouted as he took off through the woods.
Arthur, Elanor, and Morgana ran after Simon. Frollo took off
in a different direction, crying like a baby. Simon ran toward
two trees, hoping the spiders couldn't squeeze between

them. However, he was stopped there, unable to move — as if stuck to an invisible tennis net.

With some effort, Simon managed to turn his head. He saw his magicmates stuck in place, too. Worse — he saw another group of giant banana spiders easing slowly toward them through the woods. The scary creatures stopped a dozen feet away. The largest, about ten feet tall, stepped out of the group and came even closer. The young Magicals all screamed in fear.

The leader of the spiders struck his front pair of legs together. The force caused a great bang and a flurry of sparks. The magicmates fell silent. "It wouldn't do to spin visible webs for you to destroy, would it, Simon Peppercorn?" the great spider said. "Your silly games in Hard Space caused us much harm and loss there." The other spiders hissed angrily. "It is easy to be caught off guard and devoured by a vicious bird when detracted by the tedious task of weaving a web," the leader continued.

"*I'm sorry!*" Simon pleaded. "I just wanted to clear them from my path. I didn't want to get a big, icky…, I mean a, a spider in my face."

The spiders hissed again. "Were you ever attacked by one of our kind? Did you never think we may be there for a purpose? To protect wood fairies, for example?" the big spider said. "Now we are weakened by your play, our power to exist in Magic Space diminished."

"I really am sorry," Simon said, desperate. "If you're going to eat me, let my friends go. They didn't hurt you."

"We are not as primitive as you. I would prefer to eat a

stinkbug. You shall all be released, but your magic is required to restore our power," the spider said. He turned toward a bush twenty feet away. A dim, narrow ray of red light shot weakly from between his eyes and hit the bush. A few of the leaves burned and crumbled to the ground.

"That is the extent of my force — others are even weaker," said the spider. "We know you have some command of Wandfire, Simon Peppercorn. You must use it to recharge the organ of power between our eyes." He turned to the other spiders. "Release them." Some of the captors crawled to the magicmates and gnawed at the invisible strings that held them.

Elanor and Arthur hid behind Simon. Morgana stood a little to the side, ready to pull her wand. Simon worried about his control of Wandfire. What if he *roasted* one of the spiders? They would probably have to fight it out, and it wasn't even the spiders' fault. But he was determined to do his best. The leader knelt before him, his head bowed.

Simon saw a deep red spot between the spider's eyes. He pointed his wand at it, concentrating and visualizing a streak of lightning. A fiery surge shot out of the wand and hit its target on the spider's head. After a moment Simon sensed that the organ of power was fully charged — he cut off the electrical flow.

The spider stood erect. The spot between his eyes glowed ruby red. He took aim at the same bush as before. A bright, red light flashed from the organ of force like a bullet and totally incinerated the bush. The other spiders took turns bowing in front of Simon. As they rose, they tested their powerful beams on nearby trees, setting them ablaze. Elanor, Arthur, and Morgana used there wands to blow out the fire with Extinguio spells.

After all the spiders were recharged and finished with their laser display, the leader spoke up. "It is best to leave this place. Much smoke has risen into the air — we will escort you elsewhere." He knelt low and told Simon to climb onto his back. The other kids mounted three other spiders.

"I never thought I'd go for a spideyback ride," Elanor said.

Later, on the way, Morgana thought of Frollo. "Where do you think that helpless troll got off to?" she asked.

"Don't worry," Simon reassured, "he's probably trailing behind us somewhere."

After about half an hour, the spiders stopped in a large clearing. The magicmates were surprised by the sight of several creatures suspended in the air, some flapping their wings frantically, unable to move. The animals looked suspiciously like polecattoflies, but were a solid bright green on the back.

"Regular Cattoflies," Morgana said, dismounting from her ride.

"Trapped on invisible webs," Arthur said.

"We would be happy to share our dinner with you," said the spider leader.

"That's very gracious, but we need to move on," Simon said, hoping his host didn't insist. "Our master is probably looking for us. Could you just point out —" Suddenly, a large drop of blood dropped onto Simon's arm. He saw another drop land on the back of the giant spider. Great drops of blood were splattering everywhere as wide shadows swept across the clearing. Everyone turned their head toward the sky.

"*Harpies!*" said the spider leader. Humongous vultures, with the ugly, hideous heads of sinister hags, circled overhead. Their noses were hooked beaks — their skin was warty and wrinkled like prunes. Tears of blood dripped from their dark, sunken eyes.

Three of the harpies swooped down on the company below. The spider leader blasted one with a spider ray. The harpy began to smolder. It then burst into fire and crashed into a tree. The second monster snatched up one of the smaller spiders and flew away, tearing into its prey with its powerful beak. The third harpy was caught in a crossfire of thin, red beams from several spiders.

Then the sky went nearly black, shielded by a mass of the horrible, swarming creatures. The spiders fired recklessly into the air. The magicmates stood back-to-back with their wands drawn. The harpies soon swooped down in greater numbers. Many were blasted out of the air with spider rays. The young Magicals helped by knocking the harpies off balance with Stupidus and Spazz Out spells. Simon used Mortis Simulatis to drop a few of the beasts.

Seemingly from nowhere, a giant among the harpies flew low with a huge rock in her claws and dropped it on the spider leader — it crushed him to the ground. Simon fired a bolt of Wandfire at the flying monster as many spiders blasted it with their ruby red rays. The giant vulture hag exploded into thousands of soggy pieces.

After seeing the loss of their leader, the outnumbered spiders retreated back into the safety of the thick forest, firing off occasional blasts through the tree limbs. "Those stinking cowards," Arthur said. "Why don't they stay here and fight?"

"You can stay and be a dead hero," Elanor said, "but I'm getting out of here." The young Wicked Witch Hunter took off across the clearing for the safety of the trees — Arthur tailed close behind.

Simon reached the clearing soon thereafter. He immediately looked back for Morgana — she was thirty yards back, running like the wind. Morgana looked back over her shoulder and tripped on the uneven ground. She dropped her wand. "*Morgana!*" Simon screamed. He ran to his friend and pulled her up.

"You're so stupid, Simon Peppercorn," Morgana said. Before Simon could respond, one of the hideous harpies swooped down and grabbed his hood in its sharp claws. Simon flinched and dropped his wand. Another harpy snatched up Morgana — the two beasts swept up into the air with their prey.

Soon a vast swarm of harpies was flying over the forest. Before long, the terrain began to change. Simon noticed that they were soaring over high, rolling hills. The hoard of harpies thinned out along the way to less than a dozen. After a while, Simon felt the claws of his captor loosen. Before he knew it, he was falling through the air, fearful of how far below the ground was. Luckily — or not — the fall wasn't so bad. He dropped into a large nest of sticks. Morgana dropped in beside him.

"I don't know where we are, but it smells awful!" Simon said.

"We're on a tree root sticking out from a cliff," said Morgana. "It's a harpy's nest — I saw it from the air."

"We have to figure out a way to get out of here," Simon said.

"Without our wands?" said Morgana. "We can't fight. You've got that swan cape, but those harpies would rip you to pieces."

"For once I wish I had a cell phone," Simon said. He sank down in the nest to think up a plan. Several harpies circled overhead. Nightfall soon crept across the sky without an attack. Simon fell asleep, shivering from the cool of the higher altitude. He woke up once to find Morgana snuggled up to him, sound asleep.

In the morning, Simon woke up unrested. Morgana had climbed up to the top of the deep nest and was leaning over the rim. Simon climbed up to her. "There's a river down below," Morgana said. "If we jump, our bodies might wash out to sea."

Simon wondered if that was Morgana's way of trying to be funny. "I think I'll take my chances with the beautiful bird ladies," he said. "Maybe we can buy our way out of this."

As if summoned by Simon's remarks, a large, extra-ugly harpy rose up from under the nest to face the couple. "You're not worth eating," said the hag face. "And your little pocketful of shinies is nothing compared to the treasure you're worth to me."

"Our master can raise any ransom you demand. Just let us go find him," Simon said, stalling for time. Actually, he didn't think Dogbert would have any treasure at all, unless he made *him* kill a giant for it.

"Gold and silver are useless to me, idiot. What would I do — sit on it mindlessly like a ridiculous dragon?" said the harpy. "But the soul of a Warrior Wizard will buy me great favors in Hades." She nudged Simon back with her smelly beak. "And I have a deal with a great alchemist to do the extraction, though it's beyond me why he would want the rest of you."

Simon was disappointed to be so poorly appraised. However, he didn't have time to dwell upon it. A great explosion echoed through the sky, and a small fireball struck one of the harpies that circled above. The beast burst into flames and corkscrewed downward out of sight. Simon's captor flapped away in the direction from which the fireball had come. Simon and Morgana climbed up and sat on the rim of the nest.

Three round objects flew from the distance toward the magicmates. A fireball shot from one of them and blasted the ugly harpy who wanted Simon's soul. "There's her ticket to Hades," Simon said. The strange flying objects approached ever closer, evading the furious vulture hags.

"*Miss Beetle!*" Simon shouted.

To Simon's amazement, his bus driver was hovering in front of him in what resembled a big ladybug with some kind of machine-gun mounted on it. She was wearing the robe of a Wicked Witch Hunter, just like Morgana's, and her eyes were covered with large, funky goggles. "Miss Beetle!" Simon said again, in disbelief. The driver of the battle-bug lifted her goggles.

"I am Beatrice!" she said in that strange tone that seemed to be common to Wicked Witch Hunters.

"What are you doing here?" Simon said, still befuddled. "You're my bus driver!"

"Even in Hard Space you saw me as a chariot driver at times, Simon. Always trust your imagination. Now hop in. You're lucky Master Dogbert knew where to search for you."

The two riderless ladybugs eased up to the harpy's nest. Hard flaps slid open on their backs, revealing seats for Simon and Morgana to climb into. The three Magicals flew off, but vengeful harpies dived through the air, snatching at the kids. A small slot opened on Simon's bug just in front of him. A gun like Beatrice's popped up and swiveled around. Simon grabbed hold of the grips and put his finger on the trigger.

He glanced around to find Morgana — she was also armed with a fireball gun. As he looked her way, a flaming orb zoomed out of her barrel and whizzed just over his head. He looked up to see a flaming harpy dropping toward him. His ladybug banked hard and evaded the falling enemy.

The three Magicals zipped through the air, shooting down the disgusting vulture hags, whose burning flesh smelled worse than polecattoflies. The sky filled with plumes of smoke and streaks of fire. The harpies soon thinned greatly in number. The remaining few finally gave up and flew away over the high hills, screaming horribly. The triumphant trio smiled widely and gave each other the thumbs up.

Beatrice led the ladybugs into a rugged, hilly area. They all landed on a smooth spot at the edge of the forest. Elanor,

Arthur, and Frollo ran out of the woods to meet them. Simon and Morgana jumped to the ground and ran to their friends. Beatrice blew them all a kiss and flew off with her little beetle squadron without a word. Simon watched her fly off, disappointed that she didn't stay.

"How did you get here? How did you know where to find us?" Morgana asked.

"Master Dogbert finally came after us on a flying carpet," said Elanor. "We'd done found Frollo in the woods, so he flew slow and let Frollo run along behind us."

"We camped here last night, but he was gone when we woke up. Here — take these," Arthur said. He gave Simon and Morgana their wands. "We picked them up for you after the harpies left."

"Wow, thanks!" Simon said. He took his wand and looked it over. "I could have used that."

"Where'd Master Dogbert go? Is he coming back?" asked Morgana.

"He looked rough," said Elanor. "I think he's been fighting a lot, but he wouldn't tell us about it." Simon cringed. He suspected that Dogbert was acting to protect him. "He said for us to stay on the trail," Elanor continued. "There're some towns along the way where we can make ourselves useful."

"That's what our Venture is about," said Morgana. "How are you, Frollo?" The poor troll's hair looked as if it needed a new do — his tee shirt was torn and dirty.

"I fell down when I ran from the spiders," Frollo said. "Troll caves are always full of spiders. I'm afraid of them."

Morgana and Elanor fixed Frollo up again. This time they put him in a Katy Perry tee shirt.

During an early apple lunch, Simon and Morgana told the others about the adventure with the harpies. Frollo almost ran away just hearing about it. Soon they were up and moving again. Arthur led the way for a short distance through the woods in the direction Dogbert had told him.

Before long, the company was on the main trail, though it soon left the forest and brought them back into the sparsely wooded hill country. It was the first time they walked in the open since the Venture began. The only other person the youngsters met was an old man pulling a cart loaded with pots and pans. He said the ware had magical qualities and offered to sell the whole lot, cart and all, for a hundred golden shinies. When the magicmates refused his generous offer, the old man mumbled something about trolls and continued on his way.

Simon, for one, was happy not to meet anyone else. He suspected they would have plenty of interaction soon enough. It became apparent where that would be when the troupe climbed to the top of a small hill just off the trail. Down below was a small town surrounded by a stone wall, though it didn't appear to be very well protected.

Simon pointed his wand toward the town. "ZOOM IN!" he spelled. The town suddenly magnified before the magic-mates. The buildings looked as if they were in bad need of repair. Tiles were missing from the roofs, and there were dark blotches where chunks of plaster had fallen off the walls. Even the Magic Space flag was worn and tattered.

Frollo explained with excitement that his hills were just beyond the next town.

"Looks kind of drab," said Arthur, "but maybe we can get a real, hot meal. I'm sick of cold apple pizza."

"Why don't you turn into a squirrel and chew on some acorns?" Simon said, angry. He was very proud of his gift from Swanwhite and was easily offended when someone else showed a lack of appreciation. He Zoomed Out the buildings before leaving the hill. The rest of the walk to the town was rather quiet, which no one seemed to mind. Frollo had to remain behind under the shade of one of the sparse trees, in case the townspeople didn't like trolls.

A withered old man sat in something resembling a ticket booth before the main gate. "You must pay to enter our town," he said. "One golden shiny per head."

"Hey, that's crazy. We're not bringing in goods to sell," Arthur said. The old man lifted a bell as if to sound an alarm.

"Just shut up and let's give him the money," Simon said decidedly. Elanor had been given coins by the other magic-mates to hold as a joint fund. She pulled out three golden and two silver shinies and gave them to the toll collector. The young Magicals passed through an open door in the gate and walked the narrow streets in search of an inn. Some of the buildings had boarded-up windows. The people in the narrow lanes wore tattered clothes — their children had no shoes on their feet. Even the Magic Space IceCreamery was boarded up. Simon wondered what Dogbert could have wanted them to do here.

On the market square, where only a few merchants hawked their meager wares, Simon spotted a desolate inn. The magicmates quickly entered, glad to take their eyes off the pleading faces outside. There were no customers in the room, and it looked as if there hadn't been in a long time.

The kids all pulled rickety stools from a table and sat down. The innkeeper didn't turn to face them until he heard the jingle of gold and silver coins that Arthur tossed around in his hand. The miserable man finally shuffled up to the table, still polishing a mug that probably hadn't been used in ages. "We used to have plenty of those," he said.

"Well, here's a few more. What can we get to eat for them?" Arthur said smugly.

"A few onions and a rat. But you'll have to catch the rat yourself," said the innkeeper.

"Eeeyew! That's disgusting," Elanor said.

"Where's all the food?" Simon asked, concerned.

"We have been reduced to poverty," came a voice from over the boy's shoulder. Simon turned to see that several people had entered the inn — probably curious about the young Magicals.

"Aye, we used to be a very prosperous town, indeed," said a man in the crowd, who wore an elegant, but patched-up cloak. "We all got so rich that we forgot how to work for ourselves, unless it was out of habit — like old Thaddeus here." He shoved a thumb toward the innkeeper.

"What happened?" asked Elanor. She had begun to feel sorry for the motley lot.

"For many generations," Thaddeus picked up, "we had a magic harp of solid gold. If played by a maiden of pure heart, precious jewels would flow from the girl's mouth as she sang." The innkeeper seemed to drift off in remembrance.

An old woman continued. "Then years ago the chosen maiden was seduced by a Wicked Wizard. He taught her dark magic and turned her into a hag," she said. "He wanted our harp, but she proved smarter than him."

"It was the greed he infected her with," said Thaddeus, snapping back to his surroundings. "She cast a spell on the harp. Anyone who heard its music, save the player, would be lulled into a deep sleep for a century."

"You couldn't do anything to get it back?" Simon asked.

"Ah, she offered it," said another sad voice from the growing crowd. "She'd give it back if anyone could answer three simple questions she put forth. If not, she'd play them a lullaby."

"She worked that trickery on her master and then turned it against us," said the old woman who spoke before.

"Oh, that sounds easy," Arthur said brashly. "Anyone could answer a little riddle."

"True, indeed — for the first two questions. They are always the same, as are the answers," said Thaddeus. "But the third question always changes, and it is always *impossible* to answer. Several wizards have gone to her cave to try, but not one has returned. Now you see what has become of us." Tears rolled down the innkeeper's face.

Arthur leapt to his feet, beaming. "We'll take the challenge," he bellowed. "My friend Simon Peppercorn can outsmart an old hag any day." The little crowd cheered with joy. Simon wanted to slide under the table and slip out the door, but he knew there was no way out. He *had* to help the poor town.

The magicmates set off immediately to cross the next hill and find the witch's cave. Simon hoped she might not even be there. Morgana remained in the town to distract the witch should she show up.

While the others munched on their apples — they had passed up on the onions and rat — Simon mulled over the first two of the hag's questions and answers. "What is the name of the wizard who made me a witch? Gruden is his name. What is the instrument that makes my treasure grow? A harp of gold it is," Simon thought over and over. But what about the third question? Would it be random? What if he got it wrong?

"Simon."

What if the witch put him to sleep?

"Simon!"

He couldn't chance using his wand. She might start playing before he got a shot at her.

"Simon Peppercorn!" shouted Elanor. She hit Simon over the head with her wand. Sparks nearly scorched his hair.

"*Ouch!*" Simon cried out. "What'd you do that for?"

"I done called your name five times," Elanor said, exasperated. "I swear, you can be so deaf sometimes. How are you even going to hear that old hag's questions?"

"Very funny," Simon said. "Very…, hey! *That's it*. I know how to beat her." He picked up two pebbles from the ground and pointed his wand at them. "TRANSFORMUS EARPLUGS!" he spelled. Simon held two spongy earplugs in his hand.

"I was just about to suggest that," Arthur said.

"Whatever," Simon replied. He stuck the plugs in his ears and watched Arthur's moving lips. "If I can't hear that big mouth," he said, "I'll *never* hear a harp." Simon pulled the plugs out and was bombarded by Arthur's plans to fight the witch.

"Shut up, you wererat. Let Simon talk," Elanor shouted. Simon told the others his plan. He instructed them to hide near the cave and attack the witch if things went bad and she chased him.

"And if I don't come out by dark, let Dogbert know what happened — and tell Morgana goodbye." Elanor looked at Arthur and rolled her eyes, certain that Simon was being over-dramatic.

The trio crossed over the hill and found the cave where Thaddeus had told them it would be. The ugly hag was near the entrance, stirring a bubbling cauldron (hags really love their cauldrons). Elanor suddenly had a bright idea. She put a lip-reading charm on Simon, which worked well when tested on Arthur. "That way, if the third question's an easy one, you'll know what she said and can answer it. Then you'll win the harp back without a fight," Elanor explained.

"*Sweet dreams*," Arthur said.

Elanor and Arthur watched from behind some boulders

while Simon walked boldly up to the hag, earplugs smugly in place.

"Evil witch — I've come to challenge you for the golden harp!"

The ugly woman turned in surprise. "Ha! A baby Warrior Wizard. Hasn't even won his sword yet. And you dare to challenge *me*?" Simon couldn't hear a word the witch said, but he understood everything from her weathered lips. The witch quit her stirring and entered the cave — she waved for Simon to follow.

By the light of a burning torch, Simon saw the witch take up the beautiful golden harp from a silver, jeweled chair upon which she then sat. A huge pile of assorted gems, golden and silver shinies, and varied precious objects covered the cave floor. Simon looked around and saw the shapes of several wizards lying stiffly, eyes closed, apparently in a deep slumber.

He looked back to the witch and read her lips. "Let us begin, foolish boy — you have chosen your fate. What is the name of the wizard who made me a witch?"

"Gruden is his name," Simon said.

"You did your homework, I see," said the hag. "What is the instrument that makes my treasure grow?"

"A golden harp it is," said Simon.

"Very nice — very nice," said the hag. She moved one hand toward the front of the harp. Simon flinched. "What do I have..." The witch shifted the magical instrument on her lap. Simon couldn't see her mouth. *He was stricken with fear*. So much for an easy win, though he never really believed the evil woman would give up a magic harp without a fight.

"I — I don't know. Please give me another chance," he said, pretending.

"You must play by the rules, my sweet. Hear the song of my golden harp. Perhaps you will win your sword when you awaken — in a hundred years!" The hideous witch glared at Simon. Her long, crooked fingers streamed across the strings of the delicate harp. The music would have actually sounded very sweet and dreamy had Simon heard it, but the earplugs worked perfectly. Simon let his eyelids droop closed. He bent his knees, threw his arms out to the sides, and slid to the floor of the cave. He hoped his deceptive swoon looked real enough.

The Wicked Witch ended her lullaby and set the harp down on the fabulous silver chair. She bent over Simon and rubbed her hands together in delight. "Maybe you won't get that sword, after all. A bit of tender Warrior Wizard in my stew would be sooooo delicious."

Simon didn't hear those words, but he did feel the hag's hot, stinking breath on his forehead. The smell was so disgusting that his face screwed up into an awful grimace. "*What's this?*" the witch screamed. "Not asleep, eh?" "What magic is at play?" she stood straight and pulled a sharp dagger from her robe.

Simon whipped out his wand as the hag raised the blade high to strike.

"PROPELLO!" he spelled. The witch flew back against the cave wall — her head banged hard against the rock.

The dagger slipped from her hand as she crumpled to the ground. Simon ran to the golden harp and grabbed it up from the chair. He turned toward the witch and ...

"MORTIS SIMULATIS!" the witch spelled with her wand from where she fell. Simon froze in his tracks — his fingers gripped the harp tightly. The hag put away her wand and took up her dagger.

Simon repeated the Restore spell over and over to himself. He felt it slowly releasing his muscles. Then the word suddenly exploded in his head. "RESTORE!" Elanor spelled from the cave entrance. Simon's grip on the harp loosened as he regained motion. "Play the harp, Simon. *Play it!*" Elanor said. Simon didn't move a finger. He knew that Elanor would be put to sleep along with the witch. He just couldn't do it.

The hag stepped closer to Simon, torchlight reflecting off the dagger blade with a menacing glint. The witch lifted her blade for the second time to murder Simon, but Elanor flung her wand like a throwing knife as hard as she could. It hit the strings of the lustrous harp. A few sharp notes reverberated through the cave. Simon then pulled his fingers frantically across the strings. The witch collapsed to the ground in a somnambulant heap.

Elanor ran to the hag and kicked her hard in the ribs, but the sleeping fiend didn't move. "She'll be out for a century," Simon said. "Let's get the harp back to town." Elanor was looking at the treasure. She didn't respond to Simon. "You've seen bling before — get your wand and let's go," Simon said.

Elanor still didn't pay attention to him. He gave her a shake. "Where's Arthur?" Simon said sharply.

"What are you shaking me for, dude?" Elanor said. She put her hands to her ears and pulled out a pair of earplugs.

"You had in earplugs!" Simon said.

"You think I was going to come in hear and get turned into Sleeping Beauty? I ain't nobody's fool," Elanor said.

"No, but I thought — oh, never mind. Why didn't Arthur come?" Simon said.

"He turned into a chicken — said it might be too crowded in here."

Trumpets blew from the town walls. The gates swung wide open, and the impoverished townspeople poured out, cheering and shouting. Simon met the crowd with the magic harp held high for all to see. Elanor followed close behind, leading a donkey by a short rope. A body in a long, black robe was hanging across the donkey's back, just in front of two straw baskets filled with treasure. The poor donkey could hardly bear the weight.

Thaddeus the innkeeper pushed his way through the crowd. "Ahh, our beautiful magic harp. You have returned it to us — you have saved our town!" he said. The townspeople began to sing and shout in joy again. Thaddeus took the rope from Elanor and led the Magicals and the donkey through the narrow streets to the town hall. Simon and the girls were ushered up the steps.

The mayor and his officials rushed out in their tattered robes. "Thank heaven — *thank heaven*! This day shall be our biggest holiday for ever more," the mayor said, clasping his hands together. "When word came to me that young Magicals would try to win back our magic harp, I cried in despair, for others have tried and, alas, sleep they will for many, many years."

The mayor ordered several of the town guards to take the baskets of gold and jewels to the treasury. "Give us the witch!" shouted members of the crowd.

"We'll burn her at the stake!" screamed a man behind Thaddeus.

There will be time to decide her fate," the mayor said. "Why, it seems she too will sleep for a hundred years."

"We don't care. We want to burn her, anyway," said a bent old woman. The crowd pressed closer. Someone bumped into Simon. He teetered on one foot, about to fall off the step. But gravity was against him. The whole crowd gasped loudly and covered their ears as the harp slipped from Simon's hands.

"LEVITATO!"

Dogbert appeared behind Simon. As he spelled, he grabbed the hood of Simon's robe and pulled his initiate to his feet. The harp hovered in the air.

"Master Dogbert Ambrosius!" said the mayor. "What a great honor to see you in our humble town again." The townspeople fell silent.

"Always a pleasure, mayor," said Dogbert.

"I'm sure we will agree that such an illustrious Warrior Wizard can help us resolve the witch's fate," said the mayor, eyeballing the suspended harp. Murmurs of agreement rose from the crowd. Dogbert released the harp to Simon's care again.

"Bring the witch to the top of the steps," Dogbert said. Thaddeus and three other frail men pulled the hag from the donkey. To everyone's amazement, the animal raised high on its hind legs, shivered like a dog shaking off water, and dissolved into Arthur Sunshine.

"I've never been so abused in my life! I'll never get over this backache," Arthur shouted.

"Arthur, you know you are required to help your magic-mates. I'm sure you knew what you were volunteering for," Dogbert said.

"*Volunteer*? Simon threatened to play the harp and put me to sleep if I didn't."

"All's well that ends well, then," Dogbert said. Arthur glowered at Simon, who smiled back and pretended to pluck a harp string.

The men carried the ugly hag up to Dogbert and laid her down. The master magus leaned over the sleeping witch. He swept both hands over her and mumbled something, but Simon couldn't make out any words.

The hag slowly began to move. She stretched her arms and yawned deeply. Then she rose unsteadily into a sitting position. Before the eyes of the crowd, the ugly old woman transformed into a beautiful young maiden. She had long blond hair, a creamy complexion, and eyes bluer than the sky. The girl's pale cheeks turned bright red when she saw the crowd gazing at her. Simon's jaw dropped.

"Quit staring, you perv," Elanor said.

"What's going on here?" the maiden asked, confused.

"You have just awakened from a long sleep filled with bad dreams," said Dogbert.

"My magic harp! Why is that boy holding my harp?" the

frightened girl asked. The mayor told her how the instrument had been saved.

"Give her the harp, Simon," Dogbert said. Simon almost stumbled down the stairs again, moving over to the maiden.

"Don't trip over your tongue, Simon," Arthur called out. Simon was embarrassed by the chuckles from the crowd.

"Simon? That's a lovely name. I owe you everything," the maiden said in a soft, sweet voice. She took the harp gently in her hands — Simon's cheeks turned redder than hers.

Dogbert touched the harp with his wand. Golden sparkles emanated from it and faded away. "You may play," he said.

"NO!" shouted an old man, clapping his hands over his ears. The pretty, young maiden pulled her fingers over the strings. A wondrous melody filled the air. The girl sang:

"Oh, golden harp of mine,
Music of my heart,
Your sound is so divine,
May we never part.
You give me treasure fine,
Gems and jewels bright.
Your music is divine,
And brighter than light."

On the last word, the angelic girl's mouth opened wide. Diamonds, emeralds, sapphires, rubies, and other gems flowed out. The precious stones cascaded down the stairs. The townspeople scrambled to pick up the jewels as the maiden continued to play.

The mayor ordered baskets to be brought, into which everyone tossed their pickings (after filling their pockets).

The maiden stopped when she tired of playing, as did the flow of gems. The last stone to come from her mouth was a large, green emerald. She caught it in her hand and held it out to Simon. "A gift for you. It has special powers — when you are ready to use them," she said. Simon took the gem and placed it in his pocket. Before he could thank the maiden, the mayor and his officials rushed up and swept the girl into the building.

"I hereby declare a three day feast!" the mayor announced. "Send out to the whole countryside for provisions. Thaddeus, make ready your finest lodgings for our guests of honor. Tidy up the square and erect the bandstand. *We are rich again*. We owe it all to Master Dogbert and his initiates."

The crowd dispersed in all directions to prepare for the feast. Dogbert took the mayor aside and lectured him on the laziness of his citizens. "You should all have occupations and be able to prepare for yourselves in time of need," he said. "And a lazy hand has a lazy mind. It makes you easier to enchant." The mayor seemed to take Dogbert's words to heart, though he rushed off to supervise the preparations.

During the banquet, the Magicals sat at a long table on a high platform with the mayor and the town elite. The table was piled high with the genuine hot food the kids had been starving for — and it was all delicious. Simon, however, ate little. He was yearning to speak with the lovely blond maiden. He hoped to ask her about the powers of the emerald she had given him, but the girl was sandwiched between the mayor and Dogbert the whole evening.

At times the maiden played the magic harp, but did not sing, and no jewels came from her mouth. It seemed to Simon that the song was necessary to make the gems flow. Way past midnight, the Magicals went back to the inn to crash. In spite of a twinge of sadness, Simon was glad to fall onto the feather bed.

He soon was dreaming that he was back in the ugly witch's cave. She was playing the golden harp, but Simon couldn't hear the music. Realizing that his ears were stopped up, he pulled the earplugs from them, worried that he would be put to sleep. Instead, he felt a tingling energy throughout his entire body. To Simon's amazement, the ugly hag dissolved into the beautiful maiden. She smiled sweetly and sang:

"Simon Peppercorn,

A Warrior Wizard of fame,

He truly was born

To win himself a great name.

He'll master Wandfire

And great dangers he will face.

But he shall not tire

Until he saves Magic Space."

The maiden stopped stroking the harp strings, and the echoes slowly died away. She put her hand to her mouth and brought forth a large, green emerald. "A gift for you, Simon," the delicate girl said. "It has special powers — when you are ready to use them."

"What powers?" Simon asked.

"*With this stone you can raise the dead*!" The beautiful maiden's eyes suddenly took on a sinister glow, and she laughed madly. Simon stepped back in shock. The hysterical girl dissolved back into the ugly old hag. She beat violently on the harp strings. Simon covered his ears tightly with his hands — his head throbbed in agony. Then he crashed to the cave floor and drifted into a deep sleep.

CHAPTER NINE

THOMAS THICKWIG

"Simon. Simon, time to get up." Simon opened his eyes. Someone was banging on the door. From the slither of sunlight that squeezed through the shaded window, he could tell that it was early morning. "Get up, Simon!" Arthur shouted. "Master Dogbert wants us to meet downstairs."

The other magicmates and Dogbert were feasting away on leftovers from the night before. Simon dug in heartily, having eaten little at the banquet. He wanted to ask Dogbert about his dream, but decided to keep it to himself. The youngsters packed away extra food for the road. "We need to leave before anyone can insist we stay," Dogbert said.

"That'd be Simon," said Elanor. "I imagine he wants to stay here with that hoochie harp player." She looked over at Morgana, who sat in silence. "You better color your hair, girl-friend." Elanor was lucky Morgana couldn't cast a Mortis Simulatis spell with her eyes.

The door in the gate was wide open. A few sentinels were sound asleep against the wall and in the toll booth. Arthur had left earlier to fetch Frollo, who said he didn't sleep all night in fear of goblins. They joined the company outside the gate — just in time to watch Dogbert restore the Magic Space flag, which was flying over the town hall.

The initiates practiced magic under the eye of the master magus. On their way down the road, Elanor transformed Arthur into a duck — after several tries. Everyone was quite surprised when Arthur flapped, quacked, jumped into the air, and landed on his feet — still a duck.

"Not even a shape shifter can transform back until the spell wears off, or he counters it with Restore," Dogbert said. To demonstrate, he transformed Simon into a small deer. Without a Wicked Witch coming at him with a dagger, Simon was able to restore himself in a few seconds.

The duck finally turned into Arthur, after it flew on top of Frollo's head and made a terrible racket. The magicmates played with transforming and restoring for a while. Morgana even turned Frollo into a cow when a band of dwarves passed them on the road.

Simon was happiest when Dogbert let him put on his swan cape and fly around. The master transformed some boards of a broken-down cart into brooms for Elanor and Morgana, while Arthur shape shifted into a falcon. Frollo tried to keep up with them, trotting along with Dogbert on his shoulders.

The fun came to an end after the master spotted a flock of ravens. He made the youngsters return to the ground. "It's best to be cautious," Dogbert said. He wouldn't explain what he meant, but the magicmates detected a hint of concern in his voice.

The company frolicked on most of the morning until they came to a fork in the road. "Take the way to the left," Dogbert said. "You'll come to another town that could use a little help."

"You're not coming with us?" Simon asked. He was enjoying the company of his oldest friend immensely.

"I must go back and awaken the sleeping wizards in the witch's cave and speak with the mayor again," Dogbert said.

"What's another day of snoozing? Simon slept through most of Magic School," Arthur said. "We don't mind having you —" Before he could finish, Dogbert raised his hand.

"G2G!" he spelled.

The road was nearly deserted, hot, and dusty, for a group of knights passed once and kicked up a terrible cloud of dirt. Soon after, another haze swirled in from the hills and descended upon the company. Immediately, everyone began slapping at their bare skin and crying out in pain, especially Frollo, who had the most skin exposed.

"It must be a ... ouch! ouch! ... swarm of gnats. Oh, ouch!" Arthur cried, slapping his hands and neck. "They're so *tiny*, but they sting like wasps."

"They don't sting, they burn," said Frollo. The poor troll was swinging his arms like a hyper windmill. "They're drag-onflies."

"Don't be a fool. Dragonflies are big enough to see," Elanor said between slaps and howls.

"Not the ones in Magic Space," said Frollo. The magic-mates finally pulled on their hoods and drew their hands into their sleeves. The horrible bugs decided to gang up on Frollo.

Simon couldn't stand to see the troll's pain. He figured it would be easier to kill the pests if he could see them better. "ZOOM IN DRAGONFLIES!" he spelled. Suddenly, Frollo was surrounded by a huge swarm of dragons over a foot long. The flames of the miniature drakes engulfed the poor troll.

"What'd you do?" Elanor screamed. "They're roasting him!" Frollo took off running with the little dragons all around him. The magicmates followed as fast as they could, afraid to cast spells, should the troll be hit. Then Morgana stopped short.

"ZOOM OUT DRAGONFLIES!" she spelled. The beasts shrank immediately to nearly nothing, but remained visible as a swarm.

Simon remembered something Dogbert had done before. "REPELLO DRAGONFLIES!" he spelled. The cloud of vicious insects swept away into the hills. Poor Frollo was left covered with big, red spots, which he rubbed uncontrollably.

"Stop it, Frollo!" Morgana shouted. "You'll just make it worse."

"They nearly b-burned me alive," the poor troll cried. "You saw those big fl-flames."

"They only looked bigger," Simon said, "but they really weren't." Frollo did his best to obey Morgana, but whenever she wasn't watching, he rubbed away. Everyone had their own burns to tend, so the going soon became miserable and tense, until a sign of hope appeared.

A Healer Witch — in a light green robe — had a stand set up beside the road. A small sign rose above: *DRAGONFLY BALM*. Simon became very suspicious of the co-incidence, especially when the witch hastily placed a top on a clay jar and shoved it out of sight.

"Oh, dear, dear me," said the witch upon seeing Frollo. "You poor little boy — swollen to twice your size. I suspect you were attacked by dragonflies."

"That's his normal size," said Elanor, "almost, anyway."

"And the rest of you have nasty burns, too," said the witch. Simon touched the red splotches on his left hand. "I have just the thing for you — dragonfly balm. One and a half golden shinies a bottle. Guaranteed to bring instant relief."

"Let Frollo try it first," said Arthur. Morgana shut him up with a glare. She grabbed a bottle from the stand, snatched out the cork, and rubbed some of the liquid on the back of her hand. The red spots disappeared almost instantly. The other magicmates passed the bottle around while Morgana gave one to Frollo. But the suffering troll could hardly move by now.

Simon took the bottle and pointed his wand at the cork. "TRANSFORMUS SPRAY BOTTLE!" he spelled. Morgana transformed another one and helped Simon spray down Frollo.

"That'll be four and a half golden shinies," said the smiling witch. Elanor pulled out the exact amount in gold and silver.

"Keep the change," Arthur said.

Before the company got very far, Simon turned and saw the witch holding the topless clay jar. A thin, dark cloud swirled around it. Simon aimed his wand. "ZOOM IN DRAG-ONFLIES!" he spelled. His friends spun around, surprised. A multitude of miniature dragons was flying around the freaked-out witch. She grabbed her broom and took off like greased lightning, followed by the swarm of fire-breathing pests.

Once again, the magicmates and Frollo stood on a hilltop observing a town below. This one appeared to be more prosperous than the first. The tiled roofs had a newer luster, and the stuccoed walls of the buildings were clean and brightly colored. The town wall looked as if it was newly built, and the surrounding fields were well cultivated. Simon couldn't imagine what kind of troubles such a place could have. The magicmates prepared Frollo a more comfortable hiding place this time. Morgana even transformed a twig into sunglasses for him.

Simon and company headed for the town, munching on their golden apples. Frollo had already eaten everything brought from the previous town. They were surprised at how polite the gatekeeper was and pleased that he didn't ask for money to enter. As the youngsters made their way toward the market square, they heard what sounded like heavy stones being pounded on the far side of town.

"Uh, oh," Elanor said as they came into the square. "There's a crowd here, and crowds usually mean trouble."

"There's supposed to be trouble. That's why we were sent," Morgana said. In the middle of the square, a wizard stood on a wooden box, waving his arms to silence the people. His clean, white robe was covered with bright blue moons and stars. His conical hat, which barely fit over his thick, curly hair, was blue with white moons and stars.

"Listen to me — *just listen*," said the nervous wizard. "I'll go talk to him. Surely, he'll listen to reason. I'll make him an offer he can't refuse."

"You already did," shouted a man from the crowd. "And now that he's nearly finished, he'll be coming for ten of our children. You had no right to make a secret deal." The crowd angrily roared and squeezed tighter around the wizard. Again, he waved frantically for silence until the noise died down.

Someone in the assembly saw Simon and his company approaching. "Here come some young Magicals — maybe *they* can do something."

"A Warrior Wizard and Wicked Witch Hunters," someone else said. A murmur passed through the gathered. The old wizard wiped the sweat from his forehead with his freshly starched sleeve. He tried to step down from the box, but several strong men stopped him.

"Where do you think you're going?" one of them said.

"Just wanted to greet the newcomers. We Magicals have to stick together, you know," the wizard said, his thick, bushy eyebrows frowning.

"I don't think they want to stick to the bottom of the well with you," another of the men said. The magicmates were ushered through the crowd.

"Welcome. Most *graciously* welcome. Welcome — welcome! I'm Thomas Thickwig, town wizard. Truly pleased to meet others of my craft," said the uneasy man. "You may all go home now. I'll have the whole thing settled by supper-time." He made another attempt to escape.

"We're not going anywhere — and neither are you," said the first strong man.

"What's going on here? We were sent to help," Arthur said, as if the leader. A man who appeared to be a scholar stepped forward from the crowd.

"This traveling charlatan promised ten of our children to a giant in exchange for repairing our town walls. There was a great battle between hill trolls and a tribe of giants. They broke down our walls and used the stones to throw at each other. Luckily, they didn't invade the town."

"Too busy killing each other. Barely enough remained on either side to carry away their dead," said an elegant woman. She tightly clutched a little boy in her arms.

"So Thickwig suggested we hire a giant by the name of Gargantua to repair the walls quickly, lest the trolls return to attack us," said the scholar. Simon was glad Frollo had been hidden away. "He told us the giant would fix the walls for a thousand golden shinies. But he kept the money and agreed to give the giant our children."

"But I gave back the shinies," Thickwig said charitably.

"And today he will finish the last wall and come for his pay," continued the scholar.

"I told you — he *must* finish today, or he doesn't get his reward. I didn't think he could do it so soon," said Thickwig.

"Then why didn't you delay him with magic?" Morgana asked coldly.

"Exactly what I intended to do. I was in my chambers preparing a spell when these brutes burst in upon me," said Thickwig.

"*Nonsense*," said the second strong man. "He was packing a bag to escape town with. The only magic *he* knows is how to disappear."

"Go home and hide your children," Arthur said to the crowd. "We will stop the giant for you. This is Simon Peppercorn — killer of the Giant of Geen — hero of Carnac."

Simon turned as red as a beet. He wanted to kill *Arthur* more than any giant, but that would have really caused a scene. The people all gasped and whispered loudly to each other. Soon they dispersed from the square, and the strong men hauled Thickwig away. Simon decided to put off killing Arthur until Gargantua was dealt with.

Only the scholar remained in the square with the magicmates. He guided them to a place from which they could spy on the giant. The brute was thirty-two feet tall and had arms the size of oak trunks. A good part of the last wall remained to be rebuilt, but Gargantua worked tirelessly, stacking great stones on top of each other.

"How does he get all those big stones down here?" Simon asked.

"He has a magic stallion who hauls them from the hills. See? He comes now," said the scholar. The magicmates looked through the wide gap in the wall. They saw an enormous black horse in harness pulling a sled loaded with massive stones. It looked to Simon as if the load was hundreds of times too heavy for the black beast, in spite of its great size.

Gargantua kept piling the stones, and the gap in the wall grew smaller and smaller. "Somebody better think up something quick. That wall ain't getting smaller," Elanor said.

Morgana pulled out her wand. She pointed at one of the top stones and spelled, "DRAG&DROP!" The big stone slid a few inches as it followed the sweep of Morgana's wand. "DRAG&DROP!" she spelled again, sliding her wand through the air. The rock moved again as directed and slid off the wall. The giant looked at it in confusion and set it back in place. He quickly stacked two more on the wall.

"If you're trying to knock that wall down one stone at a time, you may as well forget it," Elanor said.

"Let's help," Simon said. He drew his wand and took aim. "DRAG&DROP!" Another stone slid from the wall and crashed to the ground. Arthur and Elanor pulled their wands and joined in.

Gargantua worked faster and faster until he had used up the new load of stones, in spite of the ones that fell to the ground. He paused to admire his work and scratched his head when a huge stone landed at his feet. He looked toward the town and saw the young Magicals with their wands. "*You trick me!*" he shouted, angry.

The giant picked up the large stone from between his feet and hurled it at the youngsters. As the magicmates scattered, the missile knocked down half of an old building. Simon and his friends gathered in an alley with the scholar, unseen by the giant. "That was the jail," the scholar said. "There was only one prisoner inside." Seconds later, Thickwig the Wizard ran quickly past, shaking dust from his elegant robe.

The magicmates crept back through the alley to see what the giant was doing, but he and the stallion were gone. "They went for another load," said Simon. "We'd better come up with a better plan before he gets back." Everyone sat by the wall in silence. Simon was quickly lost in thought.

"How about levitating a big stone and dropping it on his head?" Arthur said.

"How about we drop one on your head?" said Elanor. "If we missed and got him mad, he could tear this town apart." She looked toward Morgana, who stood apart, swishing her wand through the air, as if practicing a secret spell. "What do you think?" Elanor turned toward Simon. His eyes were fixed blankly on Morgana, lost in thought.

"I've got it!" Elanor shouted. Even Morgana stopped to listen. The magicmates huddled together to hear Elanor's plan.

"Oh, no — I'm not doing *that*!" Arthur said. He jumped back from the huddle.

"Why not?" Simon asked. "You've been a donkey, a bird, a giant dog. Why not this?"

"Because — it just wouldn't be me," Arthur protested.

"You will do it," Morgana said, a freaky look in her eyes.

"I'd rather be at home playing with my Play Station," Arthur mumbled.

The magicmates levitated to the top of the wall. They peaked over and saw the giant and his horse a couple hundred yards away with a load of stones. Then a beautiful white mare with a big, pink flower in her mane galloped up to the stallion and whinnied. The stallion snorted and neighed. He reared up and ripped the harness apart.

The mare ran away into the hills with the stallion following close behind. "Come back, horse! Come back!" yelled Gargantua. He took off after the animals — his pounding feet caused the town walls to shake. Several stones fell to the ground. The magicmates climbed on top of the wall. A while later, the white mare ran swiftly by the town. The great stallion followed, neighing frantically — lovesick. The mighty giant hurried by after a few minutes, unable to keep up.

Before long, night fell upon the town. The wall was not finished, and now Thickwig's deal with the giant was broken. The children were saved. The townspeople poured into the streets with torches. Everyone stood below the uncompleted wall, cheering the young Magicals.

Morgana instructed the scholar to move the congregation to the market square, in case Gargantua went back on the agreement. Several torches were mounted on top of the wall. The magicmates watched through the night as the horses passed by several times more, followed by the screaming giant.

Just at daybreak, the mare appeared over a hill, running at breakneck speed toward the town. She took a powerful leap and sprang over a gap in the wall. As her front feet hit the ground, she turned into a young boy. Arthur did several somersaults and sprawled widely on his back. The pink flower in his hair remained unruffled.

Moments later, the starry-eyed stallion flew over the same hill and ran for the same gap in the wall. "Give me a booster — Mortis Simulatis on the count of three," Simon said. Just as the black beast leapt, the magicmates aimed their wands and spelled, "MORTIS SIMULATIS!" The stallion froze in the air and fell flat on its back before the wall — all four legs pointed toward the brightening sky.

Gargantua bounded over the hill and reached the town in several long strides. The magicmates spelled together again, "MORTIS SIMULATIS!" The powerful giant flew backwards off his feet, but he flipped back up like a breakdancer.

"*My horse*! You kill my horse! I kill you! I kill all town!" Gargantua raged.

Simon pointed his wand at the ground inside the wall. "TRANSFORMUS SPONGE!" he spelled. "Jump!" The three youths leapt and bounced on the soft ground just as the giant swept his mighty arm across the top of the wall. Simon pulled out his swan cape. He transformed two burnt-out torches into brooms. "We have to get him away from town before he *does* kill everybody," he said.

The Wicked Witch Hunters hopped on the brooms and shot into the air. Simon took off after them. They fired off different spells at the infuriated giant as they buzzed around him, but none had much effect. Luckily, the enormous man forgot about the town. He chased the magicmates toward the hills, in which direction they led him.

On a hilltop, Gargantua took a wide, defiant stance. He tried desperately to knock the intrepid flyers from the air with heavy stones, or powerful swats of his flailing hands. Simon flew in ever tighter circles around the giant's head, trying to make him dizzy. Then he rose high in the air and dived straight down at the giant's huge nose to give it a walloping kick. He got closer and drew back his foot to strike. But Gargantua sniffed hard and sucked Simon's forward leg halfway up his nose. The giant pulled Simon out and held him dangling by his swan cape.

Try as he may, Simon was unable to struggle free. He was afraid his precious gift from Swanwhite would be destroyed. "Now you pay," said Gargantua. "I take you home. Feed you to baby giant."

Watching from above, Elanor circled wide and dived steeply. She flew between the giant's legs and flipped the back end of her broom upward on the pass through. Gargantua bent double, screaming in pain, but he still held tightly to Simon's cape. He raised up straight again — Simon whiplashed through the air.

"*I eat you now!*" the giant shouted. He lifted Simon over his head and opened his mouth wide, unaware of Morgana dismounting her broom down below. The pale little Wicked Witch Hunter faced off with Gargantua in her own defiant stance and pointed her wand at him.

"ELECTRO!" she spelled. A long bolt of lightning shot from her wand and struck Gargantua in the middle of the chest. Electrical waves danced up and down his enormous body — a hailstorm of sparks exploded into the air. The giant stood there stiffly, his mouth wide open. The swan cape slid from between his thumb and finger. Simon fell onto the fiend's protruding bottom lip. He bounced and leapt into the air like an Olympic diver and flew back up and around the giant.

Elanor flew rapidly toward Gargantua and kicked him in the forehead. The tiny blow toppled the huge giant to the ground. Simon and Elanor landed beside Morgana. The three of them stood for a long time and stared silently at the fallen Gargantua. They thought he was dead, but no one said it — and not one of them mentioned the Wandfire. Finally, the giant groaned and twitched.

The magicmates walked back to the town, not wanting to confront the populace, who had watched much of the scene from the town walls. However, they were swept up over the heads of the crowd that poured out to meet them and were paraded to the square.

After some time, Simon got the scholar to take him and the girls to the room where Arthur had been laid. With a lot of slapping and shaking, they managed to awaken the exhausted shape shifter. Simon poured a few drops of Japper Juice into Arthur's mouth. He and the girls also took a nip. Arthur sat up straight. "I was never so *scared* in my life!" he shouted. "That's the last time I ever shape shift against my better judgment." The pink flower fell from behind Arthur's ear and onto his lap.

"I told you that would girly you up," Elanor said. Arthur snarled in anger, but the others only laughed.

The magicmates joined the midday feast. They hoped Dogbert would show up, but he didn't. They stuffed themselves and packed away extra food, trying to keep to themselves. They had been allowed to invite Frollo to the feast. However, he had to sit outside the wall and have food lowered to him in a basket.

The townspeople were so overcome with revelry that only the scholar noticed the young Magicals slip away. Later, he would get word to them that the men of the town finished rebuilding the wall themselves. They had the aid of the black stallion, who came out of the Mortis Simulatis spell after three days. Other giants came and took away their kinsman, but they never attacked the town in revenge. Thickwig the Wizard hadn't been seen since his lucky escape.

As the little group and their cowardly friend sojourned down the rocky road, Arthur bugged the others to tell him everything that had happened while he slept. The only response he got was from Elanor, who kept transforming his hair into little, pink flowers. He didn't seem to mind it as much as he once would have. He knew that he had helped save the children of the town, and that made him feel proud and brave. "I never get to take part in the best fights," he complained.

"Cause you always try hard to avoid them," Elanor said. Arthur had nothing to worry about. Soon enough there would be plenty of action for them all.

CHAPTER TEN

FROLLO FEELS THE MAGIC

Things lightened up as the magicmates got further from the town. Simon and Morgana couldn't help but laugh at the way Elanor teased Arthur. There was a tense moment, though, when she transformed the shape shifter's robe into a polka-dotted dress. Arthur turned into a giant rat and frightened Elanor so badly she had to do a Purgo spell on herself. Quick to get even, she transformed a discarded metal bucket into a rat trap. Arthur tripped it with his tail. He transformed back to human, rubbing his butt with both hands.

Arthur thought he would get the last laugh when he lifted the huge chunk of cheese that had been transformed with the rat trap and bit into it (he had forgotten that transformed food had no nutritional value). "I'll have a morsel of that, if you don't mind," said an unfamiliar voice. Arthur thought it was Frollo trying to be funny, but the big troll shrugged his shoulders in denial.

"Who said that?" Arthur demanded, with yellow spots between his teeth. The company stopped in their tracks — Simon pulled his wand.

"You could share, you know. There's enough cheese

there for all of us, and plenty to spare," said the mysterious voice from among the boulders near the road.

"Come out, or I'll blast you!" Simon threatened. A creature about three feet tall stepped, or rolled rather, onto the road. It looked like a stone-colored blob with two bulbous eyes the size of tennis balls near the top. There were no well-defined arms or legs, though blobby protrusions did stretch out from the doughy body at times.

"What the heck are you?" Arthur asked.

"I happen to be a mushman, and a very hungry one at that," said the creature. His body stretched a foot upward and narrowed, causing his eyes to shift to the back of his head. As his mass settled again, his eyes returned to the front, though one was much lower than the other. "What about that cheese, then?"

"Forget it," said Arthur. "We may need this later. I'm not giving it to some fat blob."

"Just because you can kill a giant and knock a horse off his eight legs, you don't have the right to be greedy," said the mushman.

"What do you mean, eight legs?" Elanor said.

"What do you mean by what do I mean by eight legs?" said the snooty mushman.

"That horse was humongous, but it had four legs like every other," Elanor said.

"Don't be ridiculous," the mushman said. "I've been to the eight corners of Magic Space and I've *never* seen a horse with just four legs."

"Then you don't know how to count," Arthur said.

"Oh, *you're* such a smart one. Let's just check your math skills," said the mushman. "How many legs does a horse have in the front?"

"Two," said Arthur, rolling his eyes.

"And how many in the back?"

"Two."

"How many on the left side?"

Arthur hesitated. "Two."

"And how many on the right side?"

"Two."

"And how much is two plus two plus two plus two?" asked the mushman.

"Eight," said Arthur, puzzled.

"I don't see how you see eight legs on a horse, unless you have four eyes," Elanor said.

"I *do* have four eyes," said the mushman. He blobbed about until his eyes were level.

"Two in the front — one on the left — one on the right," Simon said, amused.

"*Finally*, two who can count properly," said the mushman. "Now, how about that cheese?"

"I don't care if there are ten of you," said Arthur. "You're not getting it!" The mushman swung a globby fist at Arthur and mushed him in the face. Arthur felt nothing but offense. He threw down the cheese and jumped at the mushman. The blob stretched out tight. Arthur bounced back and fell to the ground — the mushman pounced on him. They rolled about on the ground until Arthur was engulfed by the blobby beast.

171

The ensuing figure rose from the ground. The other magicmates and Frollo saw Arthur's head and flying fists forming out of the doughy mass. When the movement finally stopped, the blob pulled off of Arthur and rolled onto the cheese. The mushman slogged off among the big rocks with his prize — Arthur was too tired to give chase. Even Frollo got a good laugh out of this one.

"I better not here any cheese jokes," said Arthur, as the journey got underway again.

The rocky road was little traveled, though a procession of pilgrims passed on their way to the Mount of St. Michael. One of them explained that their village had been destroyed by a dragon. A Dragon Slayer had destroyed the beast, but they wanted to ask the saint's help in keeping other drakes away. The leader of the knights escorting the pilgrims warned the magicmates to be on the alert for trolls. Luckily, Frollo was hiding behind a boulder.

Before long, the terrain became even rockier and the hills much higher. Now there were no trees at all. Simon could sense that Frollo was becoming more and more nervous. "Frollo, do you know where we are?" he asked.

"In troll country. My home is near. Soon I will have to leave you," Frollo said, his voice cracking. "T-tomorrow."

"Frollo — do you think your people will attack us?" Morgana asked.

"Trolls usually don't come down this far. The knights like to kill them, even if they're not attacked. Not all trolls are bad, but people don't understand that — just because we're ugly."

"*You're* not ugly, Frollo. Not to us, anyway," Elanor said.

Frollo burst into tears. "H-home is wh-where the h-heart is," he said. "But my h-heart is here no m-more. I want to go on Ve-Venture."

"But Frollo, it wouldn't be safe," said Simon. "We'd love for you to come with us, but you're better off with your own people."

"I un-un-understand," Frollo said through sobs.

The company marched on, silent, except for Frollo's sniffles. Many standing stones were erected along the way, brooding and somber. Some looked as if they had once been carved into human shape, but had weathered into nearly formless sentinels. "We'll be mountain climbing if this road don't lead to lower ground soon," Elanor said. Arthur was already considering shape shifting into a goat to make the going easier.

"I don't like this place at all," said Morgana. "It's really creepy." Simon remained silent. He didn't want to say what the place made him think of, or that he smelled something strange in the air, something that made his nostrils burn — *something wolfish.* Finally, he suggested that they march through the night instead of camping among the eerie rocks. Maybe there would be an inn along the way, or even better, Dogbert might make a show.

Darkness had already crept up. Simon and Morgana lighted the way with their wands at times, though they tried to make their way by the moonlight. Arthur finally did shape shift into a goat. Surprisingly, he let Elanor ride on his back. The magicmates drank the little Japper Juice they had left among them. Frollo's troll nature made staying awake easy for him.

Later on, as the company emerged from a group of standing stones, a few small rocks rolled down the steep hill, pelting Elanor and Arthur. A much larger stone bounced down the hill toward Morgana. Simon leapt on her. The rock bounced over as they hit the ground. Both got up, embarrassed. "There must be landslides here," Simon said quickly. "Let's wait back there behind the standing stones. It'll be light in a couple of hours."

No one objected — the Japper Juice was wearing off, and they all were tired. Even Frollo was ready for a rest. He sprawled on the ground and leaned back against a huge vertical stone, but soon he was twitching and fidgeting uncomfortably. "Why don't you hold still for a while, Frollo? You're making me nervous," Elanor said.

"Troll stones," Frollo replied.

"*What'd you say?*" Morgana demanded.

"These are troll stones. They once were trolls," said Frollo. Simon was afraid of that, but something else bothered him worse. Before he could say a word, the hills echoed with the howl of wolves. Simon felt sickened from the smell in the air. Everyone jumped up and looked toward the hills. A pack of huge wolves stood above, howling and snarling viciously.

One of the beasts stood high on its hind legs and shape shifted into a monstrous wolfern. Simon was sure it was the one that attacked him in Hard Space. To make matters worse, three great trolls were rumbling down the hill with wooden clubs. "If they want to fight, we all take part," Simon said. "When the wolves come, Morgana and I take them on. Arthur, Elanor, Frollo…, hey, where's Frollo?" He was hiding behind a tall, upright stone, shaking like a leaf. "Oh, never mind."

Simon turned back to the hills. The trolls were now within spitting distance. Simon stood ready with his wand. "What do you want?" he asked.

"We want bad troll. We want gold," said the largest troll.

"What bad troll? What are you talking about?" Simon stalled.

"Troll with people. That bad troll."

"That's Frollo. We're helping him find his family," Simon said. He cast a look toward the wolves, who seemed to be letting the trolls do their dirty work.

"Why are you with those wolves?" Morgana asked.

"Wolfern give gold. You give gold. You give bad troll," the same troll said.

"Frollo's good," Elanor said. She whipped out her wand and aimed at the big boss. "PULSO TROLL!" The ogre's arms thrust out before him. He swung his club back hard and conked himself over the head. The ugly creature staggered back a couple of steps. He teetered backward, uprighted, and lunged forward. The three trolls charged together, swinging their clubs.

Arthur was still shape-shifted into a large goat. He power-butted the smallest troll in the belly and knocked him to the ground. The other two ogres were swinging their clubs so violently that no one could fire a wand shot at them. Arthur charged the sixteen-foot-tall boss troll from behind, but barely nudged him. The troll swung around and kicked Arthur high into the air. The flying goat landed between the magicmates with a dull thud. Arthur lay still on the ground, dissolved back into human form.

Morgana pointed her wand at the medium-sized troll — a terrible, disgusting female. "STUPIDUS!" she spelled. The ogress shivered and dropped her club. Simon did a Levitato spell on the club, but the she-troll grabbed it out of the air and began swinging again. Then a great roar and deafening howl shook the hills. The monstrous wolfern stood tall at the top of the ridge. He remained there while his wolf pack took off at full speed down the hill.

Simon felt helpless — the wolfern seemed to be peering straight into his eyes. What if the creature bit him again? Would he immediately turn into a wolf beast? Would he turn on his magicmates? Suddenly, a voice shouted out, and a bright, hot glare blinded Simon's eyes.

"CIRCULUS FLAMMEUS!" Morgana spelled. A circle of leaping flames arose around the magicmates. The heat must have aroused Arthur. He slowly climbed up from his unintentional nap.

The oncoming wolves couldn't brake their charge. The leader of the pack leapt through the ring of flames. He landed in the middle of the circle, fur ablaze. The burning wolf sprang through the opposite wall of fire and streaked into the distance, howling madly. The remainder of the pack backed off to wait for the fire to die out.

The three trolls stood back, waiting to see what the wolves would do. "Where did you learn that one?" Simon asked Morgana.

"Master Spurlock," Morgana said.

"He didn't teach me that," Elanor said.

"Of course not," said Morgana

"But I can do *this*!" Elanor said, angry. She pointed her wand at one of the wolves. "PROPELLO FIREBALL!" A fireball the size of an orange formed from the flames and shot toward the wolf. The smoldering beast ran in circles, yelping in pain. Then it took off over the hill. The magicmates all took up the spell and shot fireballs at the wolves. The burning creatures ran in flaming confusion. Finally, they followed the wolfern back over the hill. Simon was nearly faint from the stench of burning wolf.

Next, the company turned their attention to the trolls, who had become bolder as the fire burned low. The fireballs were much smaller, but hot enough to scorch troll hide. The ogres ran back up the hill out of fireball range. They hurled large stones down the slope, but the magicmates were safe behind the standing stones.

Frollo finally worked up enough courage to ease around the stone that he had hidden behind, though he was shaking uncontrollably. "Th-the b-bad trolls are planning s-something," he said, pointing up the hill. The young Magicals looked up to see the three trolls gathered in a huddle. Simon scanned the hills for a boulder large enough with which to bowl them over. What he saw instead was a small, dark cloud crawling through the sky over the distant hills.

The puffy little cloud had a silver lining. Simon put on his swan cape and flew into the sky without a word to the others.

"What the heck is he doing?" Elanor puzzled.

"Probably saving his own skin," Arthur said. Morgana shot him a freezing glare. But her eyes shifted to the trolls as they broke formation. The ogres rushed down the hill, swinging their clubs. Morgana, Arthur, and Elanor blasted Stupidus spells, which drove the attackers back.

As Simon hovered in place over the standing stones, the trolls charged again. Simon pulled his sleeve over his magic watch. "REFLECTOR!" he spelled. A round, brilliant silver disk radiated from the watch like a small shield.

Simon twisted his arm around until the disk caught the particles of light that radiated from behind the distant cloud. He turned his arm a bit more and reflected a beam at the she-troll. The ogress was bathed in a cone of the dawn light. She stopped in her tracks and looked upward at Simon. Then she looked down and saw that her legs were the hue of the rocky hill. The lifeless color crept quickly up her helpless body, which became more and more rigid. After an eternal moment of terror, she stood petrified.

Simon aimed at the smallest troll and showered him with a ray of the life-taking light. The onrushing ogre tripped over his hardened feet and crashed to the ground, quickly turning to stone. He rolled down the hill, crashed into one of the standing stones, and smashed to pieces.

The big boss troll turned to run back up the hill — probably to escape to the other side. However, he sensed that the sun was about to rise and switched directions again. He slung away his club and drew a large knife from his belt. But halfway down the hill, he stumbled to the ground. The huge troll jumped to his feet, still clutching his knife, but as he did he felt the warmth of the rising sun on his back and an icy coldness in his legs. He was so big that the stony infection inched slowly up his body.

Simon flew back to the ground beside the female troll stone. His magicmates came out into the open to feel the warmth of their shiny savior. Even Frollo peeked around a stone. Everyone watched as the great troll waved his arms in slow motion. But suddenly, the wolfern rushed over the hill with a deafening roar. He swept by the petrifying troll and grabbed the knife from his hardening hand. The vicious monster bounded down the hill at Simon, who stood frozen in fear.

Simon knew it was all over now. No amount of magic could save him from the terrible death that was speeding his way. If anything could save him, it would only be Wandfire, but he couldn't even lift his wand. Then, before any of the magicmates could react, Frollo shot from behind his hiding stone and flew up the hill in rapid bounds. The savage monster and the determined troll met with a terrific clash. They rolled and tumbled down the hill in blurry battle. Frollo locked his arm around the beast's neck and twisted with all his might. The fiendish monster slashed away at Frollo with the iron knife.

The rolling wrestlers knocked Simon over as they flipped down the hill. When the shaken boy scrambled back to his feet, he saw Frollo and the monster lying below, unmoving.

Simon joined his friends. They stood between the wolfern and the troll, looking back and forth at them in disbelief. Arthur bent cautiously over the monster, whose head was oddly contorted. "His neck's broken — I think he's dead," the shape shifter said. Simon sighed deeply in relief. As if in answer, Frollo moaned loudly. The magicmates rushed over and knelt around him.

Simon sat on the ground by Frollo's head. "*Frollo! Frollo!*" he called loudly. "You'll be alright. We'll make you better. You saved my life, Frollo." Tears welled up in Simon's eyes.

Frollo slowly opened his eyes and dimly grinned. "The Golden Wheel has risen — up on the pale, blue roof," he said with great effort. "But the power of storms gathers." Frollo took a labored breath. "The dark ones linger." Simon glanced quickly at the sky. The sun was up, and several dark, puffy clouds were floating heavily overhead.

The pitiful troll's voice grew weaker. "Frollo is so cold. The rootless — trunks — grow heavy." Elanor burst into tears. Arthur put his arm around her shoulder. Simon looked at Frollo's legs. The stony color was creeping upward. "The Sorrow Dew drips — fr… from … Frollo's heart." Morgana wept, too, at the sight of dripping blood.

"The Day Taker — comes, brings — Frollo — the Joy — of — Sleep." Frollo gasped for air. His arms and chest had turned to stone. The petrifying color crawled toward his chin. "Frollo — is — a — real — trol…" To the top of his head the color of the stony earth crept. Simon felt as if it would spread on and petrify the whole world.

"May you feel the magic," he said to his stone cold friend. He cried with the others.

The magicmates sat in disbelief. Finally, Morgana urged the company to get up and move on. Arthur started off last, but he slipped back to Frollo. He snapped off the troll's little finger and stashed it in his pocket.

Before long, Elanor felt that the silence had to be broken. "I don't understand how Frollo could turn to stone now," she said.

"You never understand anything," Morgana said. "He realized who he is."

"Who *he* is?" Simon thought. "I wonder who *I* am. A Warrior Wizard? A werewolf? Maybe a *Warrior Wolf?*" But the question would have to wait. The magicmates came to a fork in the road. Before they could decide which way to take, Masters Dogbert Ambrosius and Philomena Todd appeared before them. Behind Master Todd, it turned out, was standing Lexi Magenta.

The little, dark clouds still floated above in the sky. Had any of the Magicals looked up, they would have seen a group of black shapes fly out of them and away over the hills. Battlefang had missed his chance at Simon — all because of a troll who was afraid of his own shadow.

CHAPTER ELEVEN

HRUNTING

"I see you are all well," Dogbert said. "Where's Frollo? Has he returned home?"

Arthur spoke up and recounted everything that had happened since their last meeting. Master Todd blubbered up when she heard about Frollo and told a story about a troll family that once saved her from being turned into a frog.

Simon tried to avoid eye contact with Lexi. She was staring at him, all starry-eyed and giggly. He couldn't remember her ever looking his way before. But as he feared, she hiked from behind Master Todd and came straight to him.

"Hi Simon," she giggled, pulling the hood from her golden curls. "I'm sorry about Frollo. You must feel terrible. I keep hearing about what a hero you are." Now Simon *did* feel terrible.

"Hello, Lexi. I —"

"I am Alexis!" Her face went blank as she responded in the freaky Wicked Witch Hunter way. Simon still couldn't figure that one out.

"Ookaaay," Simon said. Alexis suddenly smiled, but before she could say anything, Master Spurlock appeared.

"Greetings Philomena, Dogbert. I see your initiates are

all in one piece. Ready to see some real magic, are they?"

"We haven't told them about splitting up yet," said Dogbert. "I'll leave that up to you and Philomena." With that, he
grabbed Simon by the arm and spelled, "G2G!"

"Couldn't you at least let me say goodbye?" Simon said.
He felt strange without his magicmates, but glad to be alone
with Dogbert again.

"I hate long goodbyes," said Dogbert, "and you haven't
got much time to get to Krakow."

"Frollo wanted to continue on the Venture with us,"
Simon said, depressed.

"I know it hurts, Simon, but Frollo was on his own Venture in a way — and he even transformed into a real warrior
by saving his friend."

"No," said Simon. "He transformed into a real mountain
troll. That's what he always wanted." After a pause, he continued, "So — why did you split us up?"

"It's time for you to take your sword," said Dogbert. "You
don't need an audience for that."

"Where are we, anyway?" Simon asked. He and Dogbert
had popped up behind a large oak tree near a huge log building. The towering roof of the magnificent hall was covered in
gold. However, the massive iron-reinforced door was broken
and leaning beside the great opening. Lots of armor and
weapons lined the long porch, but much of the battle gear was
smashed and in disarray. Warriors on horseback rode in and
out of the yard, some shouting, some singing. The master
magus surrounded himself and his initiate in a Druid's Fog.

"We're at Herot," said Dogbert. "It's the warriors' hall of King Hrothgar. A friend of mine named Beowulf had a fight here last night with a nasty wolfern named Grendel."

"*Grendel!*" Simon exclaimed. "We're in Beowulf's story?"

"We're in Magic Space — that's all," said Dogbert. "We're here to get your sword."

"You mean *I'm* here to get my sword," said Simon. "I have to fight Grendel? I saw a movie about him. He'll tear me to pieces."

"You don't have to fight Grendel — Beowulf killed him last night." Dogbert said, "That's why they're celebrating. But you do have to confront his mother."

"*Confront?* She's worse than Grendel!" Simon shouted. Some of the mounted men looked toward the tree, but didn't seem bothered about seeing no one (there are talking trees in Magic Space, after all).

"You shouldn't believe everything you see in movies," said Dogbert. "She's just another wolfern. Well, she's bigger and meaner than most, but —"

"How do you know about that movie?" Simon interrupted. "They don't let dogs in the cinema."

"Hellooo!" Dogbert said. "I'm a master magus, remember? Anyway, I was just there for the popcorn and Milk Duds. Remember the guy in the back row who laughed at all the bloody scenes?"

"Yeah, I wanted to kick his butt. So that was you?"

"Well — you're underage. You weren't even supposed to be there," said Dogbert defensively.

"Whatever," Simon said. "So what do we do now?"

"*Fly!*" Dogbert shape shifted into a swan and took off into the air. Simon slung on his swan cape and followed. Master and initiate played aerial tag over Herot for a while. Dogbert knew the flying would take Simon's mind off the danger that lay ahead. Eventually, they cruised toward the swampy lake in the distance where Grendel had dragged himself to die.

Warriors on foot and on horseback followed the bloody footprints from Herot to the lake, while others returned. All sang praises to Beowulf, or replayed the downfall of the great monster. Simon and Dogbert flew low enough to see that the water was steamy and filled with blood.

The Warrior Wizards landed behind the big oak tree again as the sun began to set. Dogbert shifted back to his master magus form and prepared camp within a new Druid's Fog. "We'll go to the lake in the morning before anybody gets up," he said. He then slipped into the mead hall and brought back a sumptuous feast, most of which he ate himself.

After supper, Dogbert told Simon what he'd heard about the battle between Beowulf and Grendel. He thought the part about the warrior pulling off the monster's arm would cheer the boy up. "A wolfern can even be whipped in a wrestling match. Just think what you can do to one with a little magic."

The great Warrior Wizard must have reassured himself well, judging from how quickly he nodded out. But Simon was unable to sleep. The noise from the building, the fear of being ripped to pieces by a horrible monster, Dogbert's hound dog snores — who could possibly sleep? Besides Dogbert. After some time, though, the partied-out soldiers fell silent. Simon transformed his master's snoring into the rolling of a gentle stream (quite a creative idea under the circumstances, he thought). And he concentrated on the Elfin Spark. It began with focusing on a burning point in his chest, though soon the burning became a strong pulsation — waves of energy that radiated from a center. But he lost track of the center — he lost track of everything.

Simon suddenly became aware of his surroundings, brought back by an incredible crash. The huge door of the mead hall, barely hanging on its hinges again, flew apart in splinters. Simon jumped up in time to see an enormous, hideous monster burst into the hall. His nose burned from the wolfish stink that wafted through the air, and his stomach churned worse than ever before. "Grendel's mother," he thought. "She's come for revenge."

A wild, chilling roar echoed through the hall. Simon heard the clanging of metal armor and weapons. Then a man screamed the most terrible and horrifying sound Simon had ever heard. Whatever happened inside the unlucky hall didn't last but a moment. The monstrous she-wolfern fled from the building. The bloody man who had screamed was flailing wildly under her powerful grip. In her other hand, she carried a huge, hairy arm. "Grendel's arm," Simon thought.

The demon stopped in the yard. She looked in Simon's direction, as if she could see him in the Druid's Fog. But she seemed to be staring through him. Grendel's mother took a step toward the oak tree, but then she quickly turned away and took off down the trail to the lake.

Simon looked over his shoulder. Dogbert was standing there with his sword held high in both hands. The master magus was glowing brighter than the creamy moon that was starting to give way to an even greater light. He slowly lowered his sword and sheathed it. "She probably figured the odds were against her," Dogbert said. "We need to leave before the warriors set out. They'll surely follow the beast." Simon suddenly felt as if he'd been struck by lightning. The full weight of what was about to come down hit him heavily. "You can still back out," Dogbert said. "Of course, you know that means —"

"NO!" Simon said. "I'm going to be a Warrior Wizard!"

Dogbert pulled out what appeared to Simon to be a less than clean handkerchief. The master pointed his wand at the fabric. "MAXIMIZE!" he spelled. The suspicious rag turned into a magic carpet. Simon started to hop on behind Dogbert, but suddenly hesitated. He touched his wand tip to the carpet and spelled, "PURGO!" Confident the rug was boogerless, he climbed aboard.

The old friends flew low over the ground, wands lit with fireballs, as the sun had barely risen. The trail led them over craggy hills and down narrow paths. Simon could hear secretive creatures stirring and rumbling below the ground. Soon they reached a clump of bent, dreary trees. The carpet threaded through the wood and brought the Warrior Wizards to a bloody, bubbling lake. The sun was now high enough to see without wandlight.

Simon noticed a bloody head perched on top of a small

boulder by the shore — a helmet and chain mail shirt lay on the ground below. The boy turned away in disgust, worried about what was soon to come.

Poisonous snakes swarmed in the water, hissing and flashing their fangs. Simon saw even scarier serpents just below the waves. Other beasts slid into the water from the shore. Dogbert aimed his wand at the lake. "TRANQUILLO!" he spelled. All the monsters in the water suddenly fell calm and rolled lazily in the waves. "That'll take care of them for a while," Dogbert re-assured.

Simon didn't feel re-assured at all. "How am I supposed to swim to the bottom and fight a monster?" he said. "Look how it's boiling, anyway."

"It's not as hot as it looks," Dogbert said, less re-assuring than before. "And you should be happy to get a warm bath for a change."

"Look who's talking," said Simon. "The fastest I ever saw you run was to get *away* from a bath."

Dogbert ignored the remark. He transformed the war helmet and the mail shirt into diving gear. "Put them on," he said.

"But that's —" Simon tried to protest.

"He'd be proud for it to be used in battle against his murderer," said Dogbert. Simon reluctantly slipped into the gear. "Her lair is at the bottom of the lake. It's in the sunken hall of an ancient king. Magic keeps it full of air and light." Dogbert stuck the mouthpiece into Simon's mouth. "There should be a really big sword hanging on the wall. Do what you must to bring it up, but I wouldn't advise a wrestling match."

Simon laughed sarcastically and slipped into the warm, bubbling waves. Several of the slimy creatures rubbed their icky bodies against him as he descended. He wanted to get this over with, however it was to end.

Soon he became disoriented in the deep, murky water. Simon threw caution to the wind — or waves — and lit his wand, surprised that the little fireball ignited. Now he could see a couple of feet ahead, but after a few strokes he came face to face with a horrible serpent. Its eyes were a dull yellow, and its huge mouth was filled with rows of sharp teeth.

"SPAZZ OUT!" Simon spelled. The nasty monster jerked and writhed and quickly passed out of sight. Simon swam down fast, but a whole swarm of ugly serpents appeared from the darkness. He fired off Spazz Out spells in every direction. Some of the creatures squirmed away in jerky spasms. Others followed Simon down a few strokes, but they all suddenly darted away. Simon looked around to see what had happened with the monsters. His heart nearly burst — Grendel's horrible mother grabbed him and dragged him deep under the water.

The boy struggled to free himself, but the giant wolfern was much too strong. She ripped the helmet from Simon's head and forced him into her sunken lair. The ruined hall was filled with a cool, sparkling light. The vengeful mother slung her prey across the room into a wall. She growled angrily and drooled as she watched Simon curiously, perplexed by the childish thing sent to her watery domain.

On the shore, Dogbert ducked behind a tree. Beowulf, King Hrothgar, and their men rode up to the lake in battle gear. The warriors dismounted and stared into the steamy water at the beasts that now squirmed angrily on the surface. Beowulf shot the largest serpent with an arrow. The soldiers poked their spears into it and pulled it onto the shore. The other creatures darted quickly into the deep.

Beowulf fastened on his helmet. Unferth, one of Hrothgar's men, strapped his own sword around the mighty warrior's waist. "I lend you Hrunting, an old and famous sword that has never failed in battle. It will bring you glory and the fame of a hero."

Beowulf made a boastful speech, but Dogbert covered his ears just in time to miss it. Finally, the great hero turned and leapt into the water. The creatures Simon had frightened off now rushed at Beowulf as he swam downward, but he hacked away at them with the great sword.

Simon slowly eased to his feet with his back against the wall — wand in hand. He shook away the air tank, appearing even smaller to the terrifying beast. Then he stretched to his full height. Bemused, Grendel's mother snorted and took a step forward. Simon thought she probably wanted to play a game of cat and mouse with him, her belly already full of soldier.

"MORTIS SIMULATIS!" The she-demon rocked back on her heels, stunned by the unexpected spell. She shook her head violently and erupted in a ghastly roar that echoed through the ancient palace. Simon spelled again, "LEVITATO!" The beast barely lifted off her heels.

Grendel's mother flashed her wolfish fangs and charged Simon before he could spell again. But the spry boy dived between the monster's legs and barely escaped her dangerous claws. He scampered a safe distance away and pointed his wand, "ELECTRO!" The electric bolt hit the wolfern mother in the belly. A zigzag of cold, bluish lines danced around her body, burning and crackling. The stink of scorching fur filled the air.

Simon felt instantly sick. He scoured the room for the sword he had come to win. The blade was hanging on the wall in a scabbard — but it was enormous. He'd have to levitate it to the surface. After blasting the chain off the hilt, he tugged at the sword with both hands, but it wouldn't budge. He looked around to see if the monster was still jolting from the shock. What he saw instead was her heavy paw swinging toward him.

The monstrous wolfern slapped Simon across the room. His head struck against a column. Dizzy, he thought the wobbly pillar was about to give way. But the solid beam was Beowulf's leg. The mighty warrior nudged Simon aside, eyeballing him — puzzled.

Simon pulled his wand and rolled aside just as Grendel's mother made a dive for Beowulf's throat. She grabbed her son's killer and tore at him with teeth and claws, but his armor protected him well. Beowulf managed to throw the fierce wolfern to the ground — but she was on top of him before he knew it. She struck at him with a dagger, which broke against his mail shirt.

Totally amazed, Simon was unsure how to strike the demon. He had to jump aside when Beowulf flung her off with a great effort of strength. The towering warrior raised Hrunting and swung the famous blade at his opponent's neck, but it bounced off dully. He threw the sword to the floor, preferring hand-to-hand combat.

Simon hit the beast with another Electro spell, but this time it only added to her fury. She took a powerful swipe at the wand bearer and knocked him across the room again. Something cushioned Simon's landing on the floor. As he hit it, a huge, hairy arm closed tightly around his neck! Grendel's arm was triggered by a nervous reflex. Simon wriggled around and saw the creepy, frozen face of the dead monster staring at him. He touched Grendel's hand with his wand and spelled, "LIBERATO!" The putrid arm sprung open and Simon rolled away. Now he felt something cold and hard beneath him. It was Hrunting.

Simon jumped up with the sword as the disgusting she-wolfern bounded toward him. But the huge beast lumbered clumsily. As she grasped for the young Warrior Wizard's puny body, he rose on his feet and thrust the sword upward. All but a foot of the blade entered the monster's body. The embedded metal melted in the foul acid of her intestines. Simon tripped backwards, holding the hilt and stub of Hrunting in one hand and his wand in the other.

The monster roared in anger and advanced toward Simon. But Beowulf gripped her around the waist from behind and slung her across the wide hall. He then bounded to the great sword on the wall and easily pulled it from the scabbard.

"Pssst!" Simon heard from the entrance of the hall. Dogbert stood there drenched, looking more mutt-like than ever. He motioned for Simon to come. The boy looked back at the monster — she flashed her wicked fangs and leapt at Beowulf.

"MORTIS SIMULATIS!" Simon spelled. Grendel's mother, now nearly exhausted, went stiff. Simon darted for the entrance as Beowulf swung the heavy sword. It cut deep into ...

Dogbert pulled Simon away. They swam swiftly to the surface, zapping slithering serpents along the way. The two Magicals surfaced through the bloody, bubbling water, out of sight of King Hrothgar and the waiting warriors. The master dried himself and his initiate with a wand flick.

"Well done, Simon — you have your sword," Dogbert said.

"This isn't even *half* a sword!" Simon said. "And it's *not* the monster's. It's Beowulf's *reject*." Simon looked at the remainders of the once powerful blade.

"That doesn't matter. It *was* whole, and you won it in battle," Dogbert said.

"Why did you make me fight such a horrible monster? There must have been an easier way to get a sword," Simon said. Dogbert ignored the question. He and Simon had already boarded the magic carpet. It sped off and away into the sky.

Simon wasn't at all thrilled with riding on a flying rug again. After all, he had a swan cape and loved the freedom of flying with it. But Dogbert was the master, and for some reason he didn't want to do a G2G. But it didn't matter to Simon. He was nearing the end of his Venture and, hopefully, close to being healed.

THE MASTER DRAGON SLAYER

The sky was more crowded than Simon had expected. A formation of Wicked Witch Hunters and Warrior Wizards on brooms swept by at a high speed. Later, Simon was sure he saw a group of Swan Maidens in the distance. He wondered if Swanwhite was among them — how nice it would be to see her again.

At one point, a huge dragon circled high over them and disappeared into the clouds. Simon didn't think much of it. He knew that pretty much anything could appear in magical skies. Finally, they landed in an area of forested hills. "Am I going to Krakow from here?" Simon asked, stretching.

"Very soon, but first your sword needs to be repaired," said Dogbert.

At that moment Simon heard a loud rustling in the woods. He turned to see Angel Ramirez with someone he didn't expect — *Waldo Burncastle*! Both wore the dark green robes of Dragon Slayers and Waldo had a long sword hanging at his side. "Waldo! A Dragon Slayer!" said Simon.

Waldo embraced Simon warmly. "Alligators are too small game for me, Simon. Dragons are a lot more fun." Dogbert took Waldo aside to confer. In the meantime, Simon and Angel exchanged adventure stories — Simon could tell that

Angel was impressed by Hrunting. The masters came back to them when Angel was in the middle of telling Simon how to make a dragonskin whip.

"Simon, you will accompany Master Burncastle to the workshop of Regin, a dwarf with magical powers," said Dogbert. "He is one of the best swordsmiths in Magic Space. Hopefully, he will return Hrunting to its former glory." Before Simon could respond, Dogbert took Angel by the wrist. "G2G!" he spelled.

"Simon, I've heard all about your Magic Space adventures. Your magic is advancing very well. And many Dragon Slayers wish they were so brave," said Waldo.

"Yeah, it's been a barrel of laughs," Simon said.

"I know about your misfortune, too. But don't worry. You'll get to Krakow in plenty of time. There are forces working in your favor that you don't know about," Waldo said. Simon wasn't much relieved, but he was happy to see his old friend. They hiked for over half an hour, and Waldo explained a lot about dragons. At a small castle, the Master Dragon Slayer was welcomed by the guards who manned the gate.

Inside, Waldo led Simon to Regin's workshop. The small blacksmith looked to Simon more like a little man than like the thick dwarves he had met before. In the smithy, Regin raised a hot, glowing sword from his anvil and thrust it into a barrel of water. Orange steam rose from the water and filled the room. When it dissipated, Regin swung the sword down at the anvil, splitting the block of iron in two. "Sharp enough for a Dragon Slayer, Master Burncastle?" Regin said, grinning.

"A sharp wit beats a sharp sword for killing a dragon," Waldo said. "That's the weapon *you* wield most effectively, Regin. Though you were never one to confront a dragon."

"I prefer a fire from my furnace — not the belly of a drake," said the dwarf. "Swords are for the foolish who seek adventure and often sacrifice more than a good sword for it."

"Looks like you're pretty good with one to me," Simon said.

"Ah, *this* beauty," Regin said, admiring his handiwork. "This is the blade of a young Warrior Wizard, not much older than you. It has bought him great revenge, but it required a bit of tuning."

"This is Simon Peppercorn," said Waldo. "He has a sword of his own — but in much need of repair. Give it to him, Simon."

Regin laid his sword aside and took the broken blade in his hands. He looked over the jagged metal and jeweled hilt carefully — his eyes widened. "How did you come to possess Hrunting?" he asked. "Unferth wouldn't let it go without a fight, and mighty combat it has seen."

Simon told Regin about the Beowulf adventure as briefly as he could.

"You are very brave for one so young," said Regin, "but this sword was made — and destroyed — with ancient magic. I will do what I can."

"At what price?" Waldo asked quickly.

"Always quick to speak of gold," said the dwarf. "Who in Magic Space could possess a greater treasure than a Dragon Slayer — except, perhaps, an unslain dragon?"

"You know I always return treasure to its rightful owners, Regin," said Waldo.

"Ah, yes, the faithful defender. Perhaps it's true," said Regin. "Still, you must pay. Not in gold, but a service." He took the sword he had been working on in his hands again. "This is Gran; it belongs to my foster son, Sigurd. He is to slay his first dragon. I ask only that you direct him, and don't let him be eaten alive."

Waldo didn't like the deal. He knew the dwarf was using the boy to get hold of a dragon's treasure. But there was too little time to argue — Simon needed to be on his way to Krakow. Regin sent for Sigurd. The young Warrior Wizard looked very powerful for a boy of seventeen years. Simon was totally baffled when Waldo asked Regin for two shovels. He was totally peeved when he had to carry them.

Sigurd led the way to where Fafnir, the dragon, had his lair. Waldo soon found the drake's tracks on a path that winded down the hill to a lake. "Now you both shall learn how hard can be the work of a Dragon Slayer," Waldo said. "Give Sigurd a shovel, Simon. Together, dig a pit about five feet deep and just as wide in the middle of the path."

The boys were stunned, but they knew they were commanded by a Master Dragon Slayer — so they dug. When they finished, Waldo told Simon to get out of the pit. He bent down to Sigurd and told him something, which Simon couldn't hear. Sigurd ducked down in the hole. Waldo pulled a wand from his robe and waved it over the pit. Suddenly, it appeared as if the hole had never been there. "It's a camouflaging spell," said Waldo. "Come — I think the dragon is stirring."

Simon and Waldo hurried to hide behind some rocks. Sure enough, the dragon soon appeared. Fafnir was over thirty feet long, dark, and scaly. He looked formidable and dangerous. Simon hoped the serpent would breathe fire, but it didn't happen. Fafnir was on his way to drink water. But he crawled over the pit and paused as his belly dragged low.

Then Simon saw the dragon shake violently and flail his head and tail about. Puffs of smoke floated from the beast's flaring nostrils. Fafnir laid his head on the ground as the life oozed out of him. Sigurd crawled out of the pit and faced the scaly creature. Gran, the sharp and powerful sword, was covered with thick, dark blood. The dragon and his slayer looked at one another. "*You are just a boy,*" said Fafnir, shocked and fearful. "Why would such a boy stick his sword in Fafnir's heart?"

"I'm a motherless boy, but a Warrior Wizard, too," said Sigurd.

Simon heard no more. Waldo took him by the arm and led him away. Soon they met Regin on the way back to the castle. "The deed is done," said Waldo. "Sigurd has done your dirty work. I'm sure he is cutting out the dragon's heart as we speak. Where is Simon's blade?"

Regin pulled a sword from under his cape. The silver blade gleamed brightly in the sunlight. The gold and jewels of the hilt glittered more spectacularly than before. The blade was perfect, but barely a foot long!

"*Are you crazy?*" Simon shouted. "I've got a hunting knife longer than that."

"What deception is this, Regin?" Waldo said. "The dragon is slain. I expect you to stick to the deal."

"You know I would not deceive a Master Dragon Slayer whose wand is as powerful as his sword," said Regin. "It took all my skills and knowledge to work the blade as I have. It would not accept foreign metal. But its ancient magic — which I do not command — is still there."

"Never trust a dwarf completely," said Waldo. "But this one is true to his craft. Take the sword, Simon." The boy took the weapon from the dwarf. In spite of his disappointment, it felt as if it belonged in his hand.

Regin pulled a scabbard from around his waist. It was on a simple leather belt, but it was made of ornamented gold. "Please accept this as a befitting home for such a noble sword, Simon Peppercorn. Remember that magic is more important than metal." Regin rushed off to find Sigurd and Fafnir.

Waldo raised his fingers to his mouth and whistled loudly. A big, shimmering brown horse galloped up almost immediately through the trees. He wore a simple bridle and saddle from which hung a round shield of iron over wood. "This is Windcharm," said Waldo. "He always answers my call — and dragon fire cannot harm him. There is no better dragon steed." Waldo swung himself into the saddle and reached a hand down to Simon. "It's time for you to see a real dragon fight," he said.

"I thought that was coming," said Simon.

Windcharm took off at a gallop, but was soon tearing up forest paths as if he knew them by heart. After a couple of hours, the four-legged speedster must have covered at least a hundred miles. Soon he slowed to a gentle gait outside of a huge castle complex the size of a small town. The encircling walls and towers were built of red brick. Many knights rode in and out through various gates. A number of Magicals flew to and from the great fortress. Boats of many shapes, some sailing, some mysteriously powered, floated on the wide river below the complex.

"I've got you closer to your destination," Waldo said. "You'll be on your way to Krakow before long."

"Are we going to watch that dragon fight?" Simon asked.

"No," said Waldo. "We're going to be in it. Someone stole some gold from the beast, and he's been taking it out on the countryside. The knights from that castle, Konibork, are too busy protecting the trade routes — or so they say."

"And they called on you to get rid of the dragon?" Simon asked.

"When they're fairly peaceful and out of the way, it's best to leave them alone, but this one has gotten out of hand. He may even attack Konibork," said Waldo. He spurred Windcharm lightly and galloped away from the castle. The great horse rode them through scorched fields and devastated villages. It didn't take long on the flat plain to locate the nearly ruined castle in which the dragon made his home.

Waldo let Simon off the horse about fifty yards from the doorless gate. "I do not want to place you in danger, Simon. Stay back and learn what you can by observation."

Waldo rode cautiously to the entrance of the stone fort. Simon watched anxiously. He knew there would be no tricks this time. The Dragon Slayer had his sword drawn and his shield raised as he and Windcharm disappeared inside. A long streak of fire flared from the ruins, but horse and rider backed out of the flame — unharmed. The angry dragon, as large as Fafnir, emerged halfway through the gate. He exhaled more fire, but Waldo was out of range. The drake lunged forward, but before he could belch again, the fearless Dragon Slayer charged. Waldo swung his sword at the massive neck, cutting a harmless gash.

The dragon raised high on its back legs and flapped its mighty wings, beating down on Waldo and Windcharm. Waldo stood in his stirrups and tried desperately to stab the beast in the soft spot of its belly. But the dragon forced the big horse to retreat. Then it leapt off the ground and spewed flames, which Waldo blocked with his shield.

Again, the dragon leapt, but this time it came down on horse and rider. Both fell to the ground. Simon eased closer, knowing that wand spells would be useless. But maybe he could draw the beast away. Windcharm circled around the drake, kicking and biting at it. But every murderous beast knows its true enemy. The dragon ignored the horse and spewed another hot blast at Waldo, this time from closer and for longer.

The iron melted from Waldo's shield — in spite of protective charms. The Master Dragon Slayer fell back to the ground, holding up a wooden disk. Another shot of fire set the thick oaken shield ablaze. Simon rushed to Waldo. "AQUASTINGUIO!" he spelled. A jet of water shot from Simon's wand and extinguished the fire on Waldo's shield.

Waldo struggled back to his knees. Simon saw the dragon's nostrils flare. He raised his left forearm. "FIRESHIELD!" he spelled. A silver disk, like the one Simon had used against the trolls, expanded from the magical watch just in time to reflect a gush of fire. The flames bounced back in the dragon's face. In fury, the creature raised high on his hind legs and spread his wings wide open. At the same moment, Waldo leapt from the ground and dashed toward the beast's underside. His sword dived deep into the dragon's belly and ripped through the vital organs inside.

Simon ran from underneath the crashing body, but the dragon's tail thrashed wildly and slapped him hard. He flew through the air and probably landed on the ground, but he was knocked out cold and didn't know what happened.

"Simon! Wake up, Simon!"

Simon heard a voice in the distance, or inside his pounding head — he wasn't sure.

"Simon Peppercorn!"

Simon slowly opened his eyes.

"You done had enough beauty sleep," Elanor said.

Simon forced his eyes wide open. Elanor and Dogbert were sitting on the side of the bed. "Where am I?" Simon asked.

"The best inn in Konibork," Dogbert said, smiling. "You even have room service." Dogbert pointed to a tray on a side table loaded with sausages, bread, slices of ham and cheese, and several fruits.

"I'm not hungry — how did I get here?" Simon said.

"Waldo brought you," said Dogbert, "but he had another job to go on." The master helped himself to a large link of sausage.

"Where're Arthur and Morgana?" Simon asked.

"You mean Morgana," said Elanor. "She made Master Todd mad and got sent off with Master Spurlock."

"What happened?" Simon asked, intrigued.

"Morgana called Alexis *teacher's pet* and turned her into a toad," Elanor said, giggling. "Master Todd thought she was making fun of *her* instead of Alexis. But Master Spurlock was snickering, so I guess he thought it was funny."

"Waldo said you saved his life and helped kill a dragon," said Dogbert, making himself a ham sandwich.

"Angel's mighty jealous. He said he ain't been let near a dragon yet," Elanor said, beaming. Simon remained silent.

"You're going to be a true Warrior Wizard — as soon as you finish up in Krakow," Dogbert said.

"Master Dogbert told me why you have to go there," Elanor said, concerned. "But I'm going with you."

"Part of the way," said Dogbert. "You have to fight your last battle in Krakow on your own."

"*Battle?*" Simon finally spoke up, suspicious. "I thought I just have to touch a crystal."

"Did I forget to tell you about Smok Vavelski?" Dogbert said, starting on another sausage. "That's one mean dragon."

CHAPTER THIRTEEN

GOLDENSTAR

The master magus and the magicmates strolled through the alleys and lanes of Konibork, checking out the fortifications and war machines. The castle complex was mostly a military bastion. Many Magicals and unusual creatures filled the lanes, along with some trained forest trolls doing construction work, and a handful of dwarf metalsmiths. Simon and Elanor were saddened by the sight of the trolls.

"I can't believe you didn't tell me about the baddest dragon in Magic Space," Simon said, "even though he lives over the one thing that can save me."

"It must have slipped my mind," said Dogbert. "Anyway, there was no need to upset you before you were ready for Krakow."

"I'm not upset *now*?" Simon said. "Of course, not. Who would be upset knowing they're going to be eaten by a vicious dragon?"

"Maybe you can use magic and slip by it some way," Elanor said, unconvinced.

"You don't know dragons! *Nobody* gets near their treasure without a fight," Simon said. "They sleep with one eye open — and they can smell an enemy a *mile* away."

"There, then. You learned well from Waldo. What could go wrong?" Dogbert said.

"How about *this?*" said Simon. He pulled Hrunting from its scabbard. "That's all the sword I have. That dragon's toenails are probably longer."

"An excellent blade. I see your point," said Dogbert, grinning. Elanor chuckled at the master's poor joke. Simon put away his blade, even more dejected.

"Simon, there are weapons mightier than a sword," Dogbert said "Focus on your goal — not your obstacles. How many times have you combined your magic with your mind to overcome enemies? If you depended on your sword alone, you would be a common knight, not a Warrior Wizard."

Simon remained silent for the rest of the sight-seeing. The Magicals watched a jousting tournament for a while, and then they visited the dungeons. Elanor was intrigued by the torture chamber and the eerie devices there. "Morgana would *love* this place," she said. Only a few of the machines were actually in use, and mostly on a few goblins.

Dogbert bought a basketful of food at an inn, and the trio went down by the river. Nearby, the local villagers were watching several knights racing overhead and doing aerial tricks on winged horses. While they ate, Elanor told Simon about her adventures with Master Todd and Alexis. They had taken on a couple of hags, including the Butt Witch, who had transformed back to her ugly, full body form. Elanor was disappointed that Simon mostly wanted to know if there'd been news about Morgana.

While the afternoon was still young, Dogbert walked the magicmates toward the forest. He gave them a lot of advice and warned them against certain dangers — but Simon didn't hear a word. He was so concerned with what lay ahead that he didn't even notice when Dogbert spelled and disappeared.

Simon and Elanor strolled peacefully through the thickening, but sun-lit, forest. Elanor's babbling helped take Simon's mind off his ordeal. The sight of brilliant and sweetly scented wildflowers along the way was accented by the rolling gurgle of a glistening stream that flowed gently near the path. The songs of feathered bards perched lazily in the towering trees also lightened the mood. But the pair of magicmates hiked on for hours. They hoped the woody way would soon bring them to the trail that led to the road to Krakow.

As they rounded one curve, Simon grabbed Elanor by the arm and put his finger to his lips. He pointed to someone several yards ahead and just off the trail. An old man was stooped over picking plants. He was dressed in a light green robe, shiny silver boots, and a broad-brimmed straw hat — a Healer Wizard.

Without looking or standing, the old man spoke in a warm voice, "Are you children lost, or strolling down lovers' lane?" Simon and Elanor took a step away from each other, lost for words. The old wizard stood straight with a bundle of green herbs in his hand. His friendly smile was illuminated by a set of radiant blue eyes that sparkled in the soft sunlight that now filtered less brightly through the forest.

"We're heading for the road to Krakow," Simon finally said. Elanor stepped closer to the wizard and stared at the plants he gently held.

"These are medicinal herbs of great power," said the wizard. "I raise horses and provide healing to wounded knights who traverse this way. My manor lies nearby."

"We haven't seen any knights," Simon said carefully.

"Don't let the quiet fool you," said the wizard. "This forest can be very dangerous, especially after dark."

"We'd better keep moving, then," Simon said.

"It will be dark soon and the road is far off," the still-smiling wizard said. "You could get lost. I invite you to be my guests. In the morning, I'll teach you to use these plants and then take you to the road." His eyes were fixed on Elanor.

"That sounds like a winner to me," Elanor said. "We've gone far enough for one day, and I want to learn about those plants."

"They heal deep cuts and dragon fire burns," said the wizard.

Elanor's mind was made up. "We're staying, Simon," she said. "I don't want to sleep in these woods if I don't have to. There might be wolves out there." Simon pretended not to twitch at the mention of wolves. He reluctantly agreed to the offer — after a weak protest.

The kindly wizard led the way. Soon they came to a large clearing in the woods. It was filled with a pretty, two-storey house surrounded by a magnificent garden, a corral, and a large barn with stables. "Come in and see the house," said the wizard. He pulled out a large brass key.

The second floor contained several ordinary, but comfortable rooms, two of which appeared to be set up as a sort of clinic. A larger room was filled with hanging plants, rows of shelves lined with jars full of dried plants, scales, utensils, mortars and pestles, and other objects that gave the impression of a laboratory. Elanor picked up a clear jar filled with small berries of multiple colors. "What are these?" she asked.

"Japper berries," said the gracious host, "but don't eat them. Unprocessed, they are very sour."

Downstairs, the wizard led the magicmates into a cozy kitchen with a large oak table standing in the middle. "You'll find plenty to eat here," he said. He laid the brass door key on the table. "I must go into the forest in search of a plant that only blooms in the wee hours. Lock the door securely and wait inside until I return. If my horses hear someone about, they may become frightened." The wizard smiled at Simon as he left.

Simon put a Firewall spell around the doors and windows. He and Elanor had a nice supper of bread with cheese and smoked ham washed down with cool, delicious milk (not horse milk, Elanor hoped). Afterwards, they climbed back up the stairs and chose neighboring rooms. Both were tired and happy to turn in. "Leave the door open — just in case," Simon said to Elanor as she levitated over the bed. But she fell sound asleep right away without answering.

Simon sank onto his bed, but couldn't sleep. Thoughts of various battles rushed through his mind: goblins, giants, dragons. At one point, he thought a troll had knocked him over the head with a club, but it was only sleep finally descending heavily upon him.

At sunrise a brilliant, golden ray of light spilled through the uncurtained window and drew Simon out of the night's slumber. He was sure it would be impossible to awaken Elanor, but to his surprise she was not in her room. Alarmed, he searched for her, calling her name. He flung open the door to the laboratory. Elanor was standing under the shelves, staring up at canisters labeled with strange words.

Simon was relieved, but angry at the same time. "Don't you disappear like that again! You know we can never be sure what we're in for," he said.

"Just chill out, Simon. We're alone here, and that old dude was cool," Elanor said. "I want to learn how to use some of his plants, anyway."

"We better eat and get out of here," Simon responded. "*I'm* the one who's got to hurry to a dragon fight." Elanor didn't answer, ashamed.

Breakfast was the same as supper, with tasty honey and strawberries added. After they tidied up, Simon decided it was time to leave. For all he knew, the old wizard may have been killed by goblins. Outside, the youngsters had to pass near the barn to get back on the path. Simon approached the old building — he liked horses a lot. In Hard Space he had often helped Waldo brush down his, and he got to ride on it sometimes.

"What are you doing, Simon?" Elanor said. "We was told not to go near the horses."

"If they were scared, we'd hear some noises." Simon eased up to the closed doors. "I don't hear anything."

"*Help! Save me!*" a voice answered from the barn.

"What was that?" Elanor asked. "It didn't sound like that old wizard."

Simon tried to open the barn doors, but they wouldn't budge. On a whim, he pulled his wand and spelled, "OPEN SESAME!" To his great surprise, the doors slowly swung open. Elanor rolled her eyes.

There were a lot of horses in stalls lining both sides of the barn. Some were young, but most were large stallions able to bear a fully armed knight. Elanor made a sour face as they entered. "Man — it smells like horse crap in here," she said.

Simon ignored her. He was fascinated by the beautiful animals. Elanor followed a step behind, fanning her nose. Suddenly, ahead of them a horse snorted loudly and called out. "Help me, Simon Peppercorn. And you must save yourself!" Simon and Elanor looked at each other. They rushed to the stall from where the voice had come. A large, white mare with a golden, star-shaped patch on her forehead was bound in chains there.

"Help me, Simon. You won't regret it," said the mare. "You are in greater danger than I."

Overcoming the surprise, Simon stepped closer. "You're magical," he said. "What are you doing here? What's the matter?"

"My name is Goldenstar. The man who posed as master of this place is a powerful Wicked Wizard," said the mare. "I met him in the forest. He fed me enchanted herbs that put me to sleep. Then he was able to slip off my magic bridle and lead me here under his spell. He has gone for the forces of the one who wants you most — one more evil than himself."

"Then why didn't he use magic against me?" Simon asked.

"I overheard him in here speaking with a horrible Wolfern Wizard. He wouldn't take a chance in harming you. Spells can go disastrously wrong sometimes — you must be delivered alive. You know that, Simon. Release me and I will take you far from harm's way."

Simon suddenly jumped in fright. Elanor had eased up beside him. "How do we know *you're* not the one up to no good?" she asked.

"You see me in chains — I am unable to move. Do you think I chose this state?" the mare said. Before Elanor could answer, a strong wind blew through the stables, and the sky outside went dark. The other horses neighed in agitation. "He is returning with a pack of fiendish beasts," the mare said, frightened. "If you will not release me, at least save yourselves."

"We're getting out of here, and so is she," Simon said to Elanor.

"Take my bridle and put it on me. My powers will be fully restored," said Goldenstar. Simon saw the bridle hanging on a post by the stall door. It was made of gold and silk threads intertwined and studded with colorful gems. Simon slipped it over the horse's head as quickly as he could. Outside, the wind picked up and lightning flashed in the sky. Elanor cried out when a bolt struck in the barnyard and exploded furiously.

"Stand back!" Goldenstar commanded. The magicmates retreated a few steps. The mare closed her eyes and neighed loudly. The iron ring around her neck shattered into pieces, and the heavy chain burst into metallic bits. Goldenstar raised high on her hind legs and crashed down on the stall door.

Out in the barnyard, Simon and Elanor saw the full majesty of the beautiful creature. She bowed low for them to mount. Simon jumped on her back and grabbed up the reigns. He held a hand down to Elanor and slung her up behind him. The terrified witch wrapped her arms tightly around Simon's waist as another lightning bolt struck an old wagon and set it on fire. Thunder roared through the air like cannon fire.

As the mare took off with incredible speed, the chilling howl of wolves echoed out of the forest. Horse and riders flew down the path. The screaming of wild beasts followed near. Goldenstar asked if the youngsters saw anything behind. Elanor turned her head. She nearly slipped off the back of the horse.

"I see a pack of huge wolves following a wolfern and that Wicked Wizard on a brown horse," she cried.

The magical mare struck the ground hard with her hoof. "Oh, Earth, mother of us all, form a thick and blinding fog," she said. A dense, cloudy mist formed behind her. She sped away, though the eerie howling rang in the darkness.

After a short while, Goldenstar spoke again, "Look back now and tell me what you see."

Elanor twisted her head, holding on to Simon as tightly as she could. The fog was nearly gone. "*Oh, mercy!*" she shouted. "They got even bigger and they're a lot closer." Elanor fumbled for her wand, nearly slipping off.

"Leave the wand," said Goldenstar. Elanor renewed her grip around Simon's waist. The powerful horse lifted her head up. "Oh, sheltering Sky, father of us all, rain stones upon our pursuers." Immediately, rocks the size of baseballs poured from the sky. The mare was nearly flying now.

The magicmates heard wolves behind them screaming in pain. Again, after a short time, Goldenstar gave voice, "Look and tell me what you see." Elanor hated to do it, but she turned her head again. Her eyes opened wider than cd's. She nearly squeezed through to the other side of Simon.

"The wolves are gone, but the Wicked Wizard and his horse are giants now!" Elanor screamed in terror. *"He's trying to grab me!"*

Goldenstar struck the ground again. "Oh, mighty Earth, who gave birth to me," she said, "open a great chasm and swallow the enemy of your child."

The Wicked Wizard reached out to grab Elanor, his long, hideous fingers inches from her throat. Then, a great hole opened up on the path. An explosion of sparks spewed up from it. The giant wizard and his giant horse tumbled into the opening. A horrible scream echoed from the deep chasm.

Goldenstar slowed to a gentle gallop and then to a halt. She appeared totally rested as she kneeled to allow the magicmates to climb off her back. Elanor, however, was breathing harder than a racehorse. Simon was reasonably calm — *he* hadn't seen what Elanor had. "That was the scariest time of my life!" Elanor said.

"You are safe now," Goldenstar said. "The earth has closed upon him. He has perished forever."

"I don't know why you were so scared," Simon said. "As tight as you were hugging me, nothing could've pulled you off."

"I wouldn't hug you if you was the last wizard in Magic Space, Simon Peppercorn!" Elanor reached for her wand.

"Silence! Enough of this play," said Goldenstar. "The Wicked Wizard is gone, but there is still trouble at the manor. I must ask your assistance, if you would assent."

"We'll do anything we can," Simon said. Elanor nodded in agreement.

"The real master of the manor was transformed into a horse — one of those in the stables. But the enchantment was by way of powerful herbs. Only another, called dandetiger, will undo it."

"We don't know about that one," said Elanor. "How can we do anything?"

"There is a witch in the forest — one of very few who would have it," said Goldenstar, "but she will not give it to me. Do not ask why."

"You think she'll give it to us?" Simon asked.

"She is of good enough heart," said Goldenstar, "but she shares a hut with a selfish sister. They are identical, but never seen together. The good one may give it to you, the other — perhaps for gold."

"We have golden shinies," Simon said. "We'll buy it from her."

"Are you sure the bad one won't do anything to us?" Elanor asked.

"You must cut a branch from a rowan tree and shape it into a wand," said Goldenstar. "Give it to the witch as a present. If the bad one tried to use it for harm it would destroy her. Such is the power of rowan on a bad witch."

"What's the dandetiger look like?" Elanor asked.

"Small, bright orange flowers — even dried they look perfectly fresh," Goldenstar said. "I will take you a little further to a rowan stand. Then I must go for water from a magical spring. Hasten back to the manor by any means. And be careful."

Goldenstar carried the magicmates a short distance and told them how to get to the rowan trees. After dropping them off, she turned and sped away. Simon and Elanor cut off the path into the woods. Before long, Elanor spotted the trees — she recognized them from a lesson on wands.

Simon walked up to one of the largest trees. He jumped up, grabbed onto a low-hanging limb, and clutched a long, narrow twig in his hand. But the tree began to shake violently. Simon lost his grip and fell to the ground. Elanor laughed loudly as Simon got off the ground rubbing his behind.

"You're supposed to ask permission," Elanor said. All the trees suddenly shook their limbs and mumbled lowly, as if agreeing.

"Oh, all right," Simon said, irritated. "Mr. Tree — may I please take a twig for a wand?" The bark of the tree scrunched into a face.

"That's *Mrs. Rowan* to you. I *suppose* you may, but only because you're with *such* a nice young witch." Simon jumped up to the limb again, but the tree shook him off once more. Elanor laughed even louder.

"Hey, what's the deal?" Simon said.

"Not *that* limb! I didn't give you permission to take from *that* limb," said Mrs. Rowan.

"Well, which one?" Simon said. "I'm in a hurry."

Mrs. Rowan bent a different limb toward Simon. "*This one*," she said. Simon snapped off a small branch that looked as if it would make a good wand.

"Thank you," he said, backing quickly away.

"Now — *go away*. We have *shade* to make," said Mrs. Rowan.

Simon pulled out Hrunting and whittled the twig into a fairly straight wand about eleven inches long as he and Elanor walked. He stopped and pointed the wand upward. Wandfire shot out the end and quickly dissolved over the treetops. Simon transformed an unknown wildflower into a tulip with it. "Works," he said.

"Put a disguising charm on it," Elanor said, "so they don't know it's rowan wood."

Simon touched the wand with his own. "SIMULATO WILLOW WAND!" he spelled. The rowan wand took on a darker color. After a short distance, Elanor nudged Simon in the side.

"The witch's hut," she whispered.

CHAPTER FOURTEEN

BABA YAGA

A head through the woods stood a small stick hut with a poorly thatched roof. A wisp of dark smoke rose from the crooked chimney. The magicmates passed through the open gate of the rickety fence and quietly approached the door. Simon raised his hand to knock, but …

"Come in, my children — don't just stand there," squeaked a kindly old voice. Simon and Elanor looked at each other and cautiously entered the hut. Straight across from them at the fireplace stood a tall, but stooped, old woman. Her hair was gray and stringy. She had sagging wrinkles, baggy eyes, and a long, crooked nose topped with a large wart. Her tattered black robe, patched in several places, hung to her bony ankles. The smiling hag was leaning over a cauldron suspended over the fire, stirring the contents with a wand.

A fat, black cat darted from between the witch's feet and leapt onto the table. It curled about itself and seemed to fall instantly to sleep. Simon noticed the open shelves that covered the upper walls. They were filled with many dusty jars, some of which contained dried plants. Others were filled with various creatures, or parts thereof — some alive —

some dried — some in liquid. One jar held a pair of lips that were twisted into an odd smile. Another possessed a pair of eyes that Simon felt was staring at him. Then he spotted a jar of bright orange flowers.

"Dandetigers," Simon thought.

"What can I do for you Lovelies?" asked the witch sweetly.

"Please, Miss, Miss —" Elanor began.

"Baba Yaga," the hag said.

"Please, Miss Baba Yaga — we came to see you."

"You came to see Baba Yaga? How very kind," the witch said with a sincere smile.

"We need your help, and we brought you a present," said Elanor. Simon held out the rowan wand.

"A present for Baba Yaga? What wonderful children, indeed!" The witch wiped her own wand on her robe and set it on the mantle. She took the new one in her hand and examined it closely. Then she pointed it at Simon — he froze completely. "Put it on the table for me, Dearest."

Simon placed the wand on the table by the fat cat, relieved. The furry creature leapt to the floor and jumped onto the window sill where it lay silently again.

"We need dandetiger flowers to help a friend. He was turned into a horse," Simon said.

Baba Yaga raised her eyebrows. "You are much too young for such high magic. Who sent you here?" she said, serious. Simon wondered if this was the bad sister after all.

"Please, Miss Baba Yaga," blurted Elanor. "Another friend, a magical horse, is helping us."

"*Goldenstar*!" Baba Yaga said. She sighed deeply and began stirring the cauldron again. "Still holds a grudge, I suppose. Still blames my whole line for the suffering of hers. She has unicorn blood, you know."

"Maybe she would've come herself," Simon said, "but there's not much time. She had to get special water while we came here."

The old witch continued stirring quietly for a while, gazing into the cauldron. Finally, she let go of her wand. It kept stirring as she crossed to the table and lifted the rowan wand. "Willow, my favorite," she said. She pointed it at the jar of dandetiger flowers Simon had seen on the shelf. "VOCO!" The jar floated down to the table as Baba Yaga directed. "You may take it, but there is a condition," said the witch. "You must bring back the unused portion. It is extremely rare and valuable. And you must tell Goldenstar I wish for a meeting. Bring back her answer."

"Oh, we will. Thank you so much — you're so kind," Elanor poured it on.

"You noobies are so naïve," said Baba Yaga as she wrapped some of the flowers in a green leaf. She handed the packet to Elanor. "Be off now — and beware."

Simon and Elanor hurried along the path back toward the manor, but before long Simon stopped and put on his swan cape. "You know Master Dogbert don't like us flying without him around," Elanor said.

"I'll see you back at the manor — if you're so scared," Simon said. "Just give me the flowers."

"Don't think you're leaving me here alone, Simon Peppercorn," Elanor threatened. She transformed a fallen branch into a broom and took off above the trees.

The view below was breathtaking. Sunbeams filtered through white, fluffy clouds and reached down into the trees like caressing fingers. Simon pointed out to Elanor a herd of what must have been gophergoats frolicking in a small clearing below. Some of them were half-sunken in holes, kicking massive amounts of dirt up between their legs. The ones with their heads visible had long horns that arched over in front of their faces — perfect for digging. Elanor was the one to spot a pair of unicorns grazing near a brook.

The thrill turned to fear when a dark shadow spread over the ground. Simon and Elanor looked up to see a large, dark cloud drifting across the sun. Several dark shapes flew out of the cloud toward them. "I hope it's not harpies," Simon shouted through the wind.

"I *told* you we're not supposed to fly, fool. What are we going to do?" Elanor shouted back.

"Stick close behind me," Simon yelled. He dived suddenly and then zigzagged over the treetops and spiraled back up into the air. Elanor followed close behind, gripping her broomstick tightly. They flew into a white cloud to hide, but came through it quickly. As they emerged from the whiteness, Simon saw the flying figures swoop down in a circle around him and Elanor.

The creatures were much larger than they had first appeared. The front of their bodies was the head and wings of an eagle. The back half was that of a powerful lion. Their wings were golden-hued, and the rest of their bodies was dappled red and white. *"Gryphons!"* Elanor said, now flying close beside Simon.

The gryphons made no effort to attack. Simon had the feeling they had been sent. Soon the magicmates drifted down on the warm air and landed in the barnyard. The gryphons circled once overhead and flew away. Goldenstar was waiting in front of a cauldron that hung on a tripod. A fire burned underneath, and steam rose from the boiling water.

"We have the dandetiger," Elanor said. She pulled out her small packet and opened it up.

"Excellent," said Goldenstar. "You had no trouble, then."

"She was actually nice," Simon said, "but she made us promise to bring back the leftover flowers — and let her know if you'll meet with her."

"Then tell her I will come in my own good time. And now, Elanor, put a third of the flowers in the cauldron." Elanor did as she was told. Plumes of red steam rose into the air. "Drop in a few more." This time Goldenstar chanted rhythmically and gazed into the cauldron. A wispy, red cloud floated from the water and dispersed in the air.

"Take your wand, Elanor, and levitate the cauldron. Guide it into the barn." Elanor obeyed.

"Stop before each horse," Goldenstar continued. "Simon, dip your wand into the water. Splash it onto the horse's forehead and say: From this black magic storm, into yourself transform." The charm produced no results on the first four horses. They came to the fifth.

"From this black magic storm, into yourself transform," Simon said. The horse shook all over. Simon stumbled back, scared. A man in mail shirt and other knightly gear fell to the floor, groaning in pain.

The knight's head and right leg were covered in bandages. "For the love of jousting!" he moaned. "I thought I would be stuck here eating straw forever. Bring my horse and shield. I'll be after the wicked one who cursed me."

"Ah, Sir Lech," said Goldenstar, "a patient of Master Stanislaw."

"Well, I *wouldn't* be," shouted Sir Lech, "if that scoundrel Sir Czech hadn't struck before I could draw my sword." The angry knight fell back in pain, still moaning.

"Master Stanislaw will continue your healing soon enough," said Goldenstar.

After several more attempts, another horse rose up on its hind legs and crumpled to the ground as a bandaged and bloody knight. He was remarkably similar to Sir Lech. "For the love of jousting!" said the knight. "I thought I would be trapped here eating hay forever. Bring my horse and shield. I'll catch the fiend who cursed me."

"Sir Czech," said Goldenstar, "another patient of Master Stanislaw."

"I *wouldn't* be, if that rogue Sir Lech hadn't struck me from behind," said Sir Czech. He fell back, moaning even louder than Sir Lech.

"The twin brother of Sir Lech. You, too, shall be healed once we have recovered Master Stanislaw," Goldenstar said.

Elanor continued from stall to stall with the cauldron, but all the horses turned into nothing but horses. Then from the opposite row came the quiet bray of a small donkey. "*It's him*! *It's him*!" Elanor shouted, excited. "Come on, Simon!"

Simon thought Elanor was crazy, but he knew she could be as mean as Morgana, so he complied. He dipped his wand and splashed the drops on the donkey. "From this black magic storm, into yourself transform."

In a flash, the donkey popped into a man. Simon and Elanor hid themselves behind Goldenstar, frightened. It was the Wicked Wizard — the same light green robe — the same long silvery hair — the same captivating smile.

"Fear not," said Goldenstar, "this is the real Master Stanislaw." The magicmates eased up to the front of Goldenstar again. This man was identical to the Wicked Wizard, except that his eyes had a different glow.

"You should think I deserve more respect than that," said Master Stanislaw. "To be turned into a mere donkey — one who raises the finest horses in Magic Space." A real donkey across the aisle brayed loudly. "Of course, I do love donkeys," he quickly added, still smiling broadly. "Thank you, Goldenstar, my old friend. I presume you have encountered the Wicked Wizard?"

"He will trouble Magic Space no more. He has been devoured by Mother Earth," said Goldenstar.

"We helped, too," said Elanor.

"And to whom else do I owe heartfelt thanks?" asked Master Stanislaw.

"Elanor and Simon," said Goldenstar. "They haven't said so — but we can be sure they are initiates of Dogbert Ambrosius. You know how well he picks them."

"Do you know him?" Simon asked.

"*Know him?*" Master Stanislaw laughed. "Who doesn't know that great master magus? Let us go inside. I'll tell you stories about old Dogbert you could blackmail him with."

"We can't stay," Simon said. "I have to get to Krakow, and we need to take back Baba Yaga's dandetiger." Master Stanislaw looked at Simon with a raised eyebrow. Elanor looked at Simon as if she wanted to kick him.

"Then off you shall be," said Master Stanislaw. "But beware of Baba Yaga — she changes like the wind."

"Why can't we just keep the dandetiger?" Elanor asked.

"We're taking it back," Simon said. He grabbed the packet from Elanor and stuck it in his pack.

"That flower will cause more harm than good if not returned," said Master Stanislaw. "Magicals must live by honor, or risk losing their power — or worse, using it for the wrong ends."

"I will bear them to the witch's hut," said Goldenstar. "That will hasten them on their way."

"I hope you can come back," said Master Stanislaw. "There is much to be learned here about the gifts of the earth. May you feel the magic!" He gave the usual thumbs up.

Simon and Elanor mounted Goldenstar again. In the barnyard, Sir Lech and Sir Czech were swinging feebly at each other with their swords, though their insults were probably more damaging than their weapons.

"They constantly fight over who will inherit their father's domain," said Goldenstar, "but it will probably all go to their younger brother, who is well versed in magic."

Goldenstar was gone in a flash. Within minutes she streaked past a large, smouldering patch of ground. Elanor winced. Later, passing travelers would call it the Devil's Hole and detour around the blackened ground in fear of being swallowed down forever.

In no time at all, Goldenstar slowed to a halt just in sight of the old, rickety hut. "Will you go see Baba Yaga?" Simon asked.

"Now is not the time," said Goldenstar. "I am called in another direction. Tell her that we shall meet when the time is right. Beware, should the second sister be there. But even she may be harmless — if you humor her."

"We won't stay but a minute, anyway," Simon said. "I want to get to the road before dark."

"As you continue on the path, take the second fork on the right. There is a trail on the left side also, but do not go that way. It leads to the hut of the third Baba Yaga."

"*Third Baba Yaga?*" Elanor said. "How many of them are there?"

"She is the last, but she is a true Wicked Witch," said Goldenstar. "Even her sisters avoid her, so keep to the path. May you feel the magic!" The fantastic mare spun around and was gone like a four-legged rocket.

Simon and Elanor approached the hut more cautiously than the first time. They were tired and hungry, but eager to be finished with old witches. Simon raised his hand to knock, but as before, a squeaky voice called out, "Come in, my children. Don't just stand there."

"It sounds like the same one," Elanor whispered.

Simon opened the door and stuck his head inside. The old witch was standing at the cauldron, stirring away. It appeared as though she had been there all morning. The fat, black cat was cuddled between her feet. It ran to the window ledge and jumped up to rest there. "Come in, my Lovelies. I see you've come to return my dandetiger."

Simon relaxed. He went inside – Elanor followed. "Have a seat, Dearies. Just a bit more stirring and this wart remover will be ready," said the sweet, old voice. "It brings a good price at market, though I don't see why anyone would want to be rid of such a lovely beauty mark." Elanor eased closer to peek into the cauldron.

"We came for just a minute," said Simon. He sat at the table and opened up his pack. "I have the rest of the dandetiger here." He reached into the bag and pulled out his golden apple. "That's not it," he said. He set the apple by the rowan wand, which still lay there. Baba Yaga wiped her wand on her filthy robe and walked behind the table.

Simon dug around and pulled out the leaf-wrapped bundle. He set it beside his apple. "How sweet of you," said Baba Yaga, "such honest children. I *must* prepare you a wonderful lunch."

"We really don't have time —" The black cat screeched loudly and jumped out the window. Much louder cat wailing reverberated from the yard. Simon and Elanor rushed to the window, but the cat was gone.

"She's always doing that," Baba Yaga said sweetly. "She chases gnomes and pixies from the yard." Simon crossed back to the table and picked up his backpack. "Do sit down. It won't take but a minute," Baba Yaga insisted. She placed a loaf of bread on the table.

"We really must go," Simon said. He picked up his apple and took a big bite, reminded how hungry he was. Immediately, his eyes rolled back in his head and he stiffened like a board.

Elanor watched as Simon fell backwards and hit the floor with a loud thud. "Simon!" she screamed, rushing to his side. "What happened to him?" She looked up at Baba Yaga. The old witch had a sinister grin on her face. She held Simon's apple in her outstretched hand.

"Oh, dear me," screeched the hag mockingly. "He must have tasted one of my enchanted apples by mistake." She broke into a wicked laugh.

"You killed him!" Elanor said. She shook Simon's body.

"He's not dead," said Baba Yaga. "What kind of stew would that make?" She dropped Simon's apple on the table and picked up her wand, but Elanor sprang up with her own in hand.

"STUPIDUS!" she spelled. The old witch flipped backwards. Elanor pointed the wand at Simon. "RESTORE!" Simon remained stiff on the floor.

The hag pulled herself up. "STUPIDUS! to you, too," she spelled at Elanor. The young Wicked Witch Hunter flew back away from Simon and hit the wall. Baba Yaga sprang from behind the table. "MORTIS SIMULATIS!" she spelled, moving in closer.

Elanor rolled away from this one, shaking off the shock

she'd just received. She aimed her wand, "EXPELLO WAND!" she spelled. The wooden rod flew from the old witch's hand and landed outside the window.

"Is that the best you have? Your little school tricks are no match for my magic," said Baba Yaga. She grabbed the rowan wand off the table.

Elanor's eyes opened wide. She puffed up boldly. "I ain't afraid of you — you stupid, old bwitch."

Baba Yaga was infuriated. She aimed the new wand at Elanor. "TRANSFORMUS TOAD!" she spelled. Instead of seeing a warty toad appear in front of her, Baba Yaga felt a powerful twitch. Her whole body went into a convulsive dance of transformation. Her skin began to tighten and turn milky white. Her hair became a full, dark, glimmering mane. Her grimy, yellow teeth took on a radiant shine. Her nose shrank to fit perfectly with the rosy cheeks and full lips that now formed a beautiful, young face.

The lovely maiden slammed the wand down on the table. "*Rowan wood*!" she screamed in terror. She fell into a chair and stared at her pretty, outstretched hands. "Look what's happened to me!" She sobbed and caressed her face with her fingertips. "I've become so ugly. *Hideous*! My powers will be gone for ages."

As the girl rubbed her face, the bulbous wart fell from her sleek nose and thudded on the table. It rolled off onto the floor with a dull plunk and was swooped up by the fat, black cat, who had returned to watch the battle from the window sill. The cat ran toward the window, pausing to swallow down the nasty blob. It immediately transformed into an ugly witch, leapt out the window, grabbed up Baba Yaga's old wand, and disappeared into the woods.

Elanor almost felt sorry for the pretty girl. "What are you gloating at?" screamed the maiden through heavy sobs.

"What have you done to Simon?" Elanor said. "How can I save him?" She broke into tears. The two young girls seemed to cry together.

"Take him and go," the maiden said, "before I take an axe and chop him to pieces."

Elanor grabbed up the rowan wand from the table. She spotted the packet of dandetiger and stuffed it in her robe pocket. Then she put Simon's magic apple in his pack, levitated him, and led him out the door with her wand. She headed down the path to the sounds of the young maiden screaming and smashing things in the rickety hut.

"Simon, how am I going to get you out of this one?" Elanor sniffled. "I bet that stupid Morgana would figure something out. I've got to get you to Master Dogbert some way. I just hope he can do something. Come, Master — *please* come."

Elanor was glad she didn't meet anyone on the trail. She was too drained for confrontation and worried sick about Simon. But her solitude soon ended. A raspy hum echoed from ahead on the trail. Elanor moved Simon into the trees. The identical twin of the witch she had just defeated rounded a bend in the trail, carrying a basketful of mushrooms. Elanor realized that it could only be the good sister. She sprang in front of the witch, who was given such a fright that her mushrooms went flying through the air.

"You tricked us!" Elanor shouted. She waved her wand threateningly. "Look what your sister did to my Simon." She twitched her wand in the floating boy's direction and pulled him out of the woods.

"Oh, my!" said Baba Yaga. "That is most unfortunate. I see my sister's hand in this."

"Yeah, and you set us up. You knew we were coming back with the dandetiger," Elanor said, angry.

"Did I know when?" asked Baba Yaga.

"I guess not," said Elanor, weakening.

"Do you think the whole world stands still for you?"

"No, but what am I going to do? *Look at him*."

The old witch turned her eyes to Simon, concerned. When she lifted the boy's eyelid a bloodshot ball stared back. She held her hand several inches over Simon's heart. "Did my sister give him something to eat or drink?"

"She slipped him a poisoned apple. But she said he's not dead," Elanor said.

"How did you escape her?" Baba Yaga asked, suspicious.

"She tried to hit me with a knockout spell, but I got her first," Elanor lied.

"I am afraid there's nothing I can do for him. We certainly can't take him back to my hut now," said Baba Yaga. "Only my second sister, Baba Yaga, can help you."

"There are *three* of you — all named Baba Yaga?" asked Elanor. She didn't want to let on that she knew there was a third sister.

"That is so," answered the witch, "but we are rarely seen together, so it matters not." It seemed to Elanor that the hag was more distant than she had been when they first met in the old hut.

"Is she more like you, or your other sister?" asked Elanor.

"She is more evil than a coven of Wicked Witches," said Baba Yaga. "But she is bound to be civil to those who come to her of their own free will."

"What if she kicked that habit?" Elanor said.

"What choice do you have?" said Baba Yaga. "Soon no one will be able to save him. You must go now." The hag shook her arm. A small, white feather floated out from her sleeve and hovered in the air. "Follow this. It will lead you to Baba Yaga's hut. Give my sister what gold you have and tell her everything that has happened. She will be pleased that you got the best of her sister."

Elanor watched the old witch move away down the trail. She turned back just in time to see the feather drifting away. She took hold of Simon's hood and pulled him through the air in pursuit. At first the going was easy, but after some time the colors faded, and the soft grass and wonderful wildflowers gave way to briars. Elanor could hardly make her way without scratching up her ankles. Finally, she pointed her wand at the feather. "CONSISTO!" she commanded. The wispy cursor halted in midair.

Elanor put one hand on Simon's belly and pushed him lightly down to waist level. She then pointed her wand at his feet and raised it about a foot. "MAXIMIZE!" she spelled. Simon's feet stretched up to Elanor's wand. "I'm sorry, Simon, but I guess you really wouldn't mind." She straddled

Simon's legs and leaned back on his feet. The feather continued on its mission.

After a while, the trees began to thin somewhat, and the sun shined more brightly. Elanor spotted a clearing ahead. The feather swished around a bit and then took off back through the woods. "I guess we're here," Elanor said. She climbed off of Simon and minimized his feet back to normal size — she hoped. She left the woods, pulling Simon along again.

Elanor couldn't believe what she found in the clearing. There was a hut, slightly larger than the previous, but this one was supported on *two huge chicken legs* and was spinning round and round! The chicken hut was surrounded by a gruesome fence constructed of human bones. The gate posts were mounted with skulls, and the lock was a set of shining teeth with a keyhole carved in it.

Elanor wasn't surprised that the gate was open. "Who'd want to get in here, anyway?" she thought. She stood in front of the spinning hut. "How do I make that thing stop?" She pointed her wand at the chicken-legged shack and closed her eyes. She said the first thing that came to mind, "Hut, hut, I say to thee, stop that spinning, with your front to me."

Elanor opened her eyes — the hut had done as she commanded. She moved uneasily toward the entrance, past a huge, rusty mortar and pestle. She reached to tap on the door, but it slammed open with a loud bang.

CHAPTER FIFTEEN

MORZMEAD

"Come in. You needn't break the door down," said a high, scratchy voice. Elanor pulled Simon in behind her. The place was similar inside to the other sisters' hut, but it seemed much larger than it appeared from the yard. A fire blazed away in a large brick oven, instead of the dusty fireplace where a dry, rusty cauldron sat. The very thin, black cat, who crouched in front of a mouse hole, didn't bother to check who had entered.

Elanor's eyes scanned the room. Her gaze passed over a shelf by the door upon which sat a honey-colored chunk of amber. Inside was what appeared to be a bee. The insect's wings were flapping rapidly. All the other shelves were lined with the usual witch stuff.

Baba Yaga sat at the table. She was the ugliest hag Elanor had seen in Magic Space. The old witch was incredibly bony. Elanor couldn't believe she could hold the pestle with which she grinded away in a small mortar. Half of her weight must have come from the hideous warts that covered her face and from the long nose that hooked over her thin lips.

But something else captured Elanor's attention. A *human hand* was levitating over the table! It held a pestle and was grinding something in its own mortar.

"Come closer, girl," Baba Yaga said. When the hag opened her mouth, Elanor noticed that she had a set of sharp-pointed iron teeth. The girl cautiously approached the table. Baba Yaga smelled so funky that Elanor wanted to do a Purgo spell on her. "Did some one send you, or have you come of your own accord?"

"We chose to come," said Elanor. "My friend needs help. He ate a poisoned apple."

Baba Yaga got up from her chair and passed her hand underneath Simon.

"And it made him float in the air?" said the hag. "I've *never* seen that."

"I levitated him — so we could move quicker," said Elanor.

"Not bad," muttered Baba Yaga. She pulled her wand and pointed it at the floating hand. "REPELLO!" she screeched. The hand flew up and bounced off the ceiling. It landed on top of the big oven. With another flick of the wand, the mortar and pestle floated up to the hand. "Rest him on the table."

Elanor pulled her wand. "DESCENDO!" she spelled. Simon settled stiffly on the table. For a moment, the two witches stood with their wands held up — their eyes met briefly.

"What makes you think I should help a nice little witch like you?" Baba Yaga spat. Elanor put her wand away and drew out the rowan wand. "I have a present for you," she said, laying the wand on the table, "and I have gold. I'll pay you if you can bring him back."

"*If?* I am Baba Yaga! I know magic beyond what you shall *ever* learn!" the angry hag said. But then she noticed the golden shinies Elanor had laid on the table. Her wicked grimace changed into a wicked grin. She grabbed the coins up in her skeletal hand and slung them into a corner of the room. The skinny cat didn't stir from her mouse-watching. "Well, well. You just might make a talented young witch some day, after all."

The old witch went to the oven and tossed in a couple of logs. "Who is this boy, and how did you come here?" she asked sweetly.

"We're schoolmates. We were going to Krakow to see the dragon there," Elanor said.

"And you met my sister — with her ridiculous apples. So elementary, the fool," said Baba Yaga.

"But then I met your other sister. She told me to come here and you'd help if I gave you gold." Baba Yaga raised her eyebrows. Elanor fell silent, feeling she had said something wrong. The old hag tossed another log into the oven.

Baba Yaga pointed her wand at Simon. Elanor's stomach churned with fear. "That flower-picking fool has no right sticking her ugly nose in my business," said the hag. "But," her tone changed quickly, "I have accepted your gold. He will be healed, and then we'll have a nice dinner." Elanor flinched.

The witch turned away from Simon and pointed her wand at another hand. It was lying on the mantle of the fireplace. Elanor hadn't noticed that one. "SERUM VITAE!"

commanded Baba Yaga. The hand floated to a high shelf, pushed aside a couple of dusty canisters, and gently took hold of a small, gold vial. It gave the container to the old witch and then hovered just behind her head.

"The Serum of Life! This formula has been lost to all but my family. It is passed only to the eldest daughter," said Baba Yaga. She placed her wand on top of the oven and then leaned over Simon and poured three drops of the thick liquid into his mouth. Elanor put her wand away. "He'll come to in a few moments," Baba Yaga continued, holding up the vial. "It requires the blood of a unicorn, but with another rare ingredient it would increase my powers a hundredfold. What spells I could do then! And I would live for *thousands* of years."

The old witch gave the vial back to the hand. It took the container and put it away on the shelf. Baba Yaga turned to Elanor with a crazed look in her eyes. "I'll give the knowledge to you if you stay as my apprentice," she said. "I'll teach you spells, potions — magic you never imagined."

Elanor stood frozen. The hag raved on. "You're ugly now, but the taste of wizard flesh will give you lovely warts and make your nose grow. When the boy awakens, I'll cut out his heart. You can eat his liver — it's the tastiest part."

Elanor wanted to hurl. She hated liver, and she wasn't about to eat Simon's. "I'd love to learn all that you know," she stalled. "I'd love to be the greatest witch in Magic Space."

"*I'm* the greatest witch in Magic Space!" shot back the old hag.

"I mean, the second best witch," said Elanor, "but I

promised not to hurt anybody. And I swore to look after Simon. He's my friend. I like him a lot." She pointed to the rowan wand on the table. "We brought you that nice present. You said you'd help us. We —"

"Silence!" screamed the hag. "You dare to defy Baba Yaga? You think that a little twig is a good trade for the Elfin Spark?" Elanor's eyes widened with fear. "Oh, yes, I know who your precious Simon Peppercorn is. I've been offered a mountain of gold for his capture. And here he is, out of sight of his Warrior Wizard protectors — and only Baba Yaga to restore his life. He belongs to me. Now shake him — he's only sleeping."

Elanor leaned over Simon, but instead of giving him a shake she pulled out her wand. "SPAZZ OUT!" she spelled. Taken off guard, the ugly hag fell into a frenzied, robotic dance. She shook, twitched, and vibrated across the room, where she quickly recovered.

Then the hand above the oven dropped its pestle and slung Baba Yaga's wand to her. The angry witch raised the lethal rod.

"STUPIDUS!" Elanor spelled, before Baba Yaga had a chance. But the old hag was quick. She spelled back, "DEFLECTO!" The spell flew back and hit Elanor. She collapsed against the table — her wand flew out of her hand.

"Stupid fool — you would duel with me? TRANSFORMUS PIG!" Baba Yaga spelled. Elanor turned into a pink oinker — she grunted frantically. Baba Yaga aimed her wand again. "LEVITATO!" The pig leveled out in the air, and the vicious hag directed her toward the blazing oven with her wand. "Then your liver will make a tasty snack." Elanor drifted closer to the fire.

Suddenly, Simon sat up. "RESTORE!" he spelled. Elanor fell to the floor just in front of the oven. She jumped up and grabbed the rowan wand off the table.

"Playing possum were you?" said Baba Yaga. "Let the games continue. APPREHENDO!" The two severed hands flew at the magicmates. One of them grabbed Simon by the throat. The other shot toward Elanor, but the skinny, black cat leapt into the air and picked it off. Cat and hand rolled on the ground until the cat got the upper hand and jumped through the window with its prey.

Elanor quickly took aim at Baba Yaga. "L-O-L!" she spelled. The warty witch bent double in hysterics. Elanor turned to Simon. His face was as red as a beet — his eyes bulged out like ping pong balls. "LIBERATO!" Elanor spelled. The hand let go and backed off a couple of feet. Elanor pointed the rowan wand at it and swept her hand through the air. "DRAG&DROP!" The hand rocketed into the shelves across the room, smashing several jars. A bunch of big eyeballs fell to the floor and rolled around. Many of them were scooped up by several five-legged lizards that had been in one of the jars.

Baba Yaga took the offensive. She spelled at Elanor, "STUPIDUS!" Elanor ducked, but the spell hit Simon. He flipped back over the table.

Elanor fired off the next spell. "EXPELLO WAND!" Baba Yaga's wand flew out of her hand and landed high on a shelf. She lunged at Elanor and grabbed hold of the rowan wand.

"You think you know something about magic? Give me that wand, you little *bwitch*!" screeched the old hag.

"What'd you call me, you skanky old hag?" said Elanor. "I'll put something on you magic can't take off!" The two determined witches pulled and shoved, struggled and tussled, until Elanor felt the burning heat of the oven on her back. Simon crawled off the floor with his wand, but he couldn't get a good aim at Baba Yaga. When the heat became unbearable for Elanor, she spun suddenly around so the old witch's back was to the oven.

Baba Yaga seemed unaffected by the heat. She tugged even harder. Then, Elanor let go her grip. The nasty hag fell back with great momentum and flipped into the flames. The fire roared up, as if in anger, and spit a cloud of sparks into the room. Elanor turned toward Simon, who stood in shock. "Let's get out of here," she said.

The magicmates headed for the door. Elanor picked up her wand. She pointed it at the chunk of amber on the shelf by the door. "LIBERATO!" she spelled. The amber dissolved away into particles of brilliant, golden light. The bumble bee who had been trapped inside hovered in midair. "You can get away, too," Elanor said. The bee flew out into the yard. As Elanor closed the door, a jar labeled *GOBLIN SALT* smashed against the wall, thrown by the remaining severed hand.

When the couple reached the gate, the hut started hopping and spinning on its spindly chicken legs. "Fried chicken won't never taste the same," said Elanor.

"Let's just go," said Simon. "Which way's the road?"

Elanor looked around in confusion. "I don't know — I came through the woods. Maybe we…" She paused as a strange buzzing came in their direction from around the hut. The sound grew louder and louder. As it did, a fuzzy spot headed toward the magicmates — it grew bigger and bigger. After a moment, an eight-foot-long bumblebee was hovering in front of Simon and Elanor. It had four eyes and two sets of double wings.

"You freed me," said the strange bee. "I can help you. I'll take you anywhere." The bee slowed his busy wings and dropped down for the magicmates to climb on. Simon slid on behind the front set of wings.

"No, you don't!" said Elanor. "You rode up front on Goldenstar — it's my turn." Simon scooted back reluctantly and put his arms around Elanor. "Who's trying to get a hug now?" Elanor said, smiling. Simon loosened his grip as the bee took off into the air.

"We're going to Krakow," Simon said over Elanor's shoulder, "if you could just get us to the road, or to an inn." The bee rose higher and then cruised just over the treetops.

Elanor noticed several large stones below them the color of the one which had encased the bee. There seemed to be something moving inside. "What are those things down there?" she asked over the low hum of bee wings.

"Goblins," said the bee. "I'm a bomberbee. We drop honey bombs on our enemies, and it hardens on them. But Baba Yaga used a spell to catch me in my own honey bomb. Then she minimized it and set me on her shelf."

Back in Baba Yaga's hut, the skinny cat was sitting on the table, gnawing on the second severed hand. Suddenly, the flames in the oven rose furiously and flared through the door. *Baba Yaga leapt from the fire!* She landed on her bony feet by the table. The well-fed cat jumped straight up, its fur standing on end, and was out the window in the blink of an eye.

The old hag's hair was scorched almost completely off of her blackened head, which made her nose appear twice as long as before. Her nasty robe was burned to tatters, but parts of it still clung to her emaciated frame. "Those little urchins haven't seen the ugly side of Baba Yaga," she said.

The smut-faced hag found her wand and rushed out the door. She jumped into the large mortar and struck it on the side with the pestle. The mortar flew quickly over the trees, faster and faster, as Baba Yaga struck it violently.

"Why did she do that to you?" Elanor asked.

"Wicked Witches use our honey in their concoctions," said the bomberbee. "When I refused to give it to Baba Yaga, she entrapped me. But now, no one has to worry about her."

"*We do!*" said Simon. He had turned his head to see what was clanging behind them.

"She's coming up on us in a big bucket."

"You must be crazy," Elanor said. But the burst of a fireball very close by changed her mind. Baba Yaga's vicious screams drowned out the low hum of the bomberbee. The hag shot another fireball from her wand, but it collided with one that Elanor shot back and exploded.

Simon aimed his wand at the huge mortar. "ELECTRO!" he spelled. A short firebolt zipped out of his wand and struck the iron mortar. Blue and red streaks of electrical power flickered around the witch's vehicle.

"Ouch, ouch, ooh, ooh — ouch!" Baba Yaga chanted, dancing gingerly. She pointed her wand at a small passing cloud. "PRECIPITATO!" she spelled. The little cloud burst into tears, filling the mortar with cool water and soaking the old witch. Black soot ran down her face like cheap mascara.

The bomberbee had flown ahead, but Baba Yaga whipped the mortar violently and soon made up lost air. She aimed her wand in the growing darkness and spelled, "MORTIS SIMULATIS!" Simon grabbed Elanor's head and ducked them both down just in time. The spell flew inches over them.

Simon turned to flick a spell at the evil witch, but he was nearly blinded by a brilliant light that streaked between him and the hag. "What the heck?" he said. The light circled around the bomberbee and cruised alongside, inches away. Simon then saw that the bright light came from the wand tip of Master Magus Dogbert Ambrosius. The old Warrior Wizard sat cross-legged on his flying carpet — Morgana and Arthur were perched behind him.

"Master Dogbert!" Elanor shouted. Instead of answering, Dogbert faced off with Baba Yaga. The hideous hag shot a glowing, red fireball toward the flying carpet, but Dogbert caught it up on the tip of his wand. The fireball grew to the size of a basketball as the master spun his wand in tiny circles. Dogbert then whipped the glowing globe at Baba Yaga.

The ball grew larger and larger as it sped through the sky, and then it encircled the ugly witch and her rusty mortar like a bomberbee's honey bomb.

Baba Yaga shot another fireball at Dogbert, but when it came into contact with the Warrior Wizard's globe, it disintegrated into billions of multicolored sparks. Dogbert pointed his wand at the glittering witchball. "GLOBUS PRO-PELLO!" he spelled. The ball of light flew high up and across the sky in a great arc. When it reached its highest point, it exploded into a great display of celestial fireworks.

The company of Magicals watched a smouldering streak continue the fiery arc. After a few seconds, it disappeared into the dark forest with a tremendous, burning crash. "Well," said Dogbert, "I see she got a blast out of that." Simon was overjoyed to see his best friend, regardless of his jokes.

The magic carpet and the bomberbee cruised over the treetops until a break in the trees revealed a long ribbon on the ground below. Dogbert led the descent onto the road to Krakow.

"You have been of great service, Meadmorz," Dogbert said to the bomberbee. "I fear they wouldn't have escaped Baba Yaga without your assistance."

"Nay, Master Dogbert. I would still be the prisoner of that worst of Wicked Witches had good Elanor not set me free," said Meadmorz. "It is I who received the greater favor."

"Then I shall request a further service on behalf of these young witchmates," Dogbert said. The girls looked at each other in surprise.

"I am at your command," said Meadmorz.

"I would be truly grateful if you would transport them to the manor of Master Stanislaw immediately," said Dogbert. He turned to Morgana and Elanor. "You shall spend some time learning about magical herbs with a great master. He will…"

"*Not me!*" said Elanor. "I have to go with Simon — I have to protect him."

Morgana rolled her eyes. She slid onto the bomberbee's back and looked at Simon. Her left eyelid dropped lazily in a gentle wink. Simon was confused.

"Do not question my commands," said Dogbert. "Time is of the essence. Now, take your place on the back of Meadmorz."

Elanor ran to Simon and threw her arms around his neck. "Don't you worry about no stupid dragon," she said. "You're a Warrior Wizard. You can beat him." She rushed to the bomberbee and muscled her way in front of Morgana. Then she raised her thumb into the air, and her magicmates did the same.

"May you feel the magic!" the youngsters said together. Meadmorz lifted above the treetops and was soon out of sight. A triangle of Wicked Witch Hunters flew out of nowhere, well lit by the nearly full moon, and followed close behind the bomberbee.

Simon hoped they would stay the night at an inn, and he'd have his own room — away from Arthur. He'd lost his dislike for the annoying shape shifter, but he was tired, and nervous about the next day. Besides that, the big-faced moon had him feeling unusually irritable.

"We'll just get off the road and make camp," Dogbert said, much to Simon's disappointment. At least he darkened the dome of the Druid's Fog so the stabbing moonbeams wouldn't disturb Simon.

Arthur, of course, just had to hear all about Goldenstar and Baba Yaga. He managed to conclude that Simon would probably be eaten by Smok Vavelski without Elanor there to protect him. But his own magic had greatly improved in the brief time they had been apart (according to his own estimates). "Master Spurlock helped me get the knack for Transformation spells, but I still can't touch Morgana," Arthur said. "You should've been there when she turned Alexis into a toad. She looked like a miniature Master Todd."

Simon finally felt like listening. "Why did she do it, anyway?" he asked, trying to sound nonchalant.

"I don't know — it happened so fast. Elanor was telling Alexis about the Harp Maiden. Alexis said you'd probably fly back there as soon as the Venture is over, cause you really like blonds. She was twirling a curl with her finger and grinning like an idiot — then all of a sudden, she turned into a toad."

"It's time to turn in to bed," Dogbert said. "Simon has a big day ahead, and we have work to do ourselves."

Simon assumed that Dogbert wanted to let him have a little time to contemplate his future, however brief it may prove to be. They had already discussed the situation, but no amount of strategy could prepare a twelve-year-old initiate to confront a horrible dragon.

Regardless of the darkened view, Simon peered upward, as if drawn by the transforming power of the moon. So many times he had watched upon the yellow orb, wishing he could walk on its surface and jump, boundless, into the air. Now it seemed to be pulling something from inside him — something that lay in wait to take over his very nature.

Simon tried the only thing that could possibly relieve the ache that twisted and churned his guts. He concentrated on the Elfin Spark. Soon his breathing became deep and slow. His focus narrowed to a pulsating point. His mind began to fill with the image of a figure in a Warrior Wizard's robe standing in front of something that gave off a bright glow.

The figure slowly turned. Simon became aware that it was he, Simon Peppercorn — Warrior Wizard. But his eyes were large and bloodshot! His face was hairy and gruesome. His teeth were long, pointed fangs.

Simon rose with a terrible start. The Darkening spell must have worn off of the Druid's Fog, for the nearly full moon was beaming overhead. Under its pale, amber light, Simon noticed Dogbert sitting cross-legged with the hilt of his sword held in both hands at his chest. The blade pointed straight up at the yellow ball in the sky.

Simon lay down again and rolled restlessly in the sort of sleep that never seems fulfilled, but veils moments of nothingness. During one of those deeper dozes, master and shape shifter must have slipped away. Simon woke up and found himself alone, more so than he had ever been in his life. Beside his head, he found a chunk of stone. It looked a lot like a stubby finger.

"I'm going to petrify Arthur," Simon said — perhaps to Frollo. He packed away the souvenir and started walking with the rising sun.

CHAPTER SIXTEEN

SMOK VAVELSKI

Krakow — at last! The walk had been eventless on the well-traveled road. Simon had transformed his robe into beggar's clothes to disguise himself. And now he stood outside the walled city in his Warrior Wizard attire, overwhelmed. He had been through so much to get here. Scenes from the Venture ran through his mind, though not for long. Perhaps the most dangerous and most important fight lurked ahead. But if successful, he would be healed — no more worrying about becoming a werewolf and being hunted down by Warrior Wizards.

The moon wouldn't be full until tomorrow night. "Plenty of time," Simon thought. "I helped Waldo kill a dragon — I can kill this one by myself." Then he placed his hand on Hrunting's hilt. "Well — maybe Smok Vavelski won't be in when I get there."

Simon didn't mind paying the one golden shiny dragon tax, for Krakow was magnificent. A small hill called Vavel rose up at the edge of the town. It was topped by a castle and a cathedral surrounded by their own wall. The wide Vistula river snaked by down below the hill. It formed a natural defense against trolls, goblins, and other invaders.

There was a great hustle and bustle in every street and lane. It reminded Simon somewhat of the Mount of St. Michael. The shops sold the same wares, though many were more exotic. Mounted knights in full armor made their way through the crowds. Carts and carriages wheeled through at a snail's pace. Simon even passed by a small cart pulled by a giant purple snail.

In one lane, Simon had to crush against a wall as a procession of richly dressed ladies-in-waiting and heavily armed guards led the way for a small, richly decorated carriage. It was powered by two six-legged ponies ("Ten-legged for a mush-man," Simon thought). A young girl with long, dark curls and a third eye in the middle of her forehead sat inside the carriage. She smiled widely at Simon as her vehicle passed.

Simon couldn't believe the size of the market square. A long, ornate building sat in the very middle. It was fronted by an arcade with stylish arches and columns where merchants sold fabulous cloth: silk, velvet, cotton, wool, fancy lace, and other wares. A couple of Warrior Wizards were checking out robes. They nodded to Simon, but he crossed back through the square, which was packed with an incredible number and variety of people and creatures.

Simon came upon the group of Arab traders he had met on the Mount of St. Michael. He almost stopped one of the veiled girls to buy a banana, but thought better of it. Instead, he took one of the side lanes, where he found a milk bar.

He didn't have much money left, but Simon was happy to be charged three silver shinies for a large plate of fruit-filled pierogis, which he washed down with a glass of warm milk and honey. As he finished his meal, a trumpet began blasting out one solemn note at a time — then it stopped abruptly.

A young man at the next table, in the faded robes of a scholar, noticed Simon's perplexed look. "It is a tradition from the time of the Tartar and Goblin Wars," said the student, smiling. He invited himself to sit at Simon's table. "Long ago Tartars and goblins invaded our land from the east. The Tartars wanted our horses and treasure, but the goblins wanted to take over Vavel Hill and dig up the chakra crystal. But when the enemy was seen in the distance, the town trumpeter climbed the stairs of the watchtower.

"He blew the alarm, but half way through, an arrow pierced his throat — shot by a Tartar warrior. Now, every day when the sun is at its peak, the town trumpeter blows his horn. He stops on the same note which sounded the death of his heroic predecessor."

"Wow!" Simon said. "But I guess you won the war, unless you're a goblin in disguise."

"Oh, yes," said the student, ignoring Simon's joke. "The trumpet was magical. The signal reached the great Warrior Wizard Dogbert Ambrosius ("That figures," Simon thought.). He arrived quickly with other Warrior Wizards. Together with many great knights and a squadron of Swan Maidens, they destroyed the enemy.

"A handful of goblins held out deep beneath the earth in the Vielichka salt mine several miles east of here. But the Warrior Wizards turned them into stalagmites. The dwarf miners pulverized them and sold off the salt to forest witches. The salt business is still outsourced to the dwarves."

"The trumpet *was* magical. You don't have it any longer?" Simon said.

"Alas, it was taken by Smok Vavelski," said the student. "He is the most dangerous dragon in Magic Space, though scholars in other regions dispute it. We must give him treasure and sheep to leave us alone."

"Why doesn't someone just kill him?" Simon asked.

"It was attempted when he first came — after the Tartar and Goblin Wars," said the young man. "My research suggests that he was attracted here by the power of the chakra. At any rate, after a Dragon Slayer and a Warrior Wizard were eaten by the beast, it was decided to leave him alone and make a deal."

"*Make a deal?*" Simon said in disbelief.

"We are a peaceful and wealthy town," said the scholar, "on a major trade route. A man-eating dragon would be bad for business. And then there's the income from the dragon tax and the tourists. It ends up a nifty profit for the town."

Simon couldn't believe his ears. "You mean people come here to watch a dragon eat sheep?"

"Oh yes," said the student proudly, "my professor of Magical Marketing developed the concept when he was a student at the Krakow Magic Academy. That was after his plan to charge admission to the Energizer Spot proved successful."

"Aren't people afraid the dragon will eat *them*?" Simon asked.

"No problem there," said the scholar. "They pay an extra silver shiny for insurance and sign a waiver. But it never comes to that. Smok Vavelski doesn't want to lose out on a good thing."

"What's an Energizer Spot?" Simon asked reluctantly. The long-winded answers were wearing him out.

"The chakra below Vavel Hill absorbs earth energy and intensifies it," said the student. "And it radiates it. Some of it concentrates at a spot behind the cathedral."

"The Energizer Spot?" Simon said.

"It has a great effect on most creatures, but especially Magicals; they are more sensitive to it," said the student. "And it's a big money-maker." Simon finally paid for his food — and the student's — then tore himself away. At least he had found out where and when the dragon feeding took place.

Simon decided he would slip into Smok Vavelski's cavern just after the show started. That should give him enough time to find his way to the chakra crystal. There was no hurry, so he had a treat at a huge Magic Space IceCreamery. Then he headed toward Vavel Hill to check out the Energizer Spot. The square was still filled like a crazy circus, but the Magical Marketing student said it was the easiest way to go.

"Simon! Simon Peppercorn!" Simon looked about. Who could be calling his name in such a crowd? He looked around and saw several heads, and twice as many hands, protruding through a row of stocks nearby.

"Thomas Thickwig!" Simon said.

"So *glad* to see you, Simon. We Magicals *must* stick together, you know. I heard about your defeat of that awful giant. I wanted to stay and help, but — well — you know the circumstances. Now, if you could just get me out of here with a Liberato spell…"

"What are you locked up for?" Simon asked.

"Oh, just a minor misunderstanding," said Thickwig. "It seems the jewels from the dragon's treasure I was selling were not altogether real. But the Magical Marketing student I got them from gave a complete guarantee."

Simon was about to take great pleasure in telling Thickwig he was where he deserved to be when several armed men approached and unlocked the stocks. "It's about time!" said Thickwig. "I see you've realized I'm friends with the heroic Warrior Wizard, Simon Peppercorn." The guards showed their respect by thrusting a shovel into Thickwig's hands. One of them shoved him forward. "Wh-where are you taking me?"

"To the viewing grounds. You're on dragon dung duty," answered the lead guard.

Simon pulled his hood low over his head and scrammed away from the protesting Thickwig. He turned off on a side street which soon brought him to the bottom of a hill. In spite of the massive stone walls and towers that loomed above, Simon sensed an incredible lightness about the hill. At the top, he entered through a gate and passed between the cathedral and castle into a courtyard. He turned left — drawn that way — and paid a golden shiny to enter a smaller square. It was less crowded than Simon had expected, but more amazing.

Three dwarves in brown robes were jumping up and down twenty feet in the air. Three others stood stiffly — like troll stones. A witch in a white robe was flying around the courtyard, and her broom was flying behind, riderless! A Warrior Wizard stood motionless by a wall to Simon's left. He held his sword straight over his head in both hands. The blade was glowing red-hot.

A dark-skinned man, dressed only in a loincloth, stood on one leg near the Warrior Wizard. His hair was in long, tight braids that dragged the ground. "He's been standing there for two years," said a voice over Simon's shoulder. A wizard in a light green robe stepped up beside Simon. He had a big, fluffy bag slung over his shoulder. The friendly old face reminded the boy of Master Stanislaw.

"How does it work?" Simon asked.

"One stands still and quiet and absorbs the energy," said the wizard.

"Why are they all by that wall?"

"There is a chapel behind it which sits over the chakra. But the chapel stays closed. The energy inside is too powerful for most."

"What's it do, besides make dwarves hop and hair grow?" Simon asked. He was already feeling tingly throughout his body.

"It enhances physical and magical power — and it can bring about healing," said the wizard. "I bring my plants to increase their potency."

"Is the dragon more powerful because of the energy?" Simon asked.

"Most true," said the wizard. "Smok Vavelski is no ordinary drake, as Vavel is no ordinary hill. There are many power places, even in Hard Space. Many people find their own, but this is one of the most important. The dragon thrives upon it." Simon remembered the place by his dear, little river where he and Dogbert had practiced spells. The wizard bade Simon farewell and left with his bundle of herbs.

A couple of pilgrims left their place by the wall. One grumbled to the other that he didn't feel different at all. "Nearly eaten by trolls, I was. Two pairs of sandals worn out getting here, a nasty fight with a mushman, two golden shinies I worked three years for, and my witch's rash ain't no better at all," he said. The ragged man's body was covered with red and green blisters that oozed a yellowish gook. He scratched himself uncontrollably.

"I told you not to rub that witch's wart at the market for good luck. I just *knew* she was a Wicked Witch," said the second rustic, who wore a beaming smile and a radiant glow on his face. "You keep it up and you'll wake up in Hard Space some day."

Simon took the pilgrims' place by the chapel door. He wasn't really certain what to do, but he stood erect and closed his eyes. A thousand thoughts fluttered through his mind like butterflies on Japper Juice. He took a few deep breaths and tried to let go of everything. Soon Simon felt a current enter through his feet and slowly surge up his body. His heart began to pound so hard that he thought it would burst into pieces. Still, he tried not to think. The pounding in his chest became a warm pulse. Then his whole body became as light as a feather.

All the atoms of Simon's body seemed to separate as when he was with the Wanding Lord, but now even the atoms seemed to separate into particles. All the vibrating particles were being powered by a single point in the middle of his chest. *"The Elfin Spark,"* he thought. And that thought pulled Simon's focus back to himself. He slowly opened his eyes.

All objects appeared to Simon as brilliant swarms of dots, which quickly took on the shapes of the things they composed. The young Warrior Wizard felt like a rocket ready to take off to Mars. He jumped up into the air far above the dwarves, who were still hopping like children on a trampoline. On the way down, he grabbed hold of the witch's broom and flew several times around the square. He passed the witch twice!

Simon jumped off the broom, still feeling like a nuclear reactor. He pulled out his wand and pointed it skyward. Wandfire shot up and forked out in the heavens in much greater bolts than what Simon had seen from the Wanding Lord. When the lightning subsided, the dwarves fell heavily to the ground. The witch flew head on into a wall and crumpled to the earth — her broom combusted spontaneously. The Warrior Wizard opened his eyes, sheathed his sword, and disappeared. The dark-skinned man standing on one leg remained where he was, unmoved.

The Wandfire finally faded, and Simon stood still, holding his wand. He felt calmer, but more powerful than before — much of the energy had dissipated with the Wandfire. The dwarves bowed low to Simon and then humbly hurried from the square. The admission booth attendant hung up a *CLOSED* sign and scurried away.

Simon saw the witch moving slowly, moaning in pain. He started toward her to see if she was okay, but the earth began to tremble. "*Smok Vavelski*," Simon thought. "It's show time." He ignored the witch, who had risen to her hands and knees, and left the square. He then crossed the castle yard and half-levitated, half-leapt to the top of the high, protective wall. Simon looked down toward the bottom of the hill and saw that Smok Vavelski had climbed partly from his lair. The dragon roared loudly and blew an enormous stream of fire into the air. A loud cheer arose from across the river where a big crowd of tourists had formed.

When the dragon climbed all the way out of the cave, Simon noticed that it was much larger than he had imagined. Green and black scales covered its body. Two long, curved horns protruded from the sides of its massive head. A ridge of sharp-pointed spines stretched from between Smok's horns, down his back, and to the end of his long tail, which was tipped with a spear-like barb. The hind legs of the giant serpent were large and powerful — the front were smaller, but functional. Each foot had three sharp claws forward and one back.

The drake stretched his head skyward and exhaled another blast of flames, much to the delight of the audience. Simon figured the beast must be at least fifty feet long. Smok Vavelski coiled his huge tail, crouched on his back legs, and pushed himself upward. At the same time, his expansive wings flapped hard and raised him into the air. Again, the tourists shouted and cheered as the dragon rose high over the river, banked, and dived swiftly toward them. He shot flames over the crowd and roared skyward again.

Simon figured the show would probably go on for a while before the sacrificial cow was even brought out. He transformed the ground in front of the cave into a mattress and jumped down, hoping the dragon didn't look his way.

Undiscovered, Simon scurried quickly into the cave and lit his wand. He found that he was in a high, wide chamber that stretched on into a narrower tunnel. On either side, another passage opened up. One of the corridors was too narrow for the dragon to pass through, so Simon decided to stick with the main tunnel. After fifty yards or more, another large tunnel forked off to the left, but Simon kept going straight. Soon, however, the passage came to an end.

Disappointed, Simon backtracked and took the other way. After some time, the floor sloped more sharply down-ward. The tunnel made a long, S-shaped curve far below the hill. Simon felt the energy begin to tingle and grow inside his body. He hoped the chakra was close ahead. As he rounded the curve of the tunnel, he saw a bright flicker. "This *has* to be it," he said aloud. But it wasn't.

Simon had stepped into an enormous chamber at the end of the tunnel. It was filled with many piles of spectacu-lar treasure. The boy had never imagined so many precious jewels and objects of gold and silver. Swords, shields, and armor ornamented with sparkling gemstones were scattered among heaps of golden and silver shinies, heavy chains of gold, magnificent tableware, and golden figurines.

As great as the treasure was, Simon was disappointed to the point of tears. What did treasure matter to one who was about to become a vicious fiend? He turned away from the wondrous bling and hurried back the way he had come. At the entrance chamber again, Simon took the second wide passage. It also winded deep and wide into the earth. He rounded several of its bends until it ended at another tunnel. Slightly confused, Simon turned right — the floor appeared to decline sharply that way.

He quickly came to a large opening whose bottom half was blocked by a yellowish barrier studded with bright jewels. "I can't believe it! More treasure! Somebody help me!" he yelled out. Then the half-wall slid back. As it did, it gave way to large, black and green scales. Smok Vavelski squirmed from the chamber entrance onto his piles of treasure. Simon had circled and wound his way back to the treasure chamber!

"Somebody *help* you? Help you steal Smok Vavelski's treasure?" said the dragon, with a loud hiss. The spectacle was obviously over.

"N-no sir, Mr. Vavelski," Simon said. "I don't want your treasure. I just want to find the chakra — that's all. I need to touch it."

"Only *I* can withstand such power," said the dragon. He hissed and swished his enormous tail — treasure scattered around Simon's feet.

"I need it to heal me," Simon continued, trying to hide his fear.

"Heal? Nothing heals like dragon blood. You want to be a famous Dragon Slayer, do you?" The drake puffed a dark cloud of smoke from each nostril.

"A wolfern bit me," Simon blurted. "My master sent me to touch the chakra crystal for a cure, or I'll turn into a demon myself."

"Wolfern?" said Smok Vavelski. "Nothing tastes more disgusting than wolfish meat. I shall help you."

Simon was overcome with joy. "You'll tell me how to get to the chakra?"

"No!" bellowed the dragon. "I'll eat you, so you don't become a wolfern!" He snorted a hot flame toward Simon, but the wise, young Warrior Wizard was one step ahead. He was already hightailing it before the fire left the dragon's mouth. Smok Vavelski climbed off his treasure in hot pursuit.

As Simon rounded the first bend in the tunnel, he felt a searing heat on his back. The whole passage lit up brightly. Simon held firmly to his wand, but he knew there was only one thing he could do — RUN! And that's exactly what he did.

Simon expected the dragon to be slow on its feet, but the ever hotter flames licking at his back proved him wrong. He timed the blasts carefully, afraid the next burning belch might be the one that barbecued him. At the right moment, he pointed his wand over his shoulder.

"GOOGLE SNOWFLAKES!" Simon spelled. The fiery flame erupted as expected, but it was met by a great flurry of snow from Simon's wand. The young Magical was pounded by a huge splash of warm water. "Thank you, Keeper of Time!" Simon said on the run. He rushed toward the mouth of the cave and put on his swan cape, but was barely in the air when the dragon emerged from the cave and took off after him. Boy and dragon flew over the river and the magical hill like fighter planes in a dog fight.

Simon did all he could to avoid the beast's fiery breath. He dived toward the ground by the viewing area, hoping the pursuing drake would crash to the earth. The only result was a chance for Thomas Thickwig to escape. The talentless wizard was shoveling dragon dung when Smok Vavelski buzzed two feet over his head. The guards ran away in fear — Thickwig took off with his shovel in hand.

On a whim, Simon decided to help the magicless magician. He swooped low over the escapee and transformed the shovel into a flying broom. Thickwig climbed on clumsily and the broom took off. Simon swept away in the opposite direction to divert the dragon from his fellow Magical. He looked back for a moment and saw the broom zigzag over the water, do a triple loop-the-loop, and bolt out of sight with Thickwig hanging on for dear life.

Simon tried to distance himself from the dragon so he could think up a plan, but the creature was swift and agile in the air. There was only one thing that might work. Simon circled close under the drake and aimed his wand at the vulnerable belly. A great, multi-fingered bolt of Wandfire shot from the wand and flickered around the dragon's whole body. Precious stones, embedded in the monster's underside from lying on the treasure, lit up like a laser show and shattered into pieces. The few tourists who still lingered in the viewing area applauded wildly, thinking this was a bonus to the entertainment.

The dragon nose-dived toward the river, skimmed his burning belly on the water, and shot straight up into the sky like an arrow, disappearing from sight. Simon circled over Vavel Hill. He hoped Smok had blasted out of the atmosphere, but just as he decided to make another attempt at the cave, the dragon reappeared over the horizon in pursuit of a tiny object. As the thing got closer and bigger, it turned into Thomas Thickwig, flailing and tossing about on his bronco broom.

"I ought to let him get roasted," Simon thought. But he took off at full speed and buzzed the dragon to distract him from Thickwig. Simon flew back over the castle and dodged around the towers. He banked sharply above the cathedral, but the wise dragon had his number by now. Smok Vavelski turned sharply behind Simon and spit a tongue of fire that set the swan cape ablaze. Simon pointed his wand over his shoulder.

"EXTINGUIO!" he spelled. A strong puff of wind killed the fire immediately, but the swan cape was half destroyed. Simon glided to the ground in a narrow alley. He edged along the buildings to avoid the dragon's sight. As he made his way to the market square, the serpent's sprawling shadow passed back and forth on the ground. Havoc reined in the square — people and creatures were running in every direction. Peddlers' carts and merchants' stalls stood in flames.

Three Warrior Wizards appeared in the middle of the square, including the one Simon had seen at the Energizer Spot. When Smok Vavelski soared overhead, they raised their swords upwards and shot into the air like bottle rockets. Their blades penetrated the soft underbelly of the drake, but missed the heart, so massive was the beast's body.

The metal of the swords melted quickly, and the Warrior Wizards fell softly to the ground. Smok Vavelski roared loudly and blew fire across the whole square. He flew toward the Warrior Wizards, who now had their wands drawn. "MORTIS DRACONUM!" they spelled in unison. The mighty dragon floundered in the air and fell toward the ground. The great sweep of his tail shattered a large statue of a king to pieces.

The vicious beast hit the cobblestones hard. The Warrior Wizards charged him, their wands transformed into swords, but the indestructible drake raised his head and sprayed the brave Magicals with a long blast of flames. Caught off guard, the Warrior Wizards were totally consumed by the fire. Their ashes blew across the square.

Smok Vavelski lifted back into the air and circled over the town. Simon knew the drake was searching for him. He had to do something — smoke was rising everywhere — the disaster was his fault. Crouching behind an arch of the cloth hall, he stuffed the remainder of the swan cape into his backpack.

Then he rummaged around inside. Maybe something there would give him an idea. A pocket knife — even a sword would be of no use. Frollo's finger — a hundred whole Frollos would be useless against such a beast. The emerald from the harp maiden — that was supposed to bring back life, not take it. The techdeck Sammie gave him for his birthday — that was a whole other world, and right now he really missed it. Simon took the little skateboard from the box and spun it between his fingers. He read his sister's silly note, "A little board for a big fly."

Suddenly, a blast of dragon fire flashed behind Simon. He dropped the techdeck. The toy hit the ground and popped into a full-sized skateboard. "A LITTLE BOARD FOR A BIG FLY!" Simon shouted. He put one foot on the board, pushed off, and ollied off the ground. The board raised about four feet and hovered there.

"*Wow!*" Simon said, "*I can fly again.* Maybe I can lure the dragon away from town." He pressed on the board with his back foot and shot out through the archway. Then he flew up behind the dragon's head and dipped close to its face. He poked at the creature's eye with his wand, but that only angered him more.

The dragon flipped in the air and lashed at Simon with his powerful tail, but the boy had already taken refuge behind the tower of the great cloth hall. Smok Vavelski flew around the square, seeking his enemy. Simon zipped quickly from behind his hiding place and balanced his board between the dragon's horns. The furious beast spiraled up in the air, trying to shake free of the pest.

Simon tilted off the horrible head and did a frontside boardslide down the spines on the dragon's back. He flipped off the pointed barb of the tail and dived sharply to avoid a stream of fireballs that zoomed out of the dragon's nostrils like double-barreled machine gun fire. Then he zig-zagged among the high gables of the market square houses.

Close behind, Smok Vavelski breathed a light flame, but instead of aiming at Simon, he sprayed a gargoyle that was perched on top of a gable. The hideous demon, with bulging eyes, pointed ears, long, sharp claws, dagger-like teeth, and wings like a bat, came to life and flew after Simon. The flying skater did a wallride along the side of a church. He spiraled high into the air when he came to the end of the building. Unable to shake off the pursuer, he did a sudden loop in midair. The gargoyle passed beneath him.

The monster turned quickly and bore down on Simon with greater speed. Simon pointed his wand and spelled, "RESTORE!" The ugly creature turned back into stone and rocketed through the air like a meteor. It struck the dragon, who was approaching stealthily from the opposite direction, and fell to the ground where it broke into pieces on the cobblestones.

Again, Simon had to dodge intensely hot fire. He dropped downward and flew through the arcade of the magnificent cloth hall, weaving in and out of the long row of arches. Smok Vavelski followed close behind, belching flame after flame.

Simon banked high again and darted down a narrow lane. His pursuer kept up overhead. As Simon dead-ended at the town wall, he rose sharply and flew toward the hills in the distance. He remembered what the Magical Marketing student had said about the Vielichka salt mine several miles east of town. If only Smok Vavelski would follow him underground, maybe he could trap the beast below the earth. What else could he do? Magic spells were useless.

The dragon followed Simon across the countryside in the late afternoon sun. He was unable to match the smaller creature's agility in the air, but he was full of anger — and full of fire. As all dragons, he was shrewd, wise, and patient. So he followed the boy who had come to steal his treasure, or his blood. How dare the young fool think he could deceive the great Smok Vavelski! No one sneaking into his lair would go unpunished.

The mighty drake lingered behind in the air, expecting the boy to tire sooner or later. In fact, Simon was *exhausted*. He began to fear that he could fall off his board and into the jaws of his enemy. Then he saw what appeared to be a long row of ants crawling out of a hole. He descended sharply and soon confirmed that the ants were an army of dwarves leaving their day's work in the salt mine. The stocky little men marched in single file. They carried picks and shovels over their shoulders. Most carried woven baskets filled with salt strapped to their backs.

Simon flew through the hills for a while and waited for the dwarves to march away. Then he banked sharply and shot through the mine entrance. The dragon entered behind him, spitting flames. Simon could easily see where he was by the light of the burning torches the dwarves had left behind. The young wizard zigzagged through stalagmites, stalactites, and carved statues of salt. After he had flown far below the earth, he circled around a large stalactite and dodged under the dragon. The beast turned quickly and continued his chase.

Simon banked down behind the statue of a knight as the

drake turned in the air. The scheming Magical pointed his wand at the statue's head. "PROPELLO!" he spelled. Then he aimed at the wounds on Smok Vavelski's belly. The salt ball flew in the direction the wand pointed. As it got inches away, Simon blasted it with a fireball. The chunk of salt disintegrated and splattered the dragon's sword wounds.

The horrid beast fell back into the cave wall, roaring loudly in pain. The spines on his back buried hard into the wall. He wiggled and twisted violently to free himself. Simon took off quickly back up the enormous shaft and headed down another, narrower, tunnel. He hoped it would be more difficult for his enemy to maneuver there. But as he zipped around a wide turn, the wheels of his skateboard caught on a stalagmite and flipped him through the air.

Simon banged against the salt wall and dropped his wand just as a shot of dragon fire engulfed the skateboard. He scurried to his wand and put the fire out. He knew the dragon would soon be upon him. Almost immediately, he felt a great surge of heat and saw a bright orange glow coming from Smok's direction. But, instead of horns and teeth following the fire, a wide, high flow of salty lava rolled down the tunnel. It oozed toward Simon as the salty walls melted.

Smaller and smaller flashes of light flickered from the dragon's way. Simon backed slowly away from the molten flow, but it soon stopped advancing. However, it piled higher and higher until Simon was faced by a wall of salt. He was trapped beneath the earth with no way out — Smok Vavelski had beaten him at his own game.

The boy knew that by the time the dwarves mined their

way to him they would find nothing but salty wolf bones. He looked at his scorched skateboard. The wheels were twisted globs. The deck was ready to crumble. Simon zapped the board with a Restore spell. It returned to reasonably good condition, but it wouldn't fly.

Simon pushed off down the hard floor of the mine, hoping to find a side shaft that might lead back to the surface. But the deeper he went, the less likely it seemed. As the last flicker of torch light faded, Simon's wheels hit something and sent him tumbling. He lit up his wand and found the board. It had flipped over beside a long-handled iron pick. Other tools, burned out lanterns, and debris lay scattered about.

With pick and board in hand, Simon went back up the tunnel. He swung away at the salt wall, knocking away a few big chips and a pile of powder. He soon sat down to rest. Then an idea struck him. "Where there's a *wand* there's a *way*," he said aloud. "TRANSFORMUS POWER DRILL!" The two arms of the pick folded back into a sharp vee with spiny teeth. The wooden handle became a sleek turbo motor. Simon pointed at the wall with his wand. "PERFORATO!" he spelled.

The motor revved loudly, and the blade spun rapidly against the wall. Simon struggled to wade through the powdered salt that flew from the narrow shaft forming in front of him. After a couple of hours, the drill busted through to the main cavern. Simon walked back up to the mine entrance. On the way, he placed his skateboard in the hands of a statue of a dwarf. "TRANSFORMUS SALT!" he spelled. The skateboard became a part of the salty monument. "That was a big fly," Simon said.

The moon was glowing brightly in the sky. Simon stood a hundred yards from the mine, wondering how he would get back to Krakow by morning. He felt a queasy, sickening sensation creeping through his body. Was this the way turning into a werewolf began? Would it get more intense over the night and next day? Or maybe it would happen instantly, like a Transformus spell.

Simon rubbed his cheeks to see if they were getting hairy. "If I make it through this, I'll never grow a beard," he thought. His dreary musings were interrupted by the distant wailing of wolves. The din grew louder and seemed to be getting closer. Simon held his wand ready. Before he could determine which way the noise was coming from, a pack of large wolves knocked him to the ground.

The struggling wizard was unable to lift his wand. The delirious animals were all over him. They licked and nipped at him playfully! With great effort, the boy managed to struggle to his feet. The wolves danced and hopped around him. "Oh, great," Simon said, "they think I'm one of them. GO AWAY!" He waved his arms, but the wolves grew even louder and more excited.

Simon swished his wand around at his fan club. "TRANS-FORMUS POODLES!" he spelled. The pack of curly-haired pooches whimpered and pranced like show dogs. "Arrrrrrr! Get out of here!" Sparks shot out of the wand — the frightened dogs took off quickly into the hills. Simon pulled the swan cape from his pack. "RESTORE!" he spelled. The charred feathers turned white again, but the whole garment barely hung below his waste. He was able to lift into the air, but neither high nor fast.

The flight back to town was slow and bumpy in the strong breeze. Simon could barely lift over the high wall. He cruised into the market square and banged on the door of an inn next to a cobbler's shop. The sleepy innkeeper opened the door a bit, holding a nearly depleted candle. "It's too late. Go away!" Simon pulled a few shinies from his pocket.

The gruff innkeeper grabbed the money without a word and showed Simon to a room behind the stairs. "You'll have to share with *them*," he said. He turned around without explanation and left Simon alone in the dark. Simon fired up his wand. Straw was scattered all over the floor. His roommates were three goats huddled together in a corner.

"Not even a bed," Simon grumbled.

"Naahhhh," one of the goats seemed to answer.

Simon took aim at the animals with his wand. "TRANS-FORMUS LION GUARDS!" he spelled. Three huge lions jumped up from the huddle in the corner and took up positions. "Better not take any chances." Simon fluffed up a pile of straw and fell upon it in exhaustion. He dreamed very briefly. He dreamed that he would never dream again. Fortunately, that was just a dream.

CHAPTER SEVENTEEN

SKUBA THE COBBLER

The three lions roared fiercely when the door swung open. Simon sat up, startled. The innkeeper's bundle of fresh straw scattered in the air. The terrified man slammed the door shut, his eyes bugging out and his hair standing on end. Simon got up and restored the goats. It was morning already.

In the common room, the nervous innkeeper served Simon fresh bread, eggs, and sausages. The boy ate ravenously, his first meal since yesterday's pierogi and ice cream. As he ate, Simon brainstormed for a way to get past the dragon. Maybe he could avoid another fight by drilling underneath the fearsome beast. He had the knack for it after boring through the salt wall.

Simon finally became aware of his surroundings again. He noticed that the other patrons were staring at him angrily — some were whispering. Then someone pulled a chair out from his table. "May I join you?" asked the student of Magical Marketing. He sat down without awaiting an answer. "Going to try your luck at Smok Vavelski's treasure again?" he smiled. "I must say, that was quite a bold attempt."

"I wasn't after the treasure," Simon said rudely. "I wanted to get to the chakra under the dragon's lair."

"Ah, the famous chakra," said the student. "Last year a graduate student of Magical Informating had a wonderful idea for it. He called it banner informating. He used trained cattoflies to pull long, silk banners through the air, informating about the chakra throughout Magic Space. It would have been a great success, but harpies kept eating the cattoflies."

Simon rolled his eyes in disgust. "Which is why I wanted to speak with you," the student continued. "I have a proposition you can't refuse." Simon wanted to transform him into some kind of speechless creature. "The firedrake returned last night and burned a few more buildings. A delegation had to renegotiate the contract with him. Now the greedy beast is to receive *twice* the tribute as before. But your return certainly complicates matters."

"What's the proposition?" Simon asked, impatient.

"It's my own graduate project," said the student. He smiled widely and rubbed his hands together vigorously. "I propose a whole new deal with Smok Vavelski. You and he could perform mock battles every day, but nothing dangerous, mind you. Just imagine: Smok Vavelski versus Simon Peppercorn — Warrior Wizard. Oh, imagine the crowds it would draw! I can just picture the informating banners now. Perhaps you could convince other Warrior Wizards to guard the cattoflies. You could have a cut of the profits, of course. Why risk stealing from a dragon?" The student's eyes flared brighter than dragonflies.

Simon jumped up from the table. "You're crazy!" he shouted. "I'm a *Warrior Wizard*, not a circus clown!" He pushed his chair away and stormed out of the inn, wondering why he hadn't transformed the student into a mushman and kicked him into one of the eight corners of Magic Space.

The market square was back to its usual frantic bustle, though the noise was rather subdued. Work crews were busy repairing damaged buildings, with the aid of Magicals and domesticated forest trolls. Simon stood in front of the inn, wondering if he could find a shop with mining tools. Passersby glared at him suspiciously and hurried away.

A boy about Simon's age sat in front of the cobbler's shop next door, sewing large pieces of sheep skin together. He smiled at Simon, who was mildly shocked to see someone act friendly toward him — other than the ridiculous student. "What are you doing? Sewing boots for a giant?" Simon asked.

"I'm going to be the one who kills the dragon," the boy said, serious.

"You don't look like a Dragon Slayer," Simon said. "What's your name?"

"I'm Skuba the Cobbler," said the boy.

"Why would you want to kill Smok Vavelski?" Simon asked. "You must make a lot of money selling shoes to the tourists. You could say they're from dragonhide and informate about them."

"I'm going to do it because it's the right thing to do," said Skuba. He pulled the thick leather thread with his teeth. "Do you want to help?"

Simon wondered if Skuba wasn't as crazy as the Magical Marketing student. "How do you plan to kill him?" Simon asked, intrigued.

"With the fattest sheep he's ever eaten," said Skuba. "I got the idea from my cousin Jacob the matchmaker."

"Are you going to marry the monster and feed it poisoned lamb chops?" Simon said, unconvinced.

"He's not *that* kind of matchmaker," said Skuba. "He puts a glob of sulfur on the end of a stick. When it dries you can make fire with it. That's called a match. I'm going to fill a fake sheep with sulfur and give it to the dragon."

Simon's jaw dropped. He was speechless. He didn't want to say aloud what he was thinking. "I'm a Warrior Wizard. I've fought giants, trolls, goblins, Baba Yaga, Grendel's mother, but this kid comes up with the most brilliant plan ever — and it's so simple! Maybe I am Simple Simon."

"Are you going to help, or not?" Skuba said.

"Sure, what can I do?" Simon asked.

"We have to take this sheephide to the sulfur mine and fill it up," Skuba said. "Then we have to take it to the feeding area." He tugged hard on the heavy thread, tied it in a knot, and snipped it off.

"Sulfur mine?" Simon said. "I just went through a salt mine, and it wasn't very sweet. I've got a better idea."

Simon and Skuba were on the river bank a few hundred yards from the viewing area. They shoveled the last few scoops of sand into the sheephide. Skuba sewed up the opening and stood back with Simon to observe their masterpiece. "It's kind of lumpy in places," Simon said.

"I heard that Hard Space girls are, too," said Skuba.

Simon laughed, but he was glad Morgana and Elanor

were not there to here the remark, though he would have given anything to see them now. Simon circled the sheep and kicked it in a few places. "That's better," he said. He pointed his wand at the creation and spelled, "ANIMATO!" The fat ewe opened her eyes and rolled slowly onto her belly. Simon and Skuba pushed as hard as they could to help their sacrificial pet to her feet.

"Baaah!" the sheep said weakly. Skuba tied a leather rope around her neck.

Finally, the co-conspirators pushed and pulled the huge sheep to the holding pen by the feeding area. Simon spoke with the wrangler and gave him a handful of shinies. The boys left their pet and went to the viewing area where many tourists were already gathered. Simon paid the admission with the last of his coins and squeezed with Skuba to the front of the crowd.

"Why do you really want to kill the dragon?" Simon asked after a while. "He doesn't eat people, and your town earns money off of him."

"That's the thing," Skuba said, "the wealth has gone to everybody's head — they're all lazy and aimless. Our traditions are dying, and most people don't feel the good energy from the chakra anymore. The dragon drains it away."

At that moment a loud roar rumbled from across the river. Smok Vavelski was rearing his head and breathing large streams of fire into the air. Simon slipped back into the crowd between two fat peasant women. He felt as if he was pushing on the back end of the sheep again as the throng of tourists pressed him forward.

While the dragon performed his usual routine of aerial acrobatics and displayed his skills at pyrotechnics, the fattened sheep was led to a spot between the river bank and the viewing area. The firedrake spotted his meal from on high. "So, they have brought forth the choicest of their beasts — a much better meal than a salty little boy," he thought. "The fools fear the wrath of Smok Vavelski. Deal, or no deal, they still have more to pay."

The mighty dragon flapped his powerful wings and spiraled upward, snorting streams of sparks in a fantastic display. Then he angled downward and swooped toward the sheep. Simon's head was wedged between the two peasant women. He tried to extend his wand, but it was stuck somewhere in the wobbly fat that was trying to engulf him. He needed to act fast, or all would be lost — but it was impossible.

Smok Vavelski dropped closer and closer toward the sheep with his jaws opened wide. *A few more feet* — Simon watched helplessly — *a foot away* — all was lost! But the fierce beast buzzed inches above the sheep and banked high into the air. "They want to see the master of fire, the guardian of great treasure. Let them have another taste," thought the dragon.

Simon wiggled to the ground when everyone in the crowd sucked in their breath for a common gasp of awe. He forced himself between the hairy legs of the fat women and squirmed up beside Skuba.

Smok Vavelski finally tired of the performance. He corkscrewed over the river through a series of fiery rings and shot down like an arrow toward the tethered sheep. From the corner of his eye, he spotted Simon. "What is this?" he thought. But dinner was feet away and his hunger was stronger than his will.

The dragon snatched the sheep off the ground as if it had been a rabbit. Simon pointed his wand. 'TRANSFORMUS SULFUR!" he spelled. The half-swallowed ewe disappeared down the dragon's throat in one mighty gulp.

The great Smok Vavelski spiraled back into the air, flew in a figure eight, and then hovered high over the crowd, breathing double smoke rings through his nose. Suddenly, he belched an enormous fireball that shot across the sky like a comet, much to the delight of the cheering tourists. Then plumes of thick, black smoke poured from his mouth, nostrils, and ears. A nasty cloud wafted over the crowd. Everyone coughed and choked from the sulfurous stink. Many ran from the viewing area.

"SIMON PEPPERCORN!" the dragon bellowed. Bright, uncontrollable flames followed the words from his mouth. The remaining tourists scattered away. Smok Vavelski leveled in the air and dived at his murderer. Simon and Skuba froze where they stood, but fifty yards away, the vengeful monster exploded into a gazillion pieces of flaming dragon flesh. Simon raised his watch shield to protect himself and Skuba from the smelly debris.

Some of the tourists slowly trickled back to the viewing area. An eerie quiet filled the air. Simon cleaned himself and his partner of dragon crud with a Purgo spell. The two fat ladies, who had tripped over each other trying to get away, lay crying on the ground covered with mud and dragon filth.

"I have to go," Simon said, "before the cave gets raided."

"At least the treasure will make up for lost tourist money," said Skuba. "Maybe the townspeople won't be so mad at you."

The cave was empty when Simon got there. He easily retraced the passages he'd been through before. There were no others to be found — and no trace of a stone radiating energy, though he did feel its power. Simon inspected the walls of the treasure chamber carefully and moved piles of bling around. Maybe there was a trapdoor underneath. But the hoard was extremely vast — it was impossible to move it all.

Simon sat down on a pile of jewels in resignation. Maybe Dogbert would show up in Krakow before the full moon was in place. The master could get him to the chakra, even if he would have to go back and stay in Hard Space. At least he wouldn't bite anybody — not with fangs, anyway. The terrible thoughts were soon interrupted by the rumble of voices far down the main tunnel. Simon jumped to his feet. He stuffed a large diamond and several other sparkling gems into his pocket and headed back down the passage. He had to squeeze through the mass of townspeople that flooded into the cave.

Evening was slowly creeping across the sky. The full moon was like a big smiley face, but it seemed to Simon that it was frowning at him. He made his way back to the road and up to the top of Vavel Hill. He couldn't find healing beneath it, but perhaps he could find solace on top of it. The only people he saw there was a group of pilgrims leaving the cathedral. They must not have heard about the treasure yet.

Simon caught hold of the church door before it swung closed and went inside where he could be alone. He walked about slowly, checking out the ancient cathedral's stark majesty, but a large portrait of the Black Madonna compelled him to stop. Simon sat before the image on a small bench. After a while, he felt rather calm. He knew he would have to accept things as they were, but he wished Dogbert would show up. "I wish I could see him as my little Doggy one last time," he thought. "I wonder if he'll ever run through the woods with me again, or will he stay in Magic Space, now that I've failed in my Venture?"

A big tear rolled from the corner of the boy's eye. He had never been so sad before. Then, through the watery haze, he saw a figure in a black robe with the hood pulled low over its face approaching him. "A monk," Simon thought. The mysterious man motioned for Simon to follow him. He went to the picture of the Madonna and slid it across the wall. A small opening appeared in front of a dark staircase. The silent guide started down the steps and nodded for Simon to follow.

The staircase led steeply below the great church and into a dark room. Simon lit his wand, hoping the monk wouldn't mind. Everything was dusty and covered with cobwebs. Simon made out a number of statues, paintings, and a carved sarcophagus. Another staircase led upward, but the monk led the boy to one that continued downward.

The dark guide motioned for Simon to continue alone. The narrow staircase took him down, down, down, below the world. The energy coming at Simon was overwhelming. The Elfin Spark throbbed in his chest. He tried to focus on it and keep from thinking. That made it easier to withstand the power. Simon finally came to a large chamber. The space was divided into sections by walls with pillared arches cut into them. A pure, white glow spread out faintly from what seemed to be the center. Simon felt as if the Elfin Spark would burst at any moment, but he tried to remain quiet and focused.

As he eased toward the nearest arch, the thump of heavy steps sounded on the stairs. Simon turned his head and saw a dark figure descending. He thought it was the monk, but the stooped being eased closer and suddenly stood straight. It was at least eight feet tall! Before Simon could react, the creature leapt and landed about three feet from him.

Battlefang threw back his hood. Simon had never seen such a hideous face. It was part human, part wolf — part vicious fiend. The contorted face was covered with thick, coarse hair. The bulging black eyes glowed red from the bloodshot veins that snaked throughout them. What frightened Simon most were the long, sharp-pointed fangs that flashed in the dim sparkle that illuminated the cavern. Scared out of his wits, Simon pulled his wand. "MORTIS SIMULATIS!" He tried one of his most powerful spells, but Battlefang barely shivered.

The monster pointed his own wand toward Simon. "STUPIDUS!" he spelled. Simon flew back against a column and slid to the ground, shaking. "Was that supposed to be a *spell?*" Battlefang laughed maniacally. "Simon Peppercorn, Warrior Wizard with an Elfin Spark. Your wimpy charms are useless against my superior magic. I have transfigured into a being beyond the reach of your minor trickery." The freaky beast laughed even more madly than before.

Simon raised up a bit. He aimed his wand at the ferocious monster. "LAUGH OUT LOUDER!" Caught off guard, Battlefang fell into a fit of ear-splitting roars. Simon kept the momentum and spelled again, "SCROLL UP!" He flicked his wand quickly upward. Battlefang rocketed off his feet — his head smashed on the stony ceiling.

The great beast dropped back to his feet, barely fazed. He put his wand away and pointed his sharp-clawed finger at Simon. "STAND!" Simon shot onto his feet, leaning against the column. His eyes focused on several large, round lengths of stone that must have been a broken pillar.

Simon aimed quickly at one of the stones and spelled, "TRANSFORMUS TIGER!" A huge saber-toothed tiger sprang from the ground. It spotted the foul Battlefang and leapt upon him, growling ferociously. The two creatures rolled and tumbled in a violent duel of teeth and claws. But just when Simon thought the tiger would bite the head off of the wolfish monster, Battlefang absorbed the tiger into himself, becoming the scariest being Simon could imagine.

The monster stood tall, growling at Simon — great tusks hung from its powerful jowls. Simon aimed his wand at the humongous thing. "ELECTRO," he spelled. The monster shuttered and stooped double. But it quickly stood tall again, fur ablaze, and eased forward. "RESTORE!" Simon spelled. The creature turned into a furry stone pillar with the sword-like teeth of a saber-toothed tiger. Simon sighed deeply with relief, but before he had completely exhaled, the pillar burst into pieces.

Battlefang stood in front of Simon again. "EXPELLO WAND!" he spelled.

Simon's wand flew out of his hand and landed across the chamber. Battlefang pulled a handful of golden shinies from his robe pocket and tossed them at the boy. "STRINGO!" he spelled. The coins transformed into heavy golden chains and wrapped around Simon's chest and the column he leaned against. Simon could wiggle his arms, but he couldn't pull them free.

Battlefang now stood two feet away. Simon felt paralyzed. Even his mind hardly moved. Great energy surged through him in the odd stillness, but it seemed to quickly empty from him to the monster. "How's this for the end to your Venture — Warrior Wizard?" Battlefang laughed.

"Aren't you going to thank me for saving you from becoming a werewolf? That's right — for you won't live to see midnight. I'll drink most of your life away and then deliver you to my master. Are you surprised to learn there is one even greater than I? It is my great honor to deliver him the Elfin Spark, and yours to provide it, though I suppose you disagree."

Simon stretched and twisted his fingers. If Battlefang got a little closer, he might be able to grab the monster's wand. "He will use it to greatly improve his powers, *and* mine. Our forces will take over Magic Space and destroy your ridiculous Hard Space," Battlefang rattled on.

Simon's flailing hand hit upon the hilt of his tiny sword. "I could try to use it as a wand," he thought, "but spells don't work much against this creep."

"I would have had you sooner," said Battlefang, "but Dogbert Ambrosius confounded my plans, seeking battle in the shadows as you and your pitiful friends went about your silly adventures. Did you feel abandoned, unprotected, by your mutty little master? What kind of a Warrior Wizard would you make, anyway, if you couldn't be left alone to take on a band of goblins, or a worthless Wicked Witch?"

Simon got a good grip on Hrunting. Any spell might help gain a little time. "But you can die in peace, knowing that your famous master magus has fought bravely to protect that precious Elfin Spark," said Battlefang. "Did I say *peace*? Well — you may be upset to learn that he and his scraggly Warrior Wizards are being finished off at this very moment. My superior force of Wicked Wizards and wolferns has them trapped."

Battlefang stepped closer to Simon and slowly leaned toward the helpless boy's neck. Simon thrashed his head about frantically as the horrible fangs neared their target. He turned his miniature sword upward, but his mind went blank with fear.

Simon froze, totally resigned to his terrible fate. Why fight it? The end was at hand. But in the stillness of his fright, his mind became crystal clear. The spell came to him as the tips of the filthy fangs pressed to his neck.

"MAXIMIZE!" Simon spelled loudly, gripping Hrunting tightly.

The lovely, jeweled scabbard shattered into tiny pieces as the little blade expanded into a five-foot-long sword. The weapon pierced Battlefang's heart and thrust out his back, blood-covered. The force of the strike jolted the monster backwards. Simon let go of the mighty Hrunting. Battlefang crashed hard to the ground. The sword tip hit the stone floor and caused the deadly blade to bounce out of the monster's body and leap several feet into the air. It twisted, turned, and fell with a clang at Simon's feet. The echoing ring gave way to dead silence.

Then feet pounded on the narrow stairs. Dogbert rushed down to Simon, followed by five Warrior Wizards." LIBER-ATO!" the master spelled. The golden chains fell away from Simon. The boy rubbed his arms as if he was cold. "Complete your Venture, Warrior Wizard Initiate," Dogbert commanded.

Simon had almost forgotten why he was there. He walked slowly through an archway, trying to still his mind with each deliberate step. Then he crossed a dozen yards and entered the inner chamber. *There it was*. A four-foot-high cube was sculpted from the carved-out cavern floor. A rough, milky white stone the size of a bowling ball sat on top of it. The simple crystal emitted the soft, gentle light that filled the whole underground space.

Simon was pulled toward the chakra. He felt as if he might expand endlessly, or shrink into an invisible dot. There was no longer a difference. His mind seemed to enter the crystal as he approached it and placed his hands upon it. At the same time, the chakra's energy entered him — it filled him completely. Then he felt the Elfin Spark pulsate in his heart. Its energy merged with that of the crystal and became one great wave of power.

Simon was but a witness to what was going on. All the atoms of his body separated into their separate particles as they had done before, swirling in a sea of light. But this time he completely lost sense of himself in the great vastness of Being.

After an eternity — or no time at all — Simon became aware again. His body reshaped, or at least he became aware of it as a body again. But now it was cleansed. He knew he was healed. He stood before the wonderful crystal for a while, trying not to return to the world of thought. Stillness of mind prevented the energy from overwhelming him.

"Retrieve your sword and wand," Dogbert said, after Simon rejoined the others. Simon picked up the two treasures of a Warrior Wizard. He stared at the lifeless body of Battlefang for a while before turning back to Dogbert.

"Simon Peppercorn — you have successfully completed your Venture," Dogbert said. "And you have freed Magic Space of a powerful and dangerous enemy. You will receive formal knighting in the Magical Order of Warrior Wizards before the Wanding Lord."

The five Warrior Wizards bowed on one knee before Simon. The boy was speechless and embarrassed. "Rise and continue your mission," the master magus said to his men. The five warriors surrounded the body of Battlefang. One of them raised his hand, and they all disappeared with the hideous corpse.

Dogbert gave Simon a big hug. Then he waved his wand around the chamber.

"RESTORE!" he spelled. Hrunting's scabbard collected back together. Simon minimized his worthy blade and sheathed it. "Let's get out of here," Dogbert said.

In the upper chamber, Simon and Dogbert found the body of the monk in black. Simon grieved to see that his silent guide sacrificed his life for him.

Outside, the full moon was shining brightly overhead. Simon and Dogbert crossed the square and met Skuba the Cobbler, who was locking up the shop. "Did you get to the dragon's lair in time to get some treasure?" Skuba asked Simon.

"I was after a different kind of treasure," Simon said. "But I did take this." He pulled the diamond and other jewels he had taken from the cave out of his pocket and held them out to his friend. "For you — so you can open your own shoe shop." Skuba was reluctant to take the stones.

"Go ahead, take them. You deserve them," said Dogbert.

"You don't know how much you did for me," Simon said.

Skuba took the jewels in his hand. "Maybe I'll buy a sword instead," he said. "I want to be a Dragon Slayer."

"I just may be able to pull some strings," Dogbert said.

The Master and the young Warrior Wizard raised their thumbs at the same time.

"May you feel the magic!"

Simon and Dogbert headed down a narrow lane, bathed in glorious moonlight.

"It's a good thing we're getting out of here," Simon said. "They're going to really hate me in this town."

"Oh, I can fix that," Dogbert replied. "I know a student of Magical Marketing. He's a public relations pro."

"*Very funny*," Simon said. "*Very funny*."

"I hope there's some place open to get some sausages," the master said. "I'm so hungry, it's *not* funny."

Simon pulled out his wand and aimed at Dogbert. "L-O-L!" he spelled. Dogbert bent forward in a fit of laughter. When he finally caught his breath, he raised his hand high.

"G2G!" The master and the young Warrior Wizard disappeared.

LaVergne, TN USA
16 October 2009
161168LV00003B/4/P